SAY *I'm* YOURS

Timing is everything.

NEW YORK TIMES BESTSELLING AUTHOR
CORINNE MICHAELS

Say I'm Yours

Editor:

Ashley Williams, AW Editing

Proofreading:

Kara Hildebrand

Janice Owen

Interior Design & Formatting:

Christine Borgford, Type A Formatting

www.typeAformatting.com

Cover Design:

Sarah Hansen, Okay Creations

www.okaycreations.com

Cover photo © Perrywinkle Photography

SAY *I'm* YOURS

Timing is everything.

DEDICATION

To my grandmothers . . .

Grandma Cory, I know you'll never see this, because you're no longer with us, but I know you watch over me. Thank you for teaching me it's good to have fun. You lived life unapologetically and gave me my love of romance novels. Thank you for putting Danielle Steel novels on the shelf I could reach, telling me highly inappropriate stories about your youth, and keeping cigarettes in the kitchen drawers for me to steal. (Even though you didn't know I did that.) I love you and miss you each day.

Grandma Mary, you've taught me so much about the woman I strive to be. I wish everyone could have a grandma half as amazing as you are. You fostered my love of reading and writing through my entire life. More than that, you've given me a light that I can find in the dark. You make me laugh, you make me smile, and you make my heart whole. I love you!

Grandma Gert, you're the pillar of strength and beauty. You've endured more in your life than I can ever imagine, yet you still loved with all your heart. Thank you for teaching me how to find a way through my struggles. I hope I can be half the woman you are. I love you!

"You're a place in my heart that no one else could have."

~ F. Scott Fitzgerald

chapter
ONE

"DON'T WALK AWAY FROM ME!" Trent calls out as I move forward. "Grace!"

My stride falters. We've done this dance a hundred times. I know the steps—two steps forward, ten steps back. We circle the floor and can never quite find our rhythm.

"I'm done," I say with my back turned. "I'm done only being good enough when it's convenient for you. I'm done being the girl who's waitin' around, hoping you'll finally admit that you love her. I can't do it anymore. You're killing me."

The sound of his approach causes my heart to race. If there's one thing I can't resist in my life, it's him. He knows what he's doing, and always has. Trent is the one thing I can't quit. My heart has always belonged to him. Each time I walk away, I find myself running right back.

Stupid, I know.

It's hard loving a man who will never love me back, though, and I've spent almost twenty years waiting for Trent Hennington to give me his heart. I've learned now that it's never going to happen. I'm finally done trying to force a square peg in a round hole.

"Please." His voice cracks on the single word. "Just don't walk away. Not this time. I'm trying, darlin'. I'm workin' so hard to get my shit straight."

His words cause my stomach to clench. The only difference between this time and when we ended things three months ago is that, unlike last time, I won't be going back. His hands grip my shoulders as he pulls me against him and drops his lips to my hair. His breath is warm, and I close my eyes. This right here, the feeling of longing and desire, is why I always go back. The way he touches me and makes my body want to melt into his and wakes every nerve in my body gives me hope. But I know that hope is a fable, fiction written to replace the reality I wasn't ready to face.

I have to walk away.

I need to let him go. Not because I don't love him, but because *this* won't ever change.

I need change.

"When you finally do, I hope you'll be happy." I turn to face him, making sure he hears the sincerity in my words. "I hope you find the girl that's worth all of your heart, but I'm not her. I've tried to be." A tear falls, and I let it. "Lord knows I have. I've given you everything I could while you haven't given me anything but scraps. It's wrecked me, and I can't let you break me again. I love you. I've *always* loved you. You're the only man I've ever pictured a life with." I was done with going hungry, and now I wanted the whole darn feast.

"Grace," Trent says as he takes a step forward.

"No." I mirror him, moving a step backward, and put my hand up, reiterating, "I refuse to be that girl anymore. It hurts too much. I told you last week it was over, but then you show up last night, and I find myself right back here again. Where you're all sweet and loving and then you pull the rug out from under me. You can't do this to me anymore. If you ever loved me, even a little bit, you'll let me go."

Trent Hennington will obliterate me if I stay any longer.

"You are that girl! You've always been that girl!" He comes closer. "You're who I want, Gracie."

"No, I'm not." I rush out of the small room he cornered me in.

"I need you," Trent calls out. "I want you."

I halt and say the words from over my shoulder. "Please, I'm beggin' you not to do this."

I don't wait for his response, I move quickly.

Once I enter the wedding reception of my best friend, Presley, I stop.

The music plays loudly, but all I hear is the echo of his words. My feet won't move forward as I stare at my friends enjoying the party. Presley and her husband, Zachary Hennington, are holding each other and you can see the joy radiating off them. This moment should've happened for them a long time ago, but here they are now. They've fought for their happiness, never taking it for granted. Of course, Presley was married before and has almost teenage boys, but they found their way. Then there's Trent's youngest brother Wyatt with his new wife, Angie. All of them are happy, while I feel like I'm shattering.

Lucky for me, my heart found the one Hennington that won't ever wise up—not.

"Don't give up, Gracie. Don't walk away from me." I hear Trent's deep voice in my ear and let out a shallow breath through my nose.

"I want that," I say, looking out at the scene before me. "I want the wedding and happily ever after. I want a love like your brothers have. I want you to love me, but you don't. You won't give me your heart."

I feel his heat against my back, and I can only imagine how close he actually is to me when he says, "You're wrong."

No. I'm not. I've given him a million chances to let me in. I've given him years that I won't ever get back. Rage fills me at his words because, once again, he's trying to hold me back. "I'm thirty-six years old, and I'm tired of waiting."

"You don't have to wait, Grace. I'm standing right in front of you."

Presley's eyes find mine, and she frowns. She starts to walk toward me, but I shake my head. It's her wedding, and the last thing she needs to do is come save me. It's high time I start saving myself.

I shift so Trent can see in my eyes that I'm not playing around. "Loving me shouldn't be this hard. I'm not some love-struck teenager anymore. We're done. We were done years ago. We were done last month when I broke it off, and we're done today. Nothing you can say will change that."

The skin around his blue eyes tightens as he grips my arms. His lips press against mine. Without my telling them to, my arms fly around his neck, and I hold on to him. Our mouths move together, but my heart is pulling away.

This is goodbye for me.

It's the very last time my lips will touch his.

I was serious when I said I was done.

The desperation in this kiss is crushing. I feel him fighting for me to hold on, but I've already let go.

He breaks away first, and leans back enough so he can search my eyes for something. "I'm going to fix this," he promises. "I'm going to show you how much we belong together. I know I've messed up. I've given you every reason to walk away. But I can't lose you."

"Why?" I ask. This is what has me baffled. Why fight for me now when, a week ago, he was so willing to throw me away? "Why now?"

Trent's hand brushes my cheek. "Because you're mine. You're my girl."

I shake my head. "That's where you're wrong." I grip his hand

and remove it before gathering all the strength I have. It's time to put "the end" on the end of our story. "I'm not yours, Trent."

My legs feel weak, but I find a way to turn and walk away. Tears fill my vision as my heart plummets. I ache with each step I take, but I keep going and let a single bead of pain slide down my cheek as I leave my past behind me.

"HERE'S TO THE BRIDE AND groom!" I raise my glass to my best friend and her new husband. Everyone repeats what I say as we drink to Presley and Zach.

When I scan the room, I fake a smile, which falls the second I meet Trent's gaze. The pain I feel inside is reflected back at me. The air in the room is gone, and I swear that time stands still. He stares at me as he runs his hands through his sandy-blond hair, shifting slightly in his seat but refusing to break eye contact. He exudes confidence and masculinity all wrapped in a whole lot of heartache.

I should look away. I should stand, walk out, and stop this right now, but I can't tear my eyes from him. I'm the definition of insanity, constantly doing the same thing and expecting a different result. There will never be a different result. I'm tired of being tired. More than anything, I'm tired of being rejected. I may be done, but old habits die hard, and he's the oldest habit I have.

"Hey," Angie, Wyatt's wife, nudges me, "stop looking at him. He's not worth another second of your time, right?"

"I know. I wish things could be different. I wish he was different." The admission hurts.

"He's never going to change," Angie reminds me.

Even though Angie and I haven't been friends very long, she knows more about what's been going on with Trent than anyone. We bumped into each other a few months ago and ended up going to lunch, which was where I told her everything. How hurt I was and how I'd considered dating someone else, which was—and still is—unbelievably dumb, considering that someone else happens to be my best friend's brother.

In my defense, it's not as if there are many choices. Growing up in Bell Buckle has its challenges, like the lack of any sort of privacy, a very small dating pool, and the inability to avoid people. Angie gets it and is probably the only soul I know who would let me say all I needed to say without judgment.

It's insane.

It's frustrating.

It's small-town living.

"I hate him," I tell Angie with tears in my eyes.

"No, you don't, but you should."

She's right. I had hoped, in some crazy part of my heart, that Trent would love me the same, but clearly, I was wrong.

"It's like he only sees me now because I've walked away for good." I grab the glass of wine and toss it back.

Angie takes my hand. "It's because you don't ever make him see anything else." She straightens in her seat. "Look, I'm far from the world's expert on men. I've been married for like, a second, but when Wyatt pushed me away to the point I couldn't endure anymore, I left. It was a way to force him to decide whether our love was worth it. You gotta do the same, babe. You can't live like this. You're freaking gorgeous and no man should treat you like less than his everything. So make him see that you're not waiting anymore."

That in and of itself is another reason I like and trust this woman. She is fiercely independent and has way more courage than I do. She and Wyatt have been through absolute hell. Their relationship went downhill, but she was so much braver than I ever could be. When Wyatt pushed her, she packed her shit and left. I wish I were that strong. However, he did right by her in the end. Wyatt gave up everything to win her back.

"I'm not like you."

She shakes her head. "You don't give yourself enough credit." Her eyes move around the room and then stop. "There's someone here who sees you. I mean *really* sees you."

I turn in my seat just enough to find who she's looking at, and I swear my stomach gives a tiny flutter. Cooper Townsend. "I can't." I turn back to her, shaking my head in negation. "We've been over this. First, he's Presley's brother!" I whisper-yell. "Second, even if I'm done with Trent, I still love him."

Her eyes fill with empathy. "I know you do. Cooper knows you do, too. It's why he hasn't pushed harder. The man isn't blind, but maybe there's a chance?"

"I don't want to hurt him."

Angie's shoulders rise and then fall. "I think Cooper is more than willing to take that chance. I think he'd have a lot of fun pissing off my brother-in-law as well. There's no love lost between those two."

That was an understatement if I'd ever heard one. Cooper and Trent may have been friends their whole lives, but they don't see eye to eye on almost anything. Over the last month, it's been even worse. I think Trent knows that Cooper's feelings for me surpass friendship. The thought makes me sigh. My life is a Southern version of a soap opera.

"Angie, you're out of your ever-lovin' mind."

"The best way to get over a guy is to get under another. That's my motto."

My jaw falls slack. "You can't be serious."

"Hell yeah I am. You're not a nun. You're not with anyone or doing anything wrong. You have every right to sleep with whomever you want. If that happens so that you can teach my new brother-in-law a lesson, good. The Hennington ego is large my friend. It's time to pop it."

I twist my head over my shoulder, and Cooper smiles at me. The best I can offer back is a tentative wave before I turn back to Angie. "And hurt Cooper in the process?"

She scoffs. "If you're honest with him, he won't be hurt."

"I think you Yankees forget how things work down here."

"So you say. I'm going to check on Presley. Don't do anything I wouldn't do. Remember, there's a really great guy who is interested in you . . ."

Angie stands, and I fight the urge to scream. Date Cooper? How would that even work? He's not my type. He's nice, caring, attentive . . . normal.

I'm into the broken and unwilling to commit type.

I watch the people move around the dance floor, thinking about how different this all could've been. Trent and I could be married, have children, and be happy, but that's not the case. He pulls away, I pull harder, and eventually, I let go. I look at Angie and Presley smiling and happy, which makes my chest ache.

Swiping the bottle of wine from the center of the table, I refill my glass and then draw a long sip of wine. "Move on." I huff. "Move on to what? It's not like there's a line of guys waiting to date a former Miss Bedford County." I shake my head and continue my tirade. "Cooper? *Pfft*. Cooper isn't interested in—"

"Not interested in what?"

Shit, shit, shit. I have the worst luck ever. Only I would get caught mid-sentence talking aloud like a crazy person. "Cooper, hi." My cheeks blaze as he grins at me. "Nothing. I was just talking to myself. You know, observing and all that."

Because I'm an idiot.

His finger brushes against my cheek, causing it to burn hotter. "So, what were you observing about me?"

"You?" I squeak and then clear my throat. "I haven't the slight-est idea what you mean. I wasn't even lookin' at you."

He smirks. "I heard you say my name, Grace Rooney."

I could crawl under this table and never get out again. Me and my big mouth. "It was nothing. I was commenting on some-thing Angie mentioned before. About you wanting . . . to buy a . . . a . . . horse," I lie. "Yup. A horse."

He chuckles. "Sure you were." Cooper grabs a chair and twists it around so he sits with it backward. "I know Angie, and she is not known for talkin' horses. Plus, she doesn't have anything to do with the horse business. So, what exactly am I not interested in?" He pushes.

My pulse quickens as I try to think of something. "It's nothing."

"Grace." His voice is warm and inquisitive.

"Ask the girl to dance, son." Mrs. Townsend appears out of thin air. "She's been sittin' here *alone* almost all night."

Great. Now my best friend's mother is setting me up. She can probably smell the desperation seeping from my pores. Thirty-six, former beauty queen, never married, and unable to seal the deal. I'm every Southern mother's dream.

"I'm sure Cooper doesn't want to dance, Mrs. Townsend. He's—"

"Actually," he corrects, standing from his seat without taking his eyes off me. "I'd be honored." He holds out his arm, palm open, waiting. I stare at him, trying to figure out what to say as my stomach clenches. It's not as if I hadn't toyed with whatever I've been feeling toward Cooper for a while now, but if we dance here, now, it'll be making a statement. One I'm not sure I'm ready to make. My heart races as I look at his extended hand "Grace?" Cooper's green eyes lock on mine.

It's just a dance. Trent isn't my boyfriend. Actually, now that I think about it, we never once—since the day I met him—put an official label on our relationship. I also just stated my ending of whatever it was, and per Angie, Presley won't be mad, so there's no reason not to, right?

Right.

I plaster on a smile and place my hand in his, saying, "I'd love to dance."

His warm hand engulfs mine as he guides me to the dance floor. We stop at a spot near the edge of the crowd, and he turns toward me. "Relax, Grace." Cooper encourages as his thick arms wrap around me. "It's only a dance, and it's me. We've danced together since we were kids."

I shake my head and grin, even though this is not the same at all. Back then, I wasn't dancing with Cooper as a single woman. He was a friend, almost a brother, and now there isn't anything sibling like about this. "I know."

"Then stop shakin' like a leaf."

"It's just that you're you . . ."

And insanely hot.

"And you're . . ."

I shrug. "Me. I've been around you since I was seven. I mean, you're Cooper! The boy who pulled my pigtails and put dirt in my sandwich."

He laughs. "That was once, and I was convinced that you were the one who wrote, 'Cooper Townsend loves to eat boogers' on the bathroom wall."

I was, but he doesn't know that. I'd convinced myself that I was in love with him, and he told all the boys that I smelled like cheese. I did the only rational thing a twelve-year-old girl would do: write it on the bathroom wall. Being in a tiny town, it didn't take long for the news of the artwork to spread. I denied it like crazy and watched Cooper set out on a mission to figure out who'd written it.

"Truth?" I grin.

Cooper's lips lift as he figures it out. "I knew it! I knew it was you." His eyes sparkle.

"Well, you were mean to me! And I had a crush on you at that time."

"You did?" he asks.

"Umm." I giggle. "Yeah. You knew that!"

He shakes his head. "I had no idea."

"It wouldn't have mattered. It only lasted about two whole days. Then you did some gross boy thing, and I was over it, but for those two days . . . it was intense. Plus, if my mom ever thought there was a chance of a you and me—I wouldn't have been able to sleep over. You weren't worth missing girl time with Presley."

I didn't *really* like Cooper. Sure, he's always been good-looking and funny, but he was always looking at me as if I were the annoying little girl. Which in all fairness, I was. However, Trent and Cooper were always together when we were younger. And by then, I developed feelings for the oldest Hennington.

Now, though, I'm done with Trent, and it's Cooper who is in front of me.

His arms are around me as he holds me close. It's striking how different he and Trent are from each other. Cooper has dark brown hair, green eyes, and his five o'clock shadow doesn't make it easy for any girl to look away. Plus, he's freaking huge. He's tall, and his body is beyond words. The farm has done his body good.

"So?" Cooper calls my attention back to him. "Have you thought any more about my offer?"

I was hoping this wouldn't come up again. My heart has been torn apart. Agreeing to a date with Cooper would change so many things. Trent and I have only been separated for a week, and I'm not even sure I'm ready to date again. I'm definitely not ready to make a decision. I just had another spat with Trent—one that ended with his lips on mine. I needed time.

"I thought about it, but I don't have an answer."

"I can wait."

I sigh, and he spins me around again, completely undeterred by my evasion. "You might be waitin' a long time."

"I've been waitin' a long time already." He moves our intertwined hands between our chests. "I can be patient when it's something worth being patient for."

The honesty hangs on every syllable.

"What if all we'll ever be is good friends? What if what you think you're feeling is wrong?"

"Well," Cooper grins, "what's the worst that happens? I get to go on a date with a hot chick." He's teasing me, but his eyes grow heated as he looks me over.

I roll my eyes. "Whatever."

"Seriously, Grace. Not every girl has dark brown hair and light blue eyes. You're like my fourteen-year-old Xena fantasy come to life."

"I'm not sure if I should be flattered or insulted." It's kind of nice to know he thinks I'm hot. "So, all I am is a conquest? A way to feel better about yourself after dating Betsy?"

Last year, Cooper dated Betsy Barker. It wouldn't be a big deal, except it's very well known that they hate each other. Always have. Betsy's mom somehow got Vivienne Townsend to send him on a blind date with her.

Of course, Presley and I knew who was on the other end of his date, but Cooper didn't, which made it all the more entertaining to watch.

He shudders. "You're a close second to the She-Devil. I'm not sure if you'll live up to that level of disgust. Although, you just might."

I slap his chest and smile. "Jerk. But seriously, I need more time to think."

Cooper's olive eyes grow serious. "That's what you need to stop doin'. You think too much, and it's time you start takin' action. Listen to your heart for once."

"And you think my heart is saying it wants you?" I ask, letting my smile fade to seriousness.

"I guess we'll have to see, won't we?"

As Cooper turns me again, my gaze meets Trent's. "Yeah." I don't break my stare. "I guess we will."

chapter
TWO

COOPER AND I FINISH OUR dance, then I head over to the bar. "So," Presley's voice comes from behind me, "you and Cooper, huh?"

I let out a heavy sigh. "It was a dance, Pres."

She puts her hands up while shaking her head. "I'm not sayin' it's a bad thing, honey."

Maybe she isn't, but it sure ain't good. I'm not sure Cooper and I can ever be anything more than what we are now. Not only because my heart definitely isn't free but also because it would cause major issues in the town if things didn't work. All our mothers are best friends, Presley is one of my best friends, Cooper deals with the Hennington boys for business . . . it's a recipe for disaster. I'd be sitting right in the eye of it all. No, thank you.

The bartender hands me the drink, and I chug it before asking for a glass of water. "It isn't happening."

"Y'all looked cute out there."

"Sure."

She looks over at him and back to me. "He's liked you for a while, you know?"

I knew that, but I didn't know that she did. "When did you figure it out?"

She grins and hooks her arm in mine. "When I first got back home, he was lookin' at you differently. Remember the night we went out after I got back to Bell Buckle?" I nod. "I noticed it then. I thought maybe it was my imagination, but when you and Trent got back together, he stopped. Then, when you made it clear you were done again, it was obvious he really liked you."

Jesus. I didn't realize it. "A while ago, when Trent and I were on a break, Cooper asked me out," I confess.

I wanted to tell her sooner. She's my best friend, and we don't have many secrets between us. My even considering dating Cooper felt so wrong, though, which was why I decided that if it felt that way, it probably was. Then it was her being a basket case with her wedding coming, Angie moving back to town—for good, and the more time that passed, the weirder I felt about telling her.

"But you said no?"

"He's your brother!" It's comical, really. "And he's friends with Trent, who is your new *husband's* brother. I mean, could we make things any more complicated?"

She looks around the room wistfully. "I learned not so long ago how precious life is. We're not promised anything. We have no guarantees that we'll get jack shit. I stand here, lookin' around, and I'm in awe. I haven't done anything life altering. I don't save lives or teach children." She nudges me with her elbow. "But here I am with two unbelievable kids and a man I don't deserve. Why are you any less deserving of happiness, Grace? Why should you have to be alone because a man you love won't get his big head out of his ass?"

I have no answer for that.

Presley continues, "I'll tell you this, if you let an opportunity pass you by, I'll kick your skinny butt."

I am mid drink at her last comment, which is so absurd coming from her that water shoots out my nose when I laugh. "Presley!"

"I'm serious!" Presley hands me a napkin as we both giggle. "You're one of my best friends, and I love you far too much to see you give up a chance. So, go date Cooper. Who knows, maybe y'all will hit it off. What if he's the man you're meant to be with?"

I look into her green eyes that gleam with love and understanding. "What if things go bad?"

She shrugs. "Well, there's no way you're going to find out if you don't try, is there?"

My eyes travel over to where Cooper is dancing with his mama. His smile is bright as he effortlessly spins her around the dance floor. I remember the feel of his strong arms under my hands, and I think about what Presley said. What if he is the guy? What if I spent all that time waiting for Trent to mature, only to miss out on a man right in front of me?

Cooper's gaze shifts to mine, and I duck my head quickly. Of course, I'd be caught—again.

I slowly lift my eyes toward my best friend, avoiding Cooper at all cost, and Presley stands there biting her lip. "Don't say a word."

She raises her hands. "My lips are sealed," she says, smiling at me.

"I'll think about it. Maybe," I relent, even though I know I shouldn't. The last thing I need right now is another man. Then add in that he's Cooper Townsend, and it makes it the dumbest idea I've ever heard.

"All right," Presley grins. "Now, let's dance!"

The music shifts to a line dance I know all too well. She grabs my hand and we rush out.

I spend the rest of the night smiling and enjoying my best friend's joy, because if anyone does deserve this day—it's her.

"GRACE!" MY MOTHER YELLS INTO the receiver. "Is that you, sugar?"

Mama went away on her girls' trip with Mrs. Kannan, Mrs. Townsend, and Mrs. Hennington. Once a year, they take a vacation, drink God only knows what, and pretend they're still young. It's adorable and a little ridiculous when they get back to show us pictures. The image of my mother getting a lap dance in New Orleans will be forever seared in my brain.

"Yes, Mama. I'm here, there's no need to yell. I'm not deaf—yet."

"Well, we're all the way down here in Mexico."

No matter how many times I tell her, she doesn't grasp that I can hear her no matter how far away she is.

"The phone works just fine in Mexico. Are you havin' fun?" I ask as I flop onto my couch.

"Of course we are!" She scoffs, as if I should know better by now. "The girls and I are going on some kind of parachute sailing tomorrow. Macie said it was either that or snorkeling. You know how I feel about gettin' my hair wet, so I said fine to the para-thingy."

I stifle a laugh. She's nuts. They all are, but for her to be more worried about her hair than being suspended in the air by a parachute *over* the water . . . I can't with her. "Well, Mama, it sounds like that was the sensible choice."

"I'm sure we'll have fun. You know us, we find trouble no matter where we go." Oh, I know that. "Since your father is off in his la-la land . . . I need a favor."

"Sure, what do you need?"

My mother has called once a day with her need for favors. Since school let out a week ago and I'm on summer break, she's turned her honey-do list over to me. I'm not sure who enjoys these trips more, her or Daddy. He takes the week she's gone and locks himself in his hunting cabin. No cell phone, no television, and no people. He calls it his slice of heaven.

I think next year I'm going with him.

"I need you to go to Vivienne's and grab somethin' from Cooper. I meant to take it when I was there before we left, but it slipped my mind."

My stomach drops. "It can't wait?"

"No, Grace." She huffs. "It can't wait. There's no reason you wouldn't want to help your mama, is there?"

I'm surprised it took this long for her to meddle. I should be happy they didn't rope me into making a thousand cupcakes. "And does Cooper know I'm comin' over to pick up this item you need?" I twirl my hair as I wait for her to produce her crappy lie.

That's the thing that gets me every time, the old women—my mother included—in this town who feel it's their civic duty to meddle in everything, and they aren't even good liars. They come up with the craziest things, and half of them don't make sense. Yet, no matter how ridiculous the plans are, the people in this town go along with them. It's insane. We're all freaking nuts.

"I'm not sure, sugar."

"Mama," I warn.

"Now, Grace. I'm asking for your help. If you're too busy, then I'll have to send smoke signals to your daddy, who will be all too unhappy to be interrupted." My head falls back as I groan internally. "If you'd like me to do that, I will, and then you can deal with him."

If guilt trips were an Olympic sport, my mother would have a gold medal. "Fine," I grumble. "I'll go over there and see Cooper to get this very important item that you still haven't mentioned what it even is."

"You're so good to me." Her voice is back to chipper. "I have to go, they're starting the karaoke party! Adios!" She disconnects before I can say a word.

It's been two weeks since Presley's wedding, and I've done a pretty damn good job of avoiding both Cooper and Trent, which in this town is a pretty difficult task. Cooper hasn't reached out at all since that day, not that I expected him to, but Trent hasn't been quiet. Then, as if my thoughts summon him, my phone beeps with a new message from the commitment phobe himself.

> *Trent: I get it. You're done, but we were friends. You were my best friend. I know you don't want to talk now, and I'll respect that. Just know if you ever need me . . . I'm here. I'll always be here.*

Why does he do this to me? I want to scream and cry and throw something, but then, in the next breath, I want to run to him. This isn't easy for me. It's especially not when he says things like that. It would be a lie to say I don't miss him. I do. I may be done waiting around for him, but I'll always love him. He's embedded in my heart and soul. The only problem is his love doesn't heal, it's toxic, and I have to eradicate it before it kills me.

I grab my keys and head over to the Townsend's. If I'm lucky, Cooper won't be there, and I can get the mystery item and be gone without seeing him.

When I pull in to the drive, I realize that, of course, luck isn't on my side. Luck is never on my side, and this time, she seems to be sitting back and laughing at me.

Cooper isn't just home. He's on the porch, shirtless, fixing the chain on the porch swing.

Great.

I exit the car, and he turns to look at me as a lazy smile forms on his lips. "Grace." Cooper's warm voice washes over me.

"Coop." I grin back as my gaze rakes over his bare chest, and I try not to drool. Dear Lord, he's even better than I imagined without a shirt. The sun, which is setting behind me, is shining over every ridge and dip on his glorious body. The man is sinful.

"Mama sent me over for something that your mama has?"

He chuckles. "You believe that load of crap?"

I look down as I shake my head. "Nope, but I knew they'd call and make sure I did it. Figure it's best to play it safe."

He steps off the ladder and moves toward me. "Don't you think we're a little old to be pushed into seeing each other?"

"I don't see you comin' around to see me," I retort.

"I thought it was your move."

"I thought you knew that wasn't going to happen."

Cooper keeps moving toward me as I stand still. I don't know what I'm supposed to say to him. I feel out of sorts and slightly uncomfortable. "I hoped." His voice is low and gravelly as he speaks.

My eyes stay connected to his. "You did?"

He pushes a piece of hair out of my eyes. "Wasn't I clear?"

I guess he was . . . he and Presley basically spelled it out. Still, I'm not used to forward. I've had over twenty years of hidden meanings and half-truths with Trent. I don't really know if my compass is pointing in the wrong direction or if I'm on the right track with men. Men say women are confusing, but I have news for them—they're no freaking better.

"All I know is that we danced. It was a lovely dance, but we had no plans after that."

His big hand wraps around my wrist. "I think we've been dancing around this for a while now."

"When did you get so bold?" I ask, trying to control the shake in my voice.

"When you became single."

That's a good answer. "Oh."

"Oh?"

I'm not sure what he expects me to say. "This is a little weird for me, Coop. I've known you forever. I remember all the embarrassing things you went through, including when you liked *NSYNC." I lift a brow, daring him to refute me. "I'm trying to wrap my head around you getting all broody male on me."

He tugs my arm and grins. "I've always been this way. You were just looking at another man. I've been biding my time."

Huh. Who would've known? Not me. I clearly missed all the signs.

"And," Cooper tacks on, "I never liked *NSYNC."

"Sure, buddy. Whatever you need to tell yourself."

A throaty chuckle escapes him. "There's a lot we know about each other, and even more that neither of us has a clue about. All I'm asking for is a chance to talk, to get to know you. There are a lot of subjects I'd like to touch on."

"I bet." When his eyes drift to my chest, it's clear that the subjects he wants to touch on aren't fishing or sports, but I let that go. I don't need to think about him touching me. "Go put a shirt on," I shake my head.

"Am I making you uncomfortable?" Cooper gleams.

"*Nooo.*"

Yes.

"Uh-huh." His eyes brighten and he gestures to the house. "Come on inside. I'll get the mystery package our mothers concocted to get us together."

I nod and thank God that Cooper let me out of this very uncomfortable exchange. Yet, it isn't so much that I feel awkward. It's that these are unfamiliar waters. Cooper is right. I don't know what he's like as an adult.

After Presley left for college I still saw him, but we never spent any time together. When we did see each other, our conversations were casual. I don't know why he stayed in Bell Buckle or why he stopped working on cars or at the rodeo. I have no clue if he still likes rock music or if he's more of a country guy now. Clearly, he doesn't like boy bands anymore, but the truth is . . . I know nothing about the man that Cooper has become.

The reality that Cooper is a mystery comes crashing around me. From one step to the next, I realize I have never really looked at Cooper as if he were an adult. My eyes flick to the sculpted flex of muscles as he walks and then to the two dimples on the small of his back. A flush crawls up my neck, and I focus on the ground in front of me instead of the man. Cooper is all grown up.

We get inside and head to the kitchen. "Here." He extends the envelope.

"*This* is what she needed me to get right away?"

"I'm thinkin' it was more about who would hand it to you," he suggests. "And I'm not a man that lets opportunities like this slip away." Cooper moves closer.

Oh shit. I'm not ready for this. I don't know how I feel about anything. It's been two weeks, well, technically three weeks since I ended things with Trent, but still! I know deep down in my heart that while I may think Cooper is hot, I don't feel like that for him, at least not right this moment. My heart is still very deeply attached to Trent. I may wish I could've severed that tie completely when I decided to end things with him, but that was impossible. It's been years that my heart has been forging that bond. It's strong and requires time to loosen its resolve.

It wouldn't be fair to Cooper—or me.

"Cooper," I warn. "Listen, I appreciate that you're being very . . . forthright in your advances. I really do. It's nice being around a man who knows what he wants for once, but I have to be honest with you."

He takes another step closer as I step back. "I know what the next words out of your mouth are gonna be."

"I doubt that."

"You're going to say that you're still in love with Trent. That it's too soon and that you're not ready for anything new. Am I close?"

Yeah, you could say that. I nod.

"I know all this. I know you're scared—"

"Hey, now! I didn't say I was scared."

He smirks. "You don't have to say it."

He has some nerve. I'm not scared. I'm doing the right thing. It isn't fair to string someone along, I *know* all about that. Plus, there are a lot of moving pieces in this possibility. It would be foolish to think people wouldn't get hurt if things went bad. Not to mention I have friendships I could lose, just like he does.

So, now, being sensible is being scared?

I don't think so.

"You know what?" I huff. "I'm doing the right thing here. You like me, or at least I think you do. And I've been the person on the receiving end of lovin' someone and not having that feeling reciprocated. I'm not scared. You don't scare me, Cooper Townsend." I jab my finger in his chest as the words tumble out. "What scares me is the idea of hurtin' you. Makin' you think there's a chance when my heart is so badly broken I don't even know if I can ever care about another man again. I'm being kind. I'm being a friend. I'm doin' the right thing for both of us."

"I'm not lookin' for a friend," Cooper grips my arms. "I'm not askin' for fair or right. I'm askin' for a chance to show you that your heart isn't broken. I know you loved Trent. I'm not deluding myself by thinking otherwise." I shake my head as his eyes hold mine captive. "I know it's still tearing you apart inside, but you can let him go. You deserve more than what he gave you. We have somethin' between us. I know you feel it."

"It doesn't mean we need to act on it, Coop." His grip loosens, and my traitorous hand moves to his chest. "The truth is that I don't know what I feel. I've been upside down for so long that I don't know what right side up is. Can you understand that?"

I wait for my words to settle in, because the last thing I want to do is hurt a friend. Life is short, and the people around you are everything. Cooper has been a part of my extended family for as long as I can remember. I don't know if what I feel for him is more than loving him like I always have, and until I figure it out, I can't move forward.

"I'm only askin' for a date. One that you promised to think about. One that you owe me for writing that crap about me on the wall."

I sigh and shake my head.

If there's one thing I know about the men around here, it's that they don't quit. Hell, I'm not even sure it was my mama who orchestrated this. For all I know, it was Cooper. The war inside me battles as I try to decide what to do. Do I go out with him? Do I hold my ground and say no?

Then I wonder, why should I say no? Cooper is single, attractive, and Presley has already given me her blessing. Because of Trent? If I'm as done as I say I am, why do I let that man still dictate my happiness?

"One date?" I ask, hesitantly.

"One date."

"As friends?"

His free arm hooks around my back. "Good friends."

Oh, Jesus. Okay, one date as friends, which is what I need this to be, and then we can move past this ludicrous idea.

"And then you'll be patient and give me some time?" I press, needing confirmation.

"And then you'll want another." Cooper's eyes gleam with victory.

"Don't get yourself too excited about this, Coop. I'm agreeing to a *friend's* night out."

His lips move closer to mine, and my heart races. He can't kiss me. No way am I ready for that.

"Relax, I'm not going to kiss you," he reassures me. His lips touch the side of my cheek, and I release a deep breath. "But if you call it a friend's night out then I'm going to assume you're refusing to call it a date because we agreed to *one* and you're saving it."

I rear back and yank my hand free. "Fine, a date it is. That way, we can get this over with, and you can see you don't really like me."

"Or you can see there's possibility here."

He's freaking relentless.

"We'll see."

Needing to make my exit before he convinces me of some other crazy idea, I push him back, grab the envelope, and walk out. Cooper being who he is doesn't let me leave in grand fashion.

"Oh, Grace?"

I turn to look at him.

"I'm workin' the next two weekends, so I'll see you in three weeks."

"All right."

"No backin' out, because I won't give up that easily."

Unsure of what to say, I shake my head. I think this is going to be a disaster. My mind spins with all the things that could go bad, and there's a hefty list. But as I look at Cooper, I see how excited he is. So maybe I'm wrong. Maybe there's a possibility of something between us, and I really was wasting my time with Trent.

Maybe Cooper has been in front of me, but I was too blind to see him.

There's no way to know unless we try.

Cooper's grin grows as if he can read my mind.

"I'll see you soon for that date."

He nods, and I walk out the door, hoping I didn't make the biggest mistake of my life.

chapter
THREE

I STAND AT THE COUNTER inside my family's general store. I thought I could run in and grab a few things for the weekend, but Mama is here with a basket of bones to pick. Thankfully, none of them are for me, but I still have to listen.

My best friend, Emily Young, arrived in town after her last music tour. She's visiting her parents, and instead of heading to the local bar, we've decided to swear off any chance of seeing Cooper or Trent. My house is the only safe place.

After scouring my kitchen for supplies, I realized I was all out of junk food, and that won't do. I need all the saturated fat and calories I can get to deal with my life.

However, Mama doesn't appear to be running out of steam regarding her issues with the clan of meddling women in our town.

"Are you even listenin'?" she asks as I watch the clock ticking.

"I heard you. Mrs. Hennington didn't call you back, and Mrs. Townsend picked an awful hymn for church on Sunday."

"Good." She sighs.

I start making a plan of the fastest way to get what I need and get home within fifteen minutes as my mother prattles on about Mrs. Kannan cheating during their last game of cards. I don't know why Mama's surprised by this, she does it every week. "And then, she had the nerve to tell me that I cheated at Bingo. How do you even claim such blasphemy?"

"I don't know, Ma." I try to move away to get what I came for, but she doesn't let up.

"You know, I have half a mind to go over there and demand she gives us our money back." She nods once in agreement with herself. "And after that, I'll let Vivienne know that her singin' needs to be louder when we're rehearsing. The Lord can't understand her mumblin'.'"

Oh, yeah, that'll work out great.

"I don't think that's such a good idea. Y'all have been friends a long time, but tellin' Mrs. Townsend her singin' isn't good enough for the Lord isn't going to go over well. Now, what really has you upset?"

My mother loves those women more than she loves my father or me. There's no way she's going in there with guns blazing over a few bucks. Mrs. Kannan cheats, Mrs. Hennington bakes, Mrs. Townsend runs the music, and Mama is the trip planner. All of them have their place and each is very passionate about what they do.

She sits back in her chair and huffs.

"Mama?" I push her.

"Your father has lost his damn mind!" She stands and throws her hands in the air. "I've had it with that man. If I didn't think he'd starve to death, I would've thrown his sorry behind out of my house a long time ago." Daddy is always on her list, but he must've really upset her this time. "He told me that if I wanted to lose weight, I should stop eatin' pie. Can you believe that? Maybe he'd look like he did when I married him if he stopped eatin' everything in my house."

Maybe my father has become suicidal, because no man should ever say something like that. Especially, when my father could be Santa's less gray haired brother. His belly is filled with more jelly than a donut.

"I'm sure he didn't mean it like that."

"Always takin' his side." Her eyes narrow on me. "By the way, what is this I hear about you and Cooper? There's a rumor goin' around that you're going out with him soon?"

That's my cue to get the hell out of here. "Emily should be at the house in a few. I need to get back, we'll talk more later."

"Avoidin' it now doesn't mean it won't come up later!" she yells as I move to the back of the store.

"Okay," I reply and get to work putting different things in my basket. I need to be out of here in two minutes if I want a chance of not having to talk about this.

Chips.

Cookies.

Beef Jerky.

M&M's.

Reese's Peanut Butter Cups.

A jar of Nutella.

I know I'm missing a lot more. I plan for her to have to roll me to bed. I have a lot of feelings that need to be eaten, but when I reach the spot where my go-to snack is usually stocked, I find bags of dried fruit. Grimacing as I put the offensively healthy food back on the shelf, I turn and yell over my shoulder. "Ma! Where are the—"

"You lookin' for these?" A deep voice vibrates from behind me as my favorite candy appears before my eyes.

The hair on the back of my neck raises and my pulse quickens. I haven't seen him in weeks. I've done well at avoiding him, and four words was all it took for my body to respond.

"Thanks." I take the bag of black licorice from him, keeping my back turned. "I couldn't find them."

"Emily's in town, I saw her car and figured what you might

be up to," he explains.

"Yeah?" I don't want to look at him. I don't need to because I see him perfectly in my head. My unwillingness to face Trent doesn't stop him from moving closer to me, and I know that if I lean back a little . . . just a smidge, I would feel all of him. But we're done, and that would be irresponsible. My hand clutches the wooden shelf in front of me, and I tighten my grip. I need to hold on to something that isn't Trent.

"I know you can't be without your licorice." His lips graze my ear when he speaks, and my grip tightens.

"I'm surprised you remember."

Trent laughs and the sound travels through me. "I know everything about you, sweetheart."

My eyes close and I force my knees not to give out. I've missed him. I hate that I've missed him.

He makes me weak.

He makes me stupid.

He makes me love him.

I turn slowly to see Trent looking at me with an unreadable expression. "You know my favorite candy; I'm not sure that counts as everything."

Trent's hand rises as he pushes the hair off my forehead before moving to cup my cheek. "I know much more than that, Gracie."

"Like what?" Part of me wants to challenge him because he doesn't know me. Or if he does, he doesn't care about me.

"I know that you love me."

"Wrong. Try again."

He gives me that crooked grin I love so much. It's a little cocky and a lot of sexy. It makes me do dumb things like think about his lips on mine, which would be really bad.

"I know that you hate the word marshmallow," Trent says, making me shudder. I really hate that word. "I know that you do *that* each time someone says it. I know you talk in your sleep, you hate spiders, and you write in your journal but pretend you don't. I know you claim you didn't keep your Miss Bedford County tiara and yet it's on the top shelf of your closet. I know that you wear it when you feel like you've eaten too much food, but I don't know why. One day you'll tell me, though."

Asshole.

"I know that when you're tired or feel like punching me in the face you bite your lip." His thumb pulls on my bottom lip. "I know when you're nervous, you do this." He brings my hand between us. "You dig your thumb nail into your palm."

I tear my hand away and try not to let his touch affect me. My skin burns where we had contact, and I crave more. "You forgot the part about where I want to be someone's world."

His eyes soften, and his hand moves down to hold my neck. I feel his thumb on my jaw, the way the callous rubs back and forth causes the pit in my stomach to grow. His body closes in, but he doesn't look away. "You forgot the part where you already are."

I shake my head, trying to make this stop. "Not yours."

Tears burn in the backs of my eyes. This is what I can't do anymore. He does this, comes to me and makes me think I'm crazy and it's all in my head. He touches me as if he's the only person that should. Trent gives me a sliver of hope that I'm what he wants. I hate him for it.

"You know that isn't true," he whispers, moving closer to me.

He's going to kiss me, and I'm going to love every damn second. But when he walks away, I know exactly what will happen.

He'll break my heart.

"Don't do this," I beg. It's my last effort to hold strong.

"I've missed you, Gracie."

"You only miss me because you don't have me," I somehow manage to say.

He lets out a low chuckle before his mouth brushes against mine. "I miss you because I hate bein' away from you."

I lock my body so that I don't push forward and kiss him, which is exactly what I want to do.

"I wouldn't have left if you didn't push me."

Trent pulls back a little and his eyes stay glued on mine. "Give me another chance, darlin'. You need me as much as I need you. Stop pushin' me away and come back where you belong."

That does it. Something inside me snaps. I turn my head quickly, and his mouth touches my cheek. I shove him off me and try to get a hold of my breathing. When I finally feel in control, I stand strong.

He doesn't see what he's done to me, and him thinking I need him is half the problem. I need a fresh start. Someone who doesn't think they can play games with my heart. Cooper may not be that guy, but he could be. He doesn't want to prove a point, he genuinely likes me—or so he says.

And I'm not pushing Trent away. He's the one who let me walk.

I owe it to myself not to fall backward. It's time to move forward. And Trent Hennington is now in my rearview mirror—where he belongs.

"I don't need you. I don't need this. I'm movin' on, and you should, too. You had all the time in the world to make me yours. You pushed me away like you always do, and givin' you another chance won't change who you are, Trent. It won't make this work, because if we haven't been able to fix it by now, we never will."

Trent's eyes fill with hurt and then it shifts to resolve. "You love me. I see it. I feel it."

"I do love you. But I love myself more. I'll see you around."

"DO YOU EVEN REMEMBER WHY you love him?" Emily asks

from the couch.

She's been living in Nashville the last three years, and I miss her terribly. I'm happy for her, she's doing amazing things and is a fantastic singer. After Presley left Bell Buckle, Emily and I grew very close. Now, she's so busy with the country music scene, I barely ever see her. Emily has been there through it all, though.

She knows the answers to her question, but I know what she wants me to do.

"Because he's a good guy. I know it's easy to forget with all the crap over the years, but it's more about how he made me feel when things were good. And then today!"

"Today?"

I told her a little about the store, but I left some parts out.

"Yes, he knows me, Em. He knows all the stupid little things, and then he said all this stuff . . ."

"Like what? What does he know that makes him so hard for you to walk away from?"

"He knows I love black licorice. He knows I hate funny words. He knows my heart!" I sound desperate, even to my own ears.

"I think I just threw up in my mouth. Who the hell likes black licorice?"

I lift my head and stare at her. "You know I eat a bag a week!"

"I never knew you liked that. It's gross. No one likes black licorice. It's the Halloween candy Mr. Meyer gave out and we all threw away."

I groan and grab the bag, popping my favorite candy in my mouth. "How have you known me since I was seven and not know my favorite candy?"

She shrugs. "I might have tried to block it out because . . . eww?"

"You're ridiculous."

"And you like nasty candy!"

"Not the point." I trade the bag of candy for my glass of

wine. "My point is that Trent knows these things. He isn't all bad. There was a lot of good. I miss the good. He's the only man I've ever seen by my side."

She grabs her beer and shakes her head. "Look, I know there's always one guy that makes us stupid. Hell, I think if Bobby ever came back to town, I'd marry him because I'm that dumb, but Trent has hurt you, Grace. A lot. He's also failed you in ways that left you broken."

The need to defend him is still strong. "And I've hurt him!"

She slowly places the bottle on the table. "How? By makin' him be an adult?"

Emily is always on my side, and if I'm honest, I did things to hurt him. I would ignore him, push him, fight with him for no reason because he wouldn't give in. More than that, I let him treat me the way he has.

"I'm just saying he wasn't the only one doing the hurtin'. Plus, he does this stuff because I let him for so long."

"Okay, sure, but tell me why it's worth all the hurt? Why the hell do you let yourself go back? Because I've seen the tears. I know that you love him, and I know he loves you, even if his foolish pride won't let himself say it. But why? *Why* do you love him?"

This isn't the first time Emily has tried to get me to see the writing on the wall. It isn't the first time that I actually have. I'm not sure how to explain what it is about him. It's deep inside me.

"Because when he allows himself to let me in, it's beautiful. He has the greatest capacity for love. He does the most selfless gestures. Trent would run through a burning building to save someone."

"I know that. All the Hennington boys are good deep down, but tell me why you think you keep holdin' on," she pushes.

I take a moment to let all the good things that I've shoved so deep, rise to the top. The things I try so hard to forget because they make it easier to overlook the bad. Over the course of almost twenty years, there have been some fantastic moments with him.

"When I was fourteen and didn't have a date to the dance, remember when Johnnie stood me up?" Emily nods. "Trent didn't hesitate to run upstairs and put on his suit. His mama didn't have to urge him. He went because he saw I was cryin'. There was the time that my horse died, and he stayed in that stall with me for twelve hours as I cried. He never complained once, he held me in his arms as I fell asleep. The first time we made love, he made sure I was comfortable, safe, and took care of me." I shift in my seat and rest my head back. "I know it sounds so dumb, but I remember how he held my eyes as we connected. We were just barely adults, but it felt like something else completely."

"And recently?"

I close my eyes and try to hold back the tears. "When my sister died, do you know that Trent stayed with me for two weeks? He took time off, drove me out to Baileyton, helped with the arrangements, he was by my side every step. I didn't have to worry, because he was there."

"I remember." Emily's eyes grow sad. "I know he held you together."

"He did more than that. He took care of everything. Not once did he complain when I was a mess. Not one single word was said that wasn't to support me," a tear falls. "I lost my world that day, and Trent made it a little easier. He held my hand, kissed my tears away, he gave me everything I needed, and I never had to ask. He knows me inside and out."

It feels like a long time ago, but it wasn't. Five years ago, my sister was taken from us. She could've had it all. She should've, but she married a man who I begged her to stay away from. William spoke with his fists, and he talked a lot. He broke the beautiful girl I played dolls with and turned her into a shell of a woman.

Scarlett was almost defiant when it came to him, though.

She saw only what she wanted and ran off as fast as she could. We begged her to listen. Daddy hated William the minute he laid eyes on him. Said he could see the anger in his eyes and that, one day, it would boil over. Scarlett thought she could save him. In the end, he killed her.

"Do you know that Trent was the one who found William?" I ask.

"I do." She grabs my hand and holds it tight. "I remember that even though he wasn't the sheriff there, he got in touch with his friends and made sure they found him."

"He promised me that he'd find a way to fix it if he could. He was so sure. I fell so deeply in love with him that week."

"Scarlett chose Bill. She loved a man who was all wrong for her. Maybe—"

My blood pressure spikes as my eyes snap to hers. "Trent has never raised a hand to me!"

"I know! I never said that, honey. Calm down. I'm saying that while Trent has never physically hurt you, he hasn't been gentle with your heart."

I take a calming breath and slow my heart rate. I know what she's trying to say, but comparing Trent to Bill isn't even close to okay. He may have hurt me but never in that way. He would rather die than raise a hand to me.

"I'm sorry I freaked out," I say to Emily.

"I didn't mean for it to come out like that. I was just sayin' that sometimes our hearts lie to us about what's really goin' on. I think we want to see the good in everyone, and it can cloud our judgment."

"I don't know what changed inside him, but he became so angry at everything. The fun, sweet, sexy man I knew disappeared. The more I tried to push him to talk to me, the more he pushed me away. The more space I gave him, the more he took until it felt like there were oceans between us."

I would break things off only to find him on my porch, begging me to give him another chance. I would give in. I know the real Trent Hennington. The guy who sits on the dirty ground while his girlfriend cries. The man who drives four and a half hours to identify your sister's body and then creates a manhunt for the husband who beat her to death. He stands by your side when you need him. He's tender, strong, sweet, broody, and so much more.

He was just never fully mine.

We'd have good runs where he would be the guy I love. We'd laugh, watch television, ride horses, and make love for hours. Then something would shift when we got too comfortable again. His entire attitude would eclipse the sun that was in his eyes and leave only darkness. I could almost watch the change happen.

No matter what I gave him, it wasn't enough to pull him out.

I swipe the tears that fall as I remember the bad times. "I wish I could save him. I wish I was enough for him to want to be saved."

Emily takes a long sip of her drink. "I think Trent is in a lot of pain. I don't know why. I don't even think his brothers know, but until that man comes to some kind of epiphany, he's only going to hurt you, honey. Who knows, maybe you goin' out with Cooper Townsend will be the thing that drives him to wake the hell up."

Which brings me back to my emergency text that I needed Emily to come here for a girl's night in. Angie and Presley are great, but they're all family . . . to everyone. Presley is obviously going to be on her brother's side, well, I'm not sure which brother now. Angie is going to side with Trent because that's the side Wyatt will land on. I'm like the lone wolf here. I need a pack. I need Emily and her advice in my life more than ever.

"I should cancel that date. It isn't fair," I say, thinking about Cooper.

"Hell no you shouldn't! Look, Cooper knows damn well how

you feel about Trent. Don't be fooled, Grace. There isn't a living person in this town that doesn't. If he wants to test the waters, I say give it a chance."

"It's just dumb! I am clearly still all messed up inside."

Her voice rings of disbelief. "I think you're makin' up any excuse you can."

"And what about when Trent finds out?" I push.

Emily's grin spreads across her face. "Well, won't that be too bad for him."

He's going to lose his mind. Full-on nuclear attack will ensue.

"I don't know . . . I feel like it's a slap in his face."

Emily rolls her eyes. "We come from a small ass town. There aren't many men floatin' around Bell Buckle. He has to expect this, and if he doesn't, that sucks for him. As for your other lame bullshit about hurting Cooper? He's a grown ass man and fully capable of decidin' for himself if he can handle it. A very fine grown man, I might add. I guess it's really a matter of if you're willin' to take a chance."

"GRACE! YOUR PHONE IS RINGING!" Mama calls from the kitchen where my purse is sitting.

She dragged me shopping all over Tennessee for the day. Now, I'm carrying in all the bags and antiques she found. I don't mind doing things like this with my parents. They're both getting older and if my helping with shopping and driving makes her life a little easier, I'll do it.

Plus, I know the more I'm around, the happier she is. My mother having to bury her baby was the hardest thing she ever did. Scarlett's death broke my parents' hearts. I want to help mend them a little. Scarlett was who wanted to own the store in town. I think it's why my mother refuses to part with it.

"Grace!" she calls again.

"I'm bringing the bags in! Give me a second, Mama!"

"Trent was over by Macie's when I was visiting with her yesterday," she informs me as I set the last bag on the counter.

"Okay." I'm not sure where this is going. She practically shoved me over to the Townsend's house a few weeks ago. Now she wants to talk about the Henningtons?"

"I'm just sayin' is all. Trent was there."

"I'm not with Trent, so what he does is really none of my business."

I should've known that her not mentioning this wasn't going to last long. She removes a few things from the bags as she smiles. "I know, sugar. Cooper and his mama talked when we got back from Mexico. He said you two were going out."

And there it is. The reason there's no such thing as a secret in this town. Cooper told his mother, who told my mother, who told Macie, who probably told Trent, and we go down the list. I'm pretty sure the mayor two towns over knows.

"As friends," I inform her.

"I always thought Cooper grew into a fine man. I didn't know you two had feelings for each other."

My mother and her crew are brilliant at finding out what they want. They're able to twist you up so you say whatever you didn't realize you were holding in. I've learned, as have all the children of their group, to offer nothing. I don't know what Cooper and I are, which is technically nothing since I haven't even been on a date with him yet. The only thing I know is that if I do tell her, we'll be talking for eight hours and I'll never be ready for tomorrow.

"It's new, Mama."

She looks at me with a grin. "Vivienne said he's had thoughts about you for a while now but didn't want to cause a stir."

"Mrs. Townsend said that?" I ask.

"She sure did."

Great. My mother and Presley's mother are thick as thieves. If these two are scheming, I'm in so much trouble. It's not like I haven't fallen victim to my mother and her posse before. Plenty of times, Presley or I would get caught in the middle. I hoped to avoid it, but it seems clear the town busy bodies are going to be in the epicenter of my relationship. I need to move the topic along.

"Mama?" I draw her attention. "Why do you think Trent and I couldn't ever make it work?" Macie Hennington tells my mother everything. If there is something, maybe she will finally tell me. "Because I want to not love him anymore. I want to find a way through all this hurt and be happy. I'm not sayin' it's with Cooper." I look her in the eyes. "I thought I'd be settled by now. I'm tired of the back and forth with Trent. So, if you know something . . ." I pause and drop my gaze to the counter. "I'm beggin' you to tell me."

She walks around the counter and touches my cheek. "There are some things love can't fix. Trent is a good man. He has a good heart and a kind soul. You know I think nothing but the best of him."

I nod. "I do."

"I also think it's time you let him go, baby. I think you've loved him for a long time, and if he loves you like I think he does . . ."

"You think he loves me?" I ask with a twinge of unwelcome hope.

Her hand drops from my face and her fingers twine with mine. "I think you know he does, which is what keeps you hangin' on. I also think you know that he ain't ever going to change his ways. You have options, sugar. Choose wisely."

chapter FOUR

Trent

"THE FUCK SHE IS!" I scream at my brother.

"Relax!" Zach pushes against my chest as I try to get out the door. "You need to calm the hell down."

"Relax?" I huff and move his hand. "You're telling me to relax? I didn't see you calming the hell down when Presley returned to town. I don't think you'd be sayin' anything close to that if she were dating someone else!"

It's only been a few weeks, and she's already going out with another guy? I just saw her in the damn store, and she failed to mention it. Bullshit. It's total fucking bullshit.

On top of that, it's not just any guy. No, it has to be someone I grew up with. One of my friends. Unreal. And what the fuck is Cooper thinking? He knows my and Grace's history. He knows that Grace is mine. "I'm going to kick his fucking ass!"

This is how it's always been with us. We break up because I'm being an idiot and then I win her back. Never has she dated someone else. And neither have I. There is no way I'm going to stand idly by and allow this shit to happen.

"Trent." Zach tries again to break through my internal rage. "You can't expect her to wait around for you. You fucked this up too many times. We all tried to tell you to get your head out of your ass. She has a right to be happy."

"Are you tryin' to help me or piss me off?"

"Neither. I'm being honest." He grabs his beer and takes a swig. I hope he chokes on it.

"Take your honesty and get the hell out of my house."

I swear to Christ. My brothers may be my best friends, but they're also assholes. Whatever happened to brothers being on each other's sides? When did we decide that we were going to take the enemy's side? Mama didn't mess around when we were kids. She taught us to always have each other's backs. No one messed with the three of us. I always felt being a Hennington was the greatest gift I received, but right now, I want to strangle my brother.

"I'm fine right here." He leans back farther. "I think you need to hear it. You've been stringing that girl along since she was in high school."

We may not be together right now, but Grace is the only girl I've ever cared about. She's the only one who gets me. I can't lose her, and I sure as fuck can't watch her date another man—not in my town where they will be in my face every day.

I grunt and move around the room. "How can she date Cooper of all people? My fucking friend? They both had to know this would be way over the line."

"It's good to see you care so much."

"What the hell does that mean?"

"It means you had your chance, and you blew it. It means that you don't get a say in who she moves on with. If you wanted a say, you should've listened to her. I'm surprised that you're so surprised."

He's right. I know that, but it doesn't help me at all. I know she thinks it was all a game to me, but it never was. I loved her the minute I kissed her. Grace saw my demons and never looked away. She wanted me to let her in. She begged me to try, but I couldn't. I still can't. There's something deep inside me that doesn't allow me to go forward. I tried to move past it. I even thought about marrying her and raisin' a family, but each time I got close . . . I couldn't.

I talked to Wyatt about it once, and he understood. Back then, he never saw himself ever getting married. He was happy sleeping around and being free. Zach was the complete opposite. He met Presley when they were kids and swore he'd marry her. Hell, I don't think he ever loved another woman. Not even when he dated the skank, Felicia. It was always Presley.

I am stuck somewhere between the two of them. I don't want to get married, but I also don't want anyone other than Grace.

"What are you thinkin'?" Zach asks.

"About a hundred different things and none of them make sense."

My brother stands and runs his hand down his face. "I hate it for you, man. I really do. I think in all your layers of bullshit you love her."

"I know what I feel."

"Do you?" he says, pushing back. "Have you ever told her?"

"Mind your own business, Zach. I wasn't sitting at your house running my mouth when you were making stupid decisions."

"So, you admit it's stupid?" Zach grins.

I could kill him. "Don't you have something important to be doin'?"

Zach walks around, places his bottle down, and smirks. "I'm helping my brother out. What could be more important than that?"

"Could you let me know when you're actually going to start helping?"

Zach has always been my best friend. Wyatt is great, but he was a clown when we were kids, plus there's more of an age gap with us, but Zach and I are alike in a lot of ways. All of us are similar in how we view family. Mama and Pa didn't love one of us more than the other. They were always fair—for the most part. They also gave us what we needed and taught us to work hard for what we wanted. I wish I had listened when Mama told me to stop letting my fears rule my life.

"What are you going to do?" Zach asks.

"What choice do I have?"

He shakes his head. "This has always been your issue, Trent. You feel like the world owes you something, but let me tell you, it doesn't. You want Grace? You love her? You lay your bullshit aside and go get her. Man the fuck up. Stop actin' like you're the only man that's ever lost a woman. Hell, you're the only one left who hasn't learned that lesson. You seem to be the only idiot left standing."

"And that doesn't make me a dick for preventing her happiness? Because I swear you said something like that a few minutes ago." I throw his words back at him.

There's no winning in this. If I fight my way back into Grace's world, who's to say I won't hurt her again? Because that's what I do to her. It isn't fair, but God, I can't stop myself. I know I love her, but I won't allow myself to give in to it.

Zach rubs the back of his neck as he leans against the wall. "Maybe. I don't know. I thought you should know they're going out so you're not blindsided."

"Thanks."

"I've gotta get back to Presley and the boys, but let me know if you want Wyatt and me to come over for cards this weekend."

I nod. "I appreciate it. I'm on duty."

Zach's eyes narrow in suspicion, but he recovers quickly. "Be safe and don't do anything reckless."

I grin. "I don't have the slightest idea what you could mean."

"Right."

"Have a great weekend, Zach. Give my love to Pres." I hurry my brother out the door. I have something I need to do, and it can't wait.

"I will, and I'll see you in a few days for our fishing competition!"

"Thanks for the reminder," I say as I close the door. "Another thing I wish I could forget about."

chapter
FIVE

Grace

"GRACE, ARE YOU OUT OF that chocolate peanut butter ice cream?" Wyatt asks, seeming frustrated.

Mama said she needed to help Mrs. Kannan with something, which is code for she wants to play bridge with the girls, so here I am at the store. I don't mind. It's better than sitting at home and thinking of all the reasons I need to run away.

"I think we had a pint left!" I call out as I come around the counter. "I know Angie has been practically buying it in bulk."

He laughs. "I don't remember this when she was pregnant last time." His dark brown hair is longer than normal, and the circles under his eyes are dark. "She's awake all night, puking all day. This is the only thing she can keep down."

He must be going crazy. That man is a fixer if I've ever met one. He can't handle not being able to *do* something to make things better. There's no way he's taking this well.

"I clearly can't talk, but I assume each pregnancy is different."

Wyatt searches through the small freezer and groans. "If I don't come back with this, I worry she'll find my shotgun and use it. Besides the tiredness, I think she's become inhabited by Satan."

Angie has been a little hostile, but I chalked it up to her

adjusting to this new life. Marriage, another pregnancy, living in Bell Buckle again . . . I can't imagine it's been easy for her. Plus, knowing her, she's most likely still making Wyatt pay for being an asshole not too long ago.

"Let me check the back, orange definitely isn't her color."

"Glad to see you're worried about me, Grace!" he calls out as I walk back.

I lift my hand and keep moving. "I'm on her side."

As I open the door to the storage room, I almost fall over. What the hell? I organized this a week ago. Boxes are piled high, things thrown around, and nothing is where it should be. In all the years we've owned this store, I've never seen it like this. My mother is methodical about knowing where her inventory is.

I'll never find anything in here.

I climb over the boxes and make it to the deep freeze. Thankfully, there are a few pints of the ice cream Wyatt is looking for on a shelf so I don't have to dig through boxes.

"You okay?" he asks as I stumble out of the storage area and shove my hair back.

"I apparently have a lot of work to do back there."

He peaks his head around and nods. "You could always call Trent."

"I know you didn't just say that."

"I heard you have a pretty interesting night comin' up." Wyatt smiles, egging me on.

This town is frustrating as all hell. I've always loved it here—until now. "Wyatt Hennington, you better get back to your wife or you're going to be full of holes."

He laughs and hands me a ten dollar bill. "I'm just sayin' is all. My brother can't be too happy if he knows you're goin' out with Cooper."

"You can just say yourself right out that door." My accent

thickens as I say it. "Your brother had plenty of time to stake his claim. He chose not to."

Wyatt, Presley, and I were all in the same grade. The three of us were partners in crime, always into some kind of trouble. Before he met Angie, Wyatt had a thing for Presley, which was awkward at times, but it was always the three of us. Then Presley fell in love with Zach, and my heart became attached to Trent. Poor Wyatt was suddenly the odd man out. Plus, his heart's desire was tied to his brother.

I always felt bad for him, but he never once felt bad for himself. Too many nights he would listen to one of us cryin' over what one of his brothers did. He'd listen, tell us we were nuts, and make us laugh.

There's no one in the world who deserves happiness as much as he does, but if he brings up his brother again, I may have to beat his ass.

"I know you've finally had enough, not like I didn't tell you to put your foot down a million times, but you know he loves you."

"I *think* he does, which is the issue."

Wyatt leans against the counter. "Well, whatever you decide, it's going to be fun to watch."

"You're such a jerk." I toss a piece of paper at him.

"Is there any way you could stop by when you're done workin'? Angie hasn't really left the house much, and I think she's ready to kill me."

"Can you blame her?" I joke.

He shrugs. "I need to help Cooper on the farm, and I don't like the idea of her home all day by herself."

Wyatt isn't an alarmist, but after all they went through last year, I can't blame him. I would probably be cautious as well. "I was going to close early . . ." I offer. I wasn't planning that, especially after the mess I found in the back, but Wyatt doesn't usually ask for help.

"I really appreciate it."

He leaves, and I decide to lock the door and focus solely on my task. If people come in and out, it'll slow my progress.

After an hour, I feel a little better. I got a lot of the boxes sorted so when I come in tomorrow, I can really get it done. I worry, though, how it got this bad. This isn't the first thing that she's had problems keeping straight recently, and as much as I don't want to, I think I'm going to have to suggest she hire some help.

Instead of driving, which would be much faster, I leave my car parked and walk to Angie and Wyatt's. Summer time in Tennessee is my favorite. I walk down the street with the sun shining and a warm breeze blowing through the sky. There is something about the freedom I feel this time of year. Plus, I don't have to go to work.

"Well, hey there stranger," a voice I would know anywhere says.

I turn with excitement as Mrs. Hennington pulls up alongside me. "Hi, Mrs. Hennington!"

"Need a lift?"

"Oh, no thank you. I'm just walking over to see Angie," I explain. "Wyatt said she isn't feeling well."

Mrs. H. shakes her head, a warm smile tilting her lips. "I don't know what my grandbaby is tryin' to do to her, but she's havin' a heck of a time. I was headin' over to check on Zach since he's watchin' Cayden and Logan today."

Oh, dear God. Presley is a brave woman for leaving Zach home with teenage boys. I'd put money on him being hogtied somewhere while they dance around him.

"I think that's probably a good idea." I giggle.

"It amazes me sometimes that my sons manage to get themselves dressed."

Macie asks me how I'm doing, and if I've been to the store. We chat a little about what she and the girls have been up to. They've apparently decided to start planning another trip. As we talk more about my mother, I debate telling her my concerns, but I decide not to. If I tell her, she'll worry or tell Mama. It's probably something I should keep to myself.

We start talking about her trip, and I pray when I'm as old as those women that I have half as much fun.

"Well, honey, I'm going to get my behind over there and make sure my boys are all alive."

"It was great seein' you." I smile.

"Grace, honey, don't you stop comin' by. I know you and Trent couldn't work things out, but you're always welcome in my home. Hell," she lets out a soft laugh, "I'll throw him out so you can visit with me, okay?"

And this is why she's my favorite person in this town. Her and Rhett. No one says a mean word about them because they're simply the best. Rhett didn't start out with money, he worked hard and provided for his family, but he was always charitable. My parents couldn't afford the horses we had, but Rhett provided them free of charge. He made sure everyone in this town had what he could give.

They're good people.

"Thanks, Mrs. Hennington."

"I'm sure I shouldn't say this, but I'm an old woman, and keepin' my mouth shut has never been my strong suit," she warns. "I'm not askin' you to give him anything. Not a damn thing, but I know my boy, and he's missin' you, sugar. Just know that."

I squeeze my hands together and close my eyes. Each time I manage to get him out of my head, something happens, and he's right back.

Stupid boy.

"I'd be lyin' if I told you I didn't miss him. But I want what you and Mr. Hennington have. I want a marriage, family, and commitment. I know Trent has some weird issue about all of it, but I would've settled for the appearance of a life. I can't keep holding out hope for something I clearly won't get."

She nods. "I think you did exactly what you needed to do, honey. I wanted you to know that he's payin' his price. He's got a lot of debt to repay. Remember that."

"I will."

"Oh, and you make sure you enjoy your big date with Cooper, now."

She's amazing. Who tells the girl their son used to date how to make it hurt him more? Macie Hennington, that's who. Seriously, she's my idol.

We say goodbye and she heads off. It takes me ten minutes to walk to Angie's, and when I get there, Wyatt's truck isn't in the driveway.

"Hello?" I knock tentatively. Last thing I want to do is wake her. "Grace?"

"Hey!" I stand outside as I see her head pop off the couch.

"The door is open! Please! Come in!"

I step inside and head toward her. Her face is pale, the circles under her eyes are dark, and I can tell she's miserable. Still, I put on a reassuring smile and crouch in front of her. "Are you okay, honey?"

She grumbles. "I swear this baby hates me. Being pregnant in your late thirties sucks ass. This baby is determined to make my life hell."

"Is there somethin' I can do to help?"

Her eyes close as she rests her head. "I wish there was. Wyatt is a wreck. He refuses to leave me for long periods, but there's nothing anyone can do. The doctor said the baby is growing and healthy, I just need to hang in there."

"Wyatt came by the store, he said you weren't able to keep much down?"

Angie shakes her head a little and then covers her mouth. Poor thing.

"I should've been comin' by more. I'm sorry, Angie."

She rolls her eyes and scoots a little. "Stop. Between Wyatt and Mama, I'm never alone. Presley's been over a lot when Wyatt has to work late. It's really fine. I wish everyone would stop worrying so much. It's only seven more months."

Her brave front isn't fooling me. I can see how worn out she is. Angie has always been the life of the party. I hate seeing her like this. "But who's counting?" I pat her leg.

"Oh, I am so counting." We both laugh before her face turns serious. "So, did you decide to go out with Cooper?"

"Don't even act like you don't know." I grin as I gently slap her arm. "There's no way it hasn't been around town and back."

She gives an impish smile. "I wanted to hear your version, though."

I fill her in on all the details about how we're going out tomorrow and how it happened. Her lips turn up when I tell her about how Mrs. Townsend and my mother concocted some package to get us talking. I express my feelings about how I'm not sure if it's a good idea and how my heart is torn. Angie doesn't say a word. She lets me spill all the thoughts I've been struggling with.

"I love Trent. I'll always love him, but I can't be hurt anymore. If he were different . . ." I wipe a tear I didn't realize fell. "I can't be disappointed time and time again. I know that walkin' away and endin' things was what we needed to do. And then there's Cooper, and he's so sweet, but I don't dream about him. I don't spend my days talkin' myself out of callin' him."

"Grace," she grips my hand, stopping me from talking. "You've spent your whole life waiting for Trent. You've given him so much more time than he deserves. Remember when he forgot your birthday? Not just forgot it was that day, but forgot the whole thing?

Seriously, you can't tell me after the years you were together he didn't know that it was your damn birthday. He doesn't deserve you if he can't remember something like that."

Angie's right. It broke my heart a little to think the man I loved didn't remember my birthday. I sat there all day waiting for him to say something, but then he remembered the Tennessee game was on and told me he'd call me later.

I spent the rest of the day alone and angry.

It took three days for him to finally remember, and I'm pretty sure it was his mama who finally told him.

"Could you walk away from Wyatt?" I ask. "With as much as you love him, could you cast him off and then date another man?"

"I don't know," she says with honesty. "I walked away from Wyatt, but after we lost Faith, Wyatt changed. He wasn't the man I fell in love with, almost as if a piece of him died with her. We'd both been through hell, but no, there was no chance that I could have been with another man. Don't get me wrong, Trent is great. He was there for me after we lost Faith, but he hasn't been there for you."

My heart hurts as she says the final words. I'd never seen Wyatt like that. He was lost, but Trent hasn't lost a child, he's scared of commitment. He's been selfish and thought he could do what he wanted because I'd take it, and he was right. I did take it. I was so worried if I pushed him that he'd walk away.

I was weak.

I was stupid.

I'm done being both.

Angie shifts and immediately I can see the discomfort painted on her face.

"Do you have any saltines?"

Angie shrugs. "I have no idea. I'm not really on my feet much."

My eyes squint a little as I try to figure out why she would say that.

"I find that being vertical means I'm puking," she explains. "I'm basically bedridden until my pregnancy isn't high risk anymore. Which means when this tiny nugget finally decides to come into the world."

"Well, you have a lot of support," I remind her, making a note to stop by here more often. "I'm going to look for some crackers. Do you want to try it?"

"I've tried almost everything, but sure, we can try. Lord knows I need some food."

I head into the kitchen and start searching. There's very little of anything in the cupboards, but I luck out on the third try and find a sleeve of saltines hidden behind a box of instant oatmeal. While in here, I fill a glass of ice water.

"Found some!" I holler to her as I walk back to the living room, but I stop short. "Cooper? What are you doin' here?"

He releases a half laugh. "Hey, Grace. Wyatt asked me to stop by and check on Angie. He was worried you might've gotten lost in the stock room?" He says it as if it's a question.

"Right. Wyatt is real helpful like that." He knew I was going to be here, and he sent Cooper over. Why do I still live here? Why don't I make friends with people a few towns over? "Always tryin' to make sure everyone is taken care of."

Angie bursts out laughing. She clutches her stomach and giggles relentlessly. "He's such an asshole. God, I love that man."

"You got the asshole part right," I grumble.

"So? We're still on for our date tomorrow?" Cooper asks as he steps forward.

"Yeah, of course," I say awkwardly.

Angie grins and squeaks a little. "What? You guys are the best entertainment I've had in weeks."

My face falls. "Happy to be of service. I really should get goin'."

"Grace has a hot date tomorrow," Cooper says from behind me. I turn to face him with my eyes wide, but he grins and steps around me. He strides to Angie and parks his butt on the couch next to her.

"Oh, I know, I hear some handsome cowboy finally got her to agree."

"Yeah, I hear he's quite a catch." He's all cocky and funny and full of charm as he says it.

They start talking as if I'm not even here. I watch as he adjusts the blanket over her and makes sure she's okay. Then he grabs the packet of crackers and hands them to her. Cooper took time out of his day, covered in sweat and dirt to check on his friend's wife. He didn't have to be here, but he is.

The part of me that is hesitant about our date fades away. This is a good man. This is the kind of man that I want to be with. Someone who does selfless things because he wants to and isn't afraid to be vulnerable. He's where I should be focusing my thoughts, and that's what I'm going to start doing.

Moving on.

chapter SIX

OF ALL THE DAYS FOR my hair not to cooperate, it has to be today? Everything has gone wrong. I dropped my cell phone in the toilet this morning, the zipper on my dress came apart, and my washing machine decided it no longer wanted to work. I'm starting to think it's a sign that I should crawl back in bed and forego tonight. In three hours, Cooper Townsend will be picking me up for our date, and if the way today is going is any indication, it's going to be a mess.

I grab my now dried out phone, and text Angie so she can, once again, reassure me this is going to be okay.

> Me: *What if my outfit isn't cute enough?*

> Angie: *Stop it right now. I know what you're doing. You look amazing, and Cooper is going to think you're perfect.*

> Me: *Says you!*

> Angie: *Do you need me to drag my sick ass off the couch and come over?*

I'm being ridiculous. But this is the first real date I've had with someone other than Trent.

> *Me: No. I'm good. Minor freak out.*

She's right. The outfit is great, but now that the issue of what to wear is resolved, I'm left to face my second issue. Trent. I have no idea if he knows, and if he does, whether he's homicidal.

Not that I'd blame him. Cooper was a longtime friend of his.

My phone buzzes in my hand, and I swipe the screen expecting a smart remark from Angie.

> *Trent: So, big date tonight?*

I drop the phone and scream. Dammit. I haven't heard from the man in a week, and now I get a text? Ugh.

Do I answer?

No.

He doesn't need a reply. Besides, what the hell would I say? *Yes, I'm getting really hot to see your old friend who I kind of like, but I still love your unworthy ass.*

I stare at the phone as it lights up again. Slowly, I bend to grab it, as if it's a bomb ready to go off. The next text flashes across the screen.

> *Trent: Grace, I know you saw that. You have those stupid read receipts on your phone. Were you planning to tell me about your date?*

I grip the phone and groan.

> *Me: Yes and no.*

There. I responded.

I wait for the next text, and my anxiety starts to grow. When it gets to be too much, I begin to pace. I know him, and that will not have appeased him. Trent demands answers, and he can be extremely pushy. One-word responses aren't going to fly, but nothing comes.

When I realize I'm being ridiculous, I toss the phone on the couch and head into my room. I need to get ready.

The outfit sits on the bed, and I run through a mental list of everything I need to do. On the bedside table, sits my tiara. I wore it today to remind myself not to eat. Then my mind flashes to Trent and his ridiculous pop quiz.

I walk over, grab it, and put it back in the closet. I want nothing to make me think of him. He isn't part of my life anymore. Sure, he may be the one thing that keeps me awake at night, but I can't control my subconscious.

I can, however, control my mind right now. And there's no way I'm going to spend another minute thinking about him.

Nope. Not one.

Tonight is about my friend date slash date, date with Cooper. He's where my mind should be.

Not five minutes later, there's a knock on the door.

My stomach plummets because I know. I can feel it in my bones. He's here.

Shit! There goes my brilliant plan. Now what do I do?

Another knock.

My heart races with each step I take. I can try to avoid him, but it won't matter. He'll find a way to see me, and I'm better off getting it over with.

With my hand on the handle, I release a deep sigh and open it.

Sure enough, there Trent stands. His hair looks slicked from being pushed back with his hands, it's messy but styled, and his blue eyes are trained on me. The air shifts as he pushes forward, and I back step away from him. He's faster, and before I can stop him, his arm wraps around my waist and he pulls me against his chest.

"Trent!" I start to protest, but his mouth crashes on mine.

My hands push against his chest, but it's no use. He's so much stronger than I am. I should try to fight him off. I think about stopping him, but instead of doing that, my hands are dragging him closer. I tangle my fingers in his hair and hold him tight. His tongue slides across my lips, and I open to him. He kisses me hard, rough, and with raw power.

I know I should stop him. I know I'm supposed to be getting ready for a date with another man, and I promised myself not more than two hours ago that I would move on. I know I should slap him and break the kiss. I know all this, but I can't find the wherewithal to stop it. Everything we've ever shared floods back, and it's too much. All I know is he's touching me, and I never want this to end.

I've missed this. I've missed him. And I hate him for reminding me.

His hands roam my body until he's fisting my hair. He tugs my head back, exposing my neck as he licks and sucks against the tender skin. I moan as he nips beneath my ear.

"So beautiful," he mutters against my skin before his mouth is on mine again.

We kiss more as I lose myself to him, and I somehow end up on my back with him on top of me. I inhale, taking in the musk scent mixed with passion. It's everything I remember and more. Trent's calloused fingers cup my neck as he pulls back. His eyes blaze as I try to catch my breath.

Trent's voice is rough and filled with heat. "Yes and no? That's what you respond? I thought I'd come by and remind you which was the right answer."

His words bring me back to the reality that he doesn't belong here anymore. We're nothing, because he isn't good for me. He's the man that cuts me with the thorns that are wrapped around his heart. I don't need any more scars from him.

"You can't do this to me!" I slap his chest, and he leans up. "You selfish son of a bitch! You came to my house so you could what? Get in my head? Could you be any more of an asshole?" I start to yell and hit him again. "Get off me, you bastard!"

"Grace," he tries to say as he rises. I'm off the couch in an instant, but he's right behind me.

"No!" I spin and make contact again. "I hate you! I hate you so much! You have no idea how much this has eaten at me, and what do you do when you find out?"

"I came over and made sure you'd remember what we were. What you are to me. What we are to each other. You can fight me, Grace, you can keep trying to rid your heart of me, but I know you love me. I know it."

Liquid fills my vision as I try to hold myself together. "And what about you? Huh? What about how you feel? You're trying to mark your territory, but I deserve more than that!"

"It's not like that," Trent defends.

"That's exactly what this is! Instead of groveling like you should, you find a way to hurt me more." A tear forms, but I fight it back. I won't cry in front of him anymore. This, though, it hurts. It's as if he's a child who doesn't know how to use his words.

Trent moves closer, and I look at him, wishing things could be different. His hand brushes my hair back. "I never want to hurt you. Never, Grace. I see it now, I don't deserve you."

We both know that's true. I don't deserve to be treated this way, but there's something that keeps me going back.

But like my mother said, I have a choice.

"Neither of us deserves this, which is why it has to be over."

Trent touches his lips to mine, and I let him. The kiss isn't full of passion or lust. It's sweet and a little sad. "I won't do this to you anymore. I'll respect your wishes. I'll let you go. Even if it's the last thing I want to do. Promise me something, will you?"

I close my eyes to get my emotions under control. How can

him giving me what I want hurt so much? This is what I asked him to do, but I feel like I'm on the verge of shattering. Loving him has been my entire life, and I don't know how to give that up. "What?" I ask as I open my eyes.

"You'll be happy."

The tears that I fought back fall. "I'll try."

He nods and runs his hand down his face. "I'm sorry. I shouldn't have come over and done this to you today. But I hope Cooper makes you happy. If he's what you want, I won't stand in your way."

Every muscle in my body tenses. I want to scream that it's him I want. I like Cooper, but Trent is my soul. He's the man I dream of every night. He's the man I want to fall asleep next to and grow old with. But he can't do that.

I have to do what's best for me, which is to watch him walk away.

"Trent," I say as he passes through the threshold. I step closer because for better or worse, Trent is worthy of love. "Promise me that you'll find whatever it is you're searching for."

He wipes the tear from under my eye. "I already had it, but I wasn't smart enough to hold on to it."

I shake my head. "If I was what you wanted, it would've been so much easier for us. It wouldn't have been years of anguish."

He cups my face, touches his lips to mine, and sighs. "You're wrong, sweetheart. It was never about you not being what I wanted. It was me not knowing that what I had was everything I needed."

Another tear falls as his hands drop. "Trent."

"No." He shakes his head. "I see it now, Gracie. I see what I've done. I put the doubt in your eyes and the pain in your voice. I was selfish to come over here. It was because I couldn't handle the idea of you with him, or any man for that matter. But it isn't my choice anymore. My brother told me once I was gonna fuck up and lose you." Trent huffs and looks away. "I did that, and I need to do the right thing now."

My voice is locked as he speaks. Inside me, a war is raging, and I'm dying. There are two parts of me that can't find the common ground. Half of me wants to beg him to stay and love me. If he would try, I could help him. However, I've been there and done that already. I fought for years and ended up failing. There's no way to help a man who doesn't want to be saved. In the end, it was me who needed the lifeline. Seeing Trent's regret and hearing the pain in his words is almost too much.

He touches my cheek and rubs his thumb across my lips. "Be happy, Gracie."

I stand like a statue as he turns and walks away. Tears continue to fall and blur my vision as I watch Trent Hennington back out of my driveway and drive down the road. Minutes pass before I move.

He's really gone.

That really happened.

How the hell am I supposed to go on a date now?

AFTER I SPENT A GOOD twenty minutes crying out all my emotions and eating half a bag of licorice, I decided to pick myself up and get myself together. The past is in the past, which includes him. There isn't anything saying Cooper will be my future, but there isn't anything saying he won't, either.

Unfortunately, my composure is harder to keep than I thought, and I keep having to take deep breaths and little breaks to get myself under control.

It's crazy how nervous I am. It isn't like a blind date where I don't already know the man. Hell, I've even seen his penis. Granted, it was when we were sixteen and solely due to a dare, but still.

My cheeks heat in the mirror as I remember in detail what it looked like. Dammit, now I'm going to end up embarrassing myself.

My mind continues down this very stupid road, and I wonder what he kisses like. What if he's heavy on the tongue or our teeth clash? What if we are so incompatible that we sit in awkward silence? What if we like each other, and I somehow screw this up? These are all the reasons I thought this was a bad idea.

If I keep going at this rate, I'll never be able to make it through tonight. I decide to lock my errant thoughts away and focus on getting ready.

Once I'm content with how I look, I head out to the living room. He should be here in a few minutes. I grab my phone and see a message from Presley.

> Presley: Have fun tonight! I love you both and can't wait to hear how it went.

> Me: Love you! I'm sure we'll talk tomorrow.

Knock, knock, knock.

Shit. Here we go.

Please, God, don't let this be Trent.

I open the door to find Cooper standing there with a bouquet of flowers. His dark hair is spiked in the front going in no real style, his deep green eyes shimmer with warmth, and the way he fills out that tight gray T-shirt leaves very little to the imagination. Jesus. He gets better and better each time I see him.

"Hey." I smile.

Cooper's grin brightens. "These are for you." He hands me the white daisies. "You look beautiful."

"Thank you." I step back and swing my arm to the side so he can enter. I love that he brought me flowers. "This was really sweet. Let me go put them in water."

I head back to the kitchen to place them in a vase, and I hear Cooper. "Your place looks great. I haven't seen it since I carried the couch in."

I laugh. "It's been a long time, Coop. I've been living here for almost seven years."

"Been that long, huh?"

"It has." I come out with the flowers and place them on the table.

"Well, you've done a lot with the place."

My house is perfect for me. I like working on projects and this place was the ultimate one. I've redone each room to be exactly like I wanted. A lot of tender love and care went into making it a home.

"Thank you. Do you want a tour?" I ask.

"Definitely."

I take Cooper through each room, showing him all the work I've done. "This was the original flooring," I explain.

"I could've used your help when I was fixin' up the farmhouse."

I duck my head at the compliment before looking back up. "I think you did a great job."

He takes my hand and gives it a gentle squeeze. "I don't mind doing the work, it was all the other crap I hated." Cooper steps closer and pushes the hair out of my eyes with his other hand. "If I had help, though, maybe it wouldn't have been so bad."

"I'll make you a deal. If you remodel a house again, I'll be happy to dictate what you should do."

He moves in closer. My breathing is shallow as I feel the heat from his body so close to mine. Cooper's eyes are warm and open and his hand rubs against my arm, leaving goose bumps in its wake. I dig my nails into my palm, hoping I can get my heart to slow.

Before I can move, Cooper takes a step back and I can breathe again. "You all right?" he asks.

"Yup. Totally fine. I'm good. I mean, I'm great. Perfect even." I start to ramble and want to punch myself in the face.

Cooper's lips turn up into a small smile. "Glad to hear it."

I need to save myself from going down the rabbit hole of mortification.

"So, where are we goin'?"

It's very out of character that I didn't ask before, but I think I was trying not to think about it. I'm a planner, and I need to have everything in order. I don't like feeling the way I have been all afternoon—out of control and very unstable. However, this is probably normal for a new . . . whatever this is.

"I figured maybe we'd head out of town for dinner? Or we can head to the café?" he offers.

"No!" The one word comes out too quickly and too loudly, and I press my lips together in embarrassment. "I mean, I think goin' out of town is a good idea, don't you?"

Could I be any more awkward?

Cooper nods. "I agree. I figure you're probably feelin' anxious enough, maybe being away from pryin' eyes is a good thing."

"I couldn't agree more."

The less chances we have of running into everyone we know—the better. Especially any of the Hennington brothers. There's no doubt Trent has already told his brothers what happened here earlier, and knowing their little posse, it isn't good for me.

My next thought is: do I tell Cooper about Trent today? I don't really need to? This is only a first date. However, nothing stays quiet in this damn town, so if Trent tells anyone, Cooper will find out. But does Cooper have a right to be upset? We're not together. This is a friend date. That's it.

I'm so screwed.

"Ready?" Cooper asks, bringing my attention back to him.

"For our friend date," I remind him.

"For our date, date."

I grab my sweater and mumble under my breath. "Whatever you need to tell yourself, buddy."

He laughs from behind me and places his hand on my back. I lock the door and then Cooper helps me into his truck. This is the reason I don't wear dresses. All the boys have these giant ass trucks, which require them to hoist you into the cab. I swear it's a conscious thing.

"Okay," he says as he gets in the cab. "No backing out now."

I shake my head and smirk. "Drive, Cooper."

"If you insist."

We head down the road and make small talk. He tells me about the herd that he needs to move tomorrow and how the farm is doing. I talk a little about how excited I am for next year. After teaching third grade for the last eight years I'm finally moving to teaching fifth grade. I'm actually looking forward to school starting because this will be fun. I get to see some of the kids I had a few years ago and teach a new curriculum.

"It sounds like you're happy," he notes.

"I really am. I've been stuck in the same lesson plans and grading scale for a long time. I love the kids, that hasn't ever been the issue, but I don't know . . ." I trail off. "I'm bored a little. Getting to find a new way to teach something excites me."

He smiles and takes my hand. "I'm glad we're doin' this. I'm glad you agreed."

"I was somewhat coerced."

"Same difference." He shrugs. "Even if I get my ass kicked," Cooper adds under his breath.

"What does that mean?"

He cracks his neck but keeps his eyes on the road. "Just that I'm sure I'll have a visit to my house pretty soon. There's no way Trent is happy about me takin' you out."

I groan. "No. He isn't."

Cooper's eyes meet mine for a second. "How do you know that?"

Shit. Now, I've kind of screwed myself into telling him. I take a few seconds to think about what exactly I want to say. "Well, he stopped by my house today."

"And?" Cooper presses.

"And he said as much." I think back to what my mother always says: less is more. I'm going to stick to the facts and leave out the whole business of my letting him maul me on the couch.

"Oh," Cooper says as his head turns back to the road. And a moment later, a loud *bang* sounds. The truck shifts, but Cooper gets it over to the side of the road safely. "Dammit!" he bellows. "I'll be right back."

He exits the truck, and I try to think of how to take back the admission of Trent coming over. I hear Cooper cuss a few times as he drops the tailgate and then slams it closed again.

This can't be good.

I get out and head back toward him as he continues to mumble.

"Everything okay?" I ask.

"Blew a tire."

"Oh, well, just change it and we can be on our way."

He huffs. "Don't have a spare."

"Why?" I'm trying really hard to hold back my amusement at the situation.

"Because I had to haul hay today," Cooper explains, obviously expecting me to connect nonexistent dots.

"And that means no tire?"

His hands grip the side of the truck so hard his knuckles turn white, and he dips his head. "It means I was in a hurry to shower and get done. It means my dumb ass forgot to put it back in. Karma for saran wrapping Presley's car has finally caught up to me."

And my self-control is gone. I lose it. Completely and utterly lose it. The giggling becomes so much that tears are falling from my eyes. I clutch my stomach and try to get a hold of myself, but

I can't. I hear Cooper start to follow suit, and then we're both hysterical.

"You," I lean forward, trying to catch my breath, "forgot the tire!" I struggle to catch my breath as I wipe the tears. "Because that's what would happen on our first date!"

Cooper comes around and grips my shoulders as I start to get myself under control. "I'll call my sister."

That sobers me. "Who will what? Have her husband come out?"

He closes his eyes. "It's better than the alternative."

This couldn't be any more comical. Our choices are: call Zach, who could quite possibly be with his brothers, or call the sheriff, who is the brother we're avoiding.

My hands rest on Cooper's chest, and I giggle again. "You have to admit this is funny."

"Maybe a little."

"Or a lot."

Cooper shakes his head. "This isn't exactly the way I thought our first date would go."

"Really?" I joke. "What did you think?"

He smirks. "For starters, we'd actually make it to dinner."

"That would've been a good start, what else?"

His eyes warm as I try to lighten the mood. "We'd have gone for a walk."

"Well, we may be doing that as it is if we don't get help out here."

He nods. "Let's make sure that part doesn't happen. I'll call Pres, and then maybe we can still salvage our night."

I'm not sure what we can save, but I appreciate that he cares. I try not to let my mind wander down the path that our blowing a tire is another sign. Considering I kissed another man tonight already, maybe the universe is trying to stop me from being a little bit of a hussy.

"All right," I acquiesce.

Cooper squeezes my arm and then heads toward the truck. I lean against the back end and shake my head. I'm pretty sure tonight should make the top list of worst dates ever. First, Trent showed up, messed with my head from all his mixed signals, and then left with such a heavy sadness in his eyes. Then I could barely breathe when I was getting ready. And sure, Cooper brought me flowers, but then this whole tire thing is unbelievable. I've been hesitant about dating anyone, but I hoped that maybe, this could be different for me.

Out of those things, Trent upsets me the most. There was something about the way he looked at me that I can't shake. It's that in all the times we've had our ups and downs, I've not once seen his eyes so sad. It was as if he were accepting our goodbye as what it was . . . the end.

A shiver runs through me, and I start to head back to the cab, but I see a car approaching. "Coop! We might be saved!"

I turn toward the back of the truck, and my stomach drops as the silhouette of a light bar comes into view.

We're not saved, we're freaking screwed.

I watch as the headlights approach and a tall form exits the car. I pray it isn't him. I'm begging God to give me Hank and not Trent.

"Everything all right here?" Trent's deep voice rings through the silence.

No. Everything is not all right. In fact, it went from bad to worse.

"Of all the places you happen to drive past tonight, this is one of them?" I ask with a little too much hostility.

Trent hooks his thumbs into his belt and cocks his head to the side. Cooper walks back, stopping short when he sees who's standing in front of me. Both men are silent as they measure each other and testosterone fills the air. This is going to go really bad, really fast.

"Cooper," I step between them, "was callin' for some assistance. Thanks for comin' out, Sheriff, but we're fine."

Trent looks over at me and then back to Cooper. "It's gettin' dark," Trent says. "Were you callin' for someone to change your tire? What? Don't want to get dirty?"

Cooper's eyes narrow slightly. "The spare is at the farm. I left a message with Zach to bring it out."

Trent's smile widens. "Well, Zach is headin' out with Presley to get a new horse, and they won't be back for a few hours."

My head falls back as I look to the heavens for support. "This can't be happening."

"Let me guess," Cooper adds. "Wyatt is busy, too?"

"Yup," Trent confirms. Bastard is a little too happy about this. "But listen, we can call a tow truck, and then I'll drive you both back home."

"Just take me back to my car, and I'll bring the spare out," I suggest.

Cooper sighs and shakes his head. "Your trunk isn't big enough."

Yes, because boys and their big ridiculous wheels. "Right."

Trent smirks and touches my shoulder. "I'm happy to give you a ride back to town."

Sure, nothing like an awkward car ride with Trent and Cooper in the cop car.

"No," Cooper says without any room for discussion.

"So, you'd rather stand out here or walk back to town?"

I would rather lightning come and strike me dead so I didn't have to be the monkey in the middle of this, but it seems I'm not going to have a choice. Trent and Cooper both keep making small movements, and my space is shrinking. All I want to do right now is go home and eat a pint of ice cream.

Rocky road has never let a girl down.

I turn slightly and place my hand on Cooper's chest. "I know we didn't expect this to happen, but I'm not really wearin' the shoes to walk back."

He looks at my strappy heels and sighs. I hate this as much as he does, but short of waiting for someone else to show up, there aren't any other choices.

"We'd appreciate a ride back, Trent." Cooper says through gritted teeth.

Trent nods and attempts to smother his delight. But I see it.

"I'll grab your stuff from the truck," Cooper says before walking away.

I stand face to face with Trent and fight the urge to slap the smug grin off his face. "Good time on your date?"

"Shut up. You could at least pretend not to look so happy about this." I huff. He seems to be enjoying every second of this.

He starts to chuckle but stops when he gets a look at my face. "Oh, please. If the roles were reversed right now, you can't say you wouldn't be the same."

"What happened to the 'be happy, Gracie'?" I say in my best impression of his.

Trent steps closer. "I want you to be happy. I just want it to be . . ."

Cooper steps behind me. "Ready."

"Great." Trent smiles. "Happy to help a resident in need."

Right.

We walk over to the car, and Trent opens the back of the cop car. "Grace can ride in front."

"I'll get—" I start to say.

"In the front," Trent ends my sentence. "Cooper wouldn't want you to be uncomfortable back there, would he?"

Way to back him into a corner on that one, Trent.

I fight back the urge to roll my eyes.

"Of course not," Cooper replies through his teeth as he slides into the cruiser. "You should ride up front."

"Problem solved." Trent slams the door closed a bit harder than he needs to.

We walk around the back of the car, and I warn him. "Don't be a jerk, Trent. I'm begging you. This is awkward for all of us."

"Not for me." He grins as he opens my door. "Get in, sweetheart. I'll have you home in no time."

Instead of arguing with him, I do as he says.

"Sorry about this, Coop," Trent says over my shoulder and then saunters around the car with a little extra pep in his step. I glare at him.

"Sure you are," Cooper mutters under his breath.

This has to be some cruel joke. My ex-boyfriend is driving my current date home in the back of a squad car. Because . . . why the hell not?

"I'll drop you off first, Gracie. That way I can take Cooper back out with his spare."

"Or you can take us *both* to Cooper's so *we* can get his spare."

"Grace," Cooper says from behind the glass. "It's fine, darlin'. We can do this another night."

Trent snorts, and I slap his leg. "Are you sure? I don't mind comin' back out so you're not alone."

"What kind of sheriff would I be if I left him stranded out there?"

"The jealous ex-boyfriend type," I mutter, seeing straight through his act.

"Don't worry, Townsend. I won't let anything hurt you out there."

I slap him again. "Can you be nice?"

"What did I say?" he asks innocently. "I'm offering to protect your date from gettin' mauled by a bear or God only knows what."

My hands tighten in my lap, and I swear this drive is taking longer than normal. Cooper looks out the back window with his head resting on his fist. It isn't anyone's fault this happened, but it still sucks. And making matters worse, Trent looks calm and relaxed. He starts to whistle and looks over to smile at me.

I loathe him.

We arrive at my house, and my stomach clenches. I shift in my seat to face Cooper. "Would you walk me to the door?" I ask.

I need to salvage even a tiny bit of tonight.

Yup. This is my life.

"I can't get out," Cooper explains after he tries and fails to open his door.

Trent clears his throat. "We don't like to let the criminals have access to an escape."

"Well," my voice grows hard, "Cooper isn't a criminal, and you bein' the helpful sheriff and all should have no problem lettin' him out so he can walk me to the door, right?"

I take a small amount of pride from being able to box him in at least once this evening. He can't say no since it isn't like anyone is under arrest, but at the same time, when he says yes, he's admitting there's no win for him. And he'll have no choice but to wait for Cooper and me to finish saying our goodbyes.

Take that, Trent Hennington.

"No problem at all."

Trent lets Cooper exit, and we head toward my door. "I'm sorry," he says looking over at Trent, who is leaning against the car watching us.

"Don't be. It wasn't like you planned this."

Cooper takes my hands in his. "I know, but this couldn't have gone any worse."

"Yeah, having to be rescued by my ex wasn't high on the list of things I wanted to do today."

"Will you let me make this up to you?"

The million-dollar question. I like Cooper. He's been a friend forever, and my accepting a make-up date isn't wrong. So, why does it feel like I'm cheating on Trent? It's insane and completely ridiculous. My eyes drift over to where he stands. Trent's eyes are unmoving as he stares at me. He doesn't have to say a word. I hear him through the silence. He's asking me to say no.

"Please?" Cooper brushes his thumb across my knuckles. "I'm not blind, Grace. I see your hesitation. I'm asking for you to give this a fraction of a chance."

Trent clears his throat, and when my eyes find him again, all pretense of relaxation has melted away from his posture. "I hate to interrupt this"—his eyes flick to where Cooper's hand is on mine—"touching scene, but I'm on duty, which means I need to get back to work."

I nod in his direction and turn back to Cooper. I'm not sure what about that statement helped me decide, but there's no way I'm turning Cooper away tonight. Who knows if things might have been great had the tire not blown. I sure as hell don't. But I do know that the man by the car has hurt me more times than I can count. I gave him a second chance and then a thirtieth chance. Cooper deserves at least one.

"I would love to try again," I say with a big smile.

chapter
SEVEN

Trent

I'VE NEVER BEEN A POSSESSIVE guy.

I had two younger brothers who stole my toys, friends, and anything else they could grab. But we lived by a code when it came to girls. We would never go after a girl the other brother dated.

I like to think of this as a man's code. Something we *all* follow. I wouldn't sleep with a married woman because that's another man's woman. It's wrong.

Cooper is breaking every goddamn man code I know.

He knows that Grace is mine.

He just doesn't give a shit.

He climbs back in the cruiser after kissing Grace on the cheek. I swear I might have used deadly force if he touched her lips. The life sentence would've been worth it.

We sit in silence as I try to assemble my thoughts. It's high time I let him know what I think. I promised Grace I'd let her be, and I won't break that promise, but I didn't say shit about him.

Once we're out of the view of her house, I throw the car in park and turn to him.

"What the hell?" he asks, trying to mask his surprise.

"I figured it was time we had a talk."

I don't know how this conversation will go, I didn't plan very far ahead, but I've got things I need to say.

"I don't have anything to say to you," Cooper glowers as he shifts in his seat. "I think we both know where we stand."

"Do we?" I push. "Because I can't imagine you know where I stand."

Cooper has been a friend for my entire life, and what he's doing is beyond fucked up. No, we're not close anymore, but the line he's crossing is unacceptable.

"I know you're pissed."

"Damn fucking right I am," I bellow. "I can't believe you would go after her. Her!"

He raises a brow and smirks. "I didn't go after her. You let her go, and I was there to catch her after you tossed her away."

Well, if that isn't the equivalent to kicking me in the nuts, then I don't know what is. He's wrong, though. I didn't toss her away—she left me. However, it doesn't change the fact that she's the girl I want. She's the girl I love. She's the girl I'm going to get back.

"You and I both know who she belongs with."

"You don't get it." He lets out a bark of incredulous laughter. "You think this is a game? That I'm trying to take something that's yours?" Cooper glares at me. "I don't think she belongs with you. I think you had your chance."

I try to slow the anger that's coursing through my body. The desire to punch him in the face is strong.

"We've been friends a long time, Coop."

He nods. "I know."

"Friends don't go after another man's girl."

For the first time since he got into the car, he looks contrite, but only for a second. "I didn't go after your girl. You guys weren't together."

Now I'm pissed. "Oh, so you waited for a fucking technicality?

You think this is going to work? That she's going to suddenly be fine with throwin' away all the years of what we've had? We may not have been together, but you're a fool if you think there aren't still feelings there."

Cooper shakes his head. "You keep holdin' on to the past, buddy. I'm not trying to be that to her. I'm lookin' toward a future."

Red clouds my vision. I clench my fists tight, trying to stop myself from ripping him out of the car and beating the piss out of him. Out of the corner of my eyes, I see him tense. Cooper knows I'm not a man who backs down from a fight, he isn't, either.

In the back of my mind, I know that would be a mistake. If I get in a fight with him, there's a chance Grace will see it different. I can't run the risk of pushing her further away because I kicked her new boyfriend's ass.

"There isn't a future for you and Grace. I think we both know that. If she had feelings for you, she wouldn't hesitate. So, why are you doin' this?"

"Why are you?" he asks with annoyance. "Because I'm not walkin' away. I like Grace. I like her a lot, and she deserves better than the shit you've given her."

I know this.

He isn't wrong, but I'm done being that man. Seeing Grace walk away that day was enough to snap me out of this. Then, knowing she's with him set my plan in motion. Watching her smile at him fucking kills me. The thought of her kissing him makes me go insane. And the mere idea of another man touching her body? You'll have to kill me before I let that happen.

She's the girl I love. The girl I've always loved but was too stupid to hold on to.

That won't happen again.

"If you care about her, you won't make this harder on her than it already is. You and I both know who she loves. And it ain't you." I growl as I point my finger at his chest.

"Do you hear yourself? You don't get to make that choice for her. I'm not the one who hurt her and fucked with her head. That's all on you, buddy."

"Fuck you."

"No, fuck you, Trent. You had all the time in the world to be with her. Even after she's done with you, you think you get a say in her life?"

"I'm not makin' a choice for her!"

Cooper folds his arms across his chest and shakes his head. "I'm not sure what to say to you. I didn't set out for any of this to happen. I really didn't. I went back and forth on whether goin' after her was the right thing to do."

I answer for him. "It wasn't."

"And what you're doin' now is?"

I'm not sure what I'm doing, but I can't stand idly by and let this happen. I can't give up on her—on us. Maybe walking away would be the noble thing, but I can't do it. I won't do it.

"No, but I don't know how to live in a world without her."

Losing Grace and knowing she was through with me was agonizing.

She has the purest heart, and I know she doesn't want to hurt anyone. I get that her not wanting to be strung along anymore has forced her to push me away. But at the same time, I don't think she will ever be done. Grace wouldn't have kissed me like that. She wouldn't tell me she loves me or be so worried about this. She needs to see that I won't ever be that man again, and she'll come back to me.

Cooper points his finger at my chest, and I see the determination in his eyes. Cooper is going to fight. "Better get used to it, my friend. I'm not givin' up. You had your chance, now it's mine."

"We're not friends," I say simply.

Needing to calm myself, I put the car in drive and focus on not causing bodily harm. When I decided to start this conversation, my intention was to let Cooper know how this would be going down, but now the part of me that's his friend, isn't sure he sees the writing on the wall. He can fight for her, but he'll lose.

I pull into his driveway on a cloud of dust and brake lights. "She won't ever love you, Coop." My words fall from my mouth as he opens his door. "I'm not tryin' to be a dick, but I know her. She's tryin' to be strong and push me away, but you don't know what we had, either." I think about how when she's happy, it can brighten the room. How her eyes would go soft right before her lips would touch mine. Grace has been hurt, but Cooper isn't the man who will fix her. "And you can try to give her what you think she wants, but at the end of the day, it'll be me she sees when she closes her eyes. So, enjoy what little time you've got now, because it won't last."

He doesn't bother responding before he slams the door shut. There's nothing either of us can say that will change anything. The person I need to convince is her, and that's what I intend to do.

chapter EIGHT

Grace

I'M DREAMING. I KNOW THIS because everything feels like it's on the edge of reality, but I refuse to open my eyes. I drank two entire bottles of wine when I got home from my disastrous date. I'm a lightweight by nature, but I let the adult grape juice flow without a care in the world.

There's something to be said about the freedom from thought. After bottle number one, I didn't give a shit about anything. My date may have gone from awkward to absolutely comical, but I survived and even agreed to try again.

As I was on the last "glass," which by then I was drinking straight from the bottle, I felt euphoric. I was wearing my pajamas and dancing myself senseless to angry white girl music.

Men. They ruin everything.

However, this hazy state of sleep is perfect. I plan to savor every second of it.

Right now, I'm dreaming I'm in Trent's arms.

I curl my body deeper into his warmth and inhale. I even got the scent right. My face glides against the pillow, as I imagine the feel of his skin. My arm tightens a little bit so I can hold on as long as I can.

"I wish it was always like this," I mumble against his body. "I wish you loved me. I wish you would come back to me the way we used to be."

"I never left." His deep sleepy voice rumbles through my head.

I keep myself in my happy place and relish this moment. I spent a long time waking up like this. Having him hold me, keep me safe, and make me feel like I'm everything to him. It's this moment I cling to. Because each day that started this way was perfect. He was just Trent. No walls, no weird commitment issues, he was open, happy, and full of love. I never had to question him in the morning.

It was as the day went on when things would change.

"You always leave," I remind him. I figure I might as well lay it all out there since this isn't real. "You take your love away and it hurts."

His arm squeezes me as he says all the things I want to hear. "It's never gone, sweetheart. I just don't want to hurt you. If I push you away, it's because I'm protectin' you. I'm not going to do that anymore, though."

I love dreamy Trent. He's sweet and is currently batting a thousand on the perfect scale.

I sigh and sink deeper. "I'm gonna hate opening my eyes."

"Why's that?" I feel his mirth flow through me.

"Because."

"That's not an answer, sweetheart."

Trent hates one-word answers. Apparently, even dreamy Trent has the same issues. I don't know how to answer him, though. Because when I wake, this will all be gone. I'll be alone and even more confused. My heart will be torn between this possibility that my mind allows me to have and the reality of the man who doesn't actually love me. He doesn't push me away because he's protecting me, he pushes me away to protect himself.

Even knowing this isn't real, I don't want to say it. The words are only thoughts, and they're mine. Admitting them aloud makes them impossible to take back. And if dreamy Trent leaves because I say something that hurts him, I'll lose all that I have.

God, I sound pathetic.

"Because I want you to stay, baby. I want to have this every day, but when I open my eyes, you'll be gone, and I'll be without you again. I don't want to be without you."

Trent's fingers make patterns on my back as he stays quiet.

I let the silence settle around us and debate opening my sleepy eyes. Minutes pass, and I move my head against his chest.

"Open your eyes, Gracie." Trent commands as his hands stop.

"No," I refuse. I'm going to stay in this freaking hallucination forever if I can.

The arm that's around me pulls me up and he rolls me on my back. *Oh, sexy time with dreamy Trent. This is good. I can work with this.* His body is braced over me as his lips touch mine.

Jesus this feels so real.

"Grace." The heat of his skin warms me. "Do you want me to kiss you, sweetheart?"

"Yes," I plead.

He doesn't hesitate. His mouth is against mine, and my legs and arms wrap around him. I press against him, eliminating any space between us. Passion explodes between us as his hard body covers mine, and my skin tingles where we touch. Still refusing to open my eyes, I kiss him as if I've never kissed him before.

I don't know if it's because of all that's happening. The confusion and change that has me desperate for him, but I don't care. Trent is mine for this minute. I'm going to take full advantage.

You don't love a man for this long and not yearn for him.

His tongue moves against mine as his hands roam my body. He pulls back, and I whimper. "Open your eyes."

"Please don't make me. I don't want to wake up." I move my

head, trying to find him again.

"You're not dreamin', sweetheart."

My eyes flash open and panic floods me. I let out a loud scream as I yank the blanket over my body. This is real? No, no, no. He can't be here. We broke up. I was dreaming, which was why . . .

Oh, God. My heart races and he cups my face.

"Grace."

I clench my eyes tighter. "This is a dream! You can't be here! This isn't real!"

His thumb rubs my cheek. "You know it's real."

This is what I get for drinking my weight in wine. I note that I have a bra and underwear on, so that's a good sign. The other thing I observe is he most definitely isn't wearing a shirt or pants. Shit. I try to retrace any memories of last night. I know I was singing, dancing around, I'm pretty sure I texted Emily. No, I called her. I told her about the date or, more accurately, that there was no date, and how Trent was the one who came to get us.

She told me to tell Trent to get lost.

And then it hits me.

I freaking called him. My foolish, drunk ass called him.

I slowly open my eyes, and sure enough, his blue eyes and unshaven face are all I see.

"This never should've happened," I tell him.

"Oh, but it did." His eyes gleam.

"Did we? I mean, we didn't, right? Because . . ."

He moves his hand lower and cups my neck. "You'd remember. Drunk or not, you'd remember."

I push him off and groan. "You had to know I didn't actually want you to come over!"

Trent flops back on the bed with his arm behind his head. I sit, taking the sheet with me to cover myself. It isn't as if he hasn't seen it before, but still. His bare chest is now on display, and I fight myself to look away. He lies there as if he belongs here. I don't know when he arrived or how he found his way into my bed. Honestly, I don't remember much about last night.

I think I sat on the couch and then . . .

His knowing grin surges my anger and I snap.

"Trent, this ain't funny!" My head starts to pound as I press my palm to my temple. "How did we end up in bed?"

He gets on his elbows and inches closer. "When you didn't answer the door, I used my key. Then—"

"I'm going to need that back." I cut him off.

"Whatever. You were passed out on the couch. I carried you in here."

"And that was your invitation to stay?"

He shakes his head and releases a heavy sigh. "You seriously don't remember?"

If I did, I wouldn't be asking him. "Clearly not."

Trent takes my hand in his. "You woke up when I laid you in bed. I didn't want to stay, Gracie. I didn't want to do this." His eyes hold mine captive for a beat. "I wanted to leave because being here fucks me up more than you know."

My breath hitches. "I don't . . ."

"No, you don't understand. You don't care that I'm goin' crazy without you, but I am. Then, to see you out with another man 'bout killed me."

"Trent." I squeeze his hand, but he doesn't stop.

"You called, and I came with no questions. Because I'll always be here for you. I'll come anytime you need me. I was tuckin' you in and your blue eyes opened. You begged me to stay. Your voice was sad, and I couldn't leave you. You told me you needed me here, that you *wanted* me to hold you, so I did. I'll do it over and over if you ask because I can't walk away from you. It's why we always find our way back here. No matter how much you think we don't work, we do. We're right for each other, and you fucking know it. Instead of seein' what we are and what we have, you're dating another man in my damn face!"

I pull my hands from his, feeling a myriad of emotions. The strongest being guilt. I'm doing the same thing he did to me for years. I'm on the edge of letting go, but can't fully. I thought I had at the wedding, but obviously, I keep hanging on.

Not fully committing to breaking a habit will end in failure, which is exactly what keeps happening.

I called him. When I was alone and without any prompting, I did this. He's the crutch I can't let go of because I'm afraid to fall.

It isn't fair to either of us. I'm hurting him, and it's selfish.

"I won't call you again," I vow. "I won't do this to you."

He looks at the ceiling and throws the covers off. Trent hops out of the bed and grabs his jeans. "You know, I thought—" He huffs. "I thought that maybe you'd see it. See what is right in front of your face. But I guess I was wrong." Trent pulls his pants up as I sit here, more confused than ever. Stunned. "You've known me a long time. Have I ever been with another woman?"

Shame creeps into my stomach and I drop my eyes to my hands. "No."

"No," Trent repeats. "Not one other woman has been in my heart or my bed. It's only ever been you."

I lift my eyes as his words sink in. He doesn't get it. It isn't about another man. It's about love. He doesn't love me. He won't say it or show it. He'll never marry me or build a family with me. Hell, he won't even move in because that's too much of a commitment. I don't want that kind of life.

"Yet, you won't love me!" I yell as he throws his shirt on. "Don't act like I'm doing some awful thing by tryin' to move on with my life. I won't live in your purgatory, Trent! I deserve a love like my parents have. I want you to come home to me, love me, build a life with me. You want a part-time lover and it ain't me anymore."

He walks over and bends so we're nose to nose. "What if that's all changed? What if I see that's not the life I want anymore?"

My heart sputters. "Why? What changed? No, you know what? Stop. You can't play games with me like this. I won't let you keep stringin' me along."

He climbs onto the bed, forcing me to lie back as he settles on top of me. "Everything changed, Grace. The minute you walked away from me at that wedding, it was like my life clicked."

"Stop," I beg with tears in my eyes.

"I saw our life flash before me. I saw you in my arms. I saw our kids, our wedding, and our life we could have. It's all there in front of us."

I try to slink out from under him, but he drops his weight on my legs. "Tell me you love me," I request. "Tell me if you want me to believe it."

He shakes his head, brushing his lips against mine. "You don't need the words, sweetheart. You need to feel it."

He's wrong.

I do need them. I need them more than anything, but before I can demand it, his lips press against mine, and my body molds to his. He holds me tight, skimming his hand up my side.

He touches me, stealing all my thoughts as the heat of his finger burns against my flesh. My hands tangle in his messy blond hair, and I keep his mouth to mine, letting his tongue sweep against mine.

I know it's wrong. I know I said I wouldn't lead him on, but I can't stop this. I won't. I need it too much.

His hand makes its way to my breast as he kneads the flesh. His thumb rolling against my nipple before tugging it.

"Feel how much your body needs me," Trent says against my lips.

I moan and arch my back when he does it again. My hands roam his body, taking his shirt off so I can feel his skin against mine. I'm like an addict getting her fix after being sober.

It's everything I remember and more.

He pushes his hand lower, skimming across my stomach. "Trent," I beg, needing him to give me more.

"What do you want, sweetheart?"

Him. I want him.

In the back of my mind, I'm screaming at myself to stop this. I'll end up hurt and alone, wishing I had pushed him away, but right now, I can't do it.

"Please." I squirm as he traces the outside of my thigh and across my belly, being careful not to touch where I need him most.

He kisses me, moves my panties to the side, and sinks his finger in. I whimper into his mouth as he fingers me. It's been weeks since he's touched me. Weeks since I've felt the warmth of his skin or had the scent of him around me.

"You're so beautiful," he says as he kisses my neck. "You're perfect. I've missed this. I've missed us."

I don't want his sweet words. I don't want to delude myself into thinking this is anything other than sex. This isn't a reunion, it's a finale. "Stop talking," I urge. "Just give me action."

And he does. Trent's finger continues to pump in and out while his mouth latches onto my breast. He sucks and circles my nipple as I writhe beneath him.

It feels so incredible. He knows exactly what I like, and he makes damn sure I remember it as he brings me to ecstasy. I climb, and the pressure builds as he starts to rub my clit.

His eyes lock on mine and I detonate.

I cry out his name as he continues to milk pleasure from my body.

As I lie here recovering, I watch him strip out of his pants.

"Tell me you want me," he commands.

My heart wants me to say the words he's asking me to say, but my head knows better.

"I need this."

He climbs on top of me, dropping his mouth back to mine. We kiss, and all the reasons I was telling myself about why I shouldn't do this . . . disappear. Sure, I will be hurt, but I don't give a shit.

Trent rubs his cock against my core, which is both a tease and a promise. "Trent." I breathe his name.

"Look at me," his voice is hard and demanding.

When I do, I begin to tremble. Seeing the emotion in his eyes causes the world around me to fade. All I see is Trent. All I feel is him. All that exists is us.

"You can't tell me you don't feel this, sweetheart. I know you do."

His blue eyes stare into mine as he enters me. I don't know if it's the last few weeks of being alone or if it's because I've ached for him, but tears form the second he's buried to the hilt.

I'm overcome with so many conflicting emotions.

I hate myself for being weak.

I love that he's here.

I hate him for making me love him.

I love how well we fit together.

I want to slap him for causing me pain.

More than anything, I want to cry.

Tears stream down my face as he starts to move. Trent doesn't say a word. He wipes them away as they continue to fall. I feel everything pass between us. There's no denying the intensity of this moment.

Trent makes love to me while my heart splinters into a thousand tiny shards. Each thrust cuts me a little deeper. I feel all that he wants me to, but most of all, I feel fear. Fear that I won't be able to keep him at arm's length anymore, that the excuse of loneliness will become much more. If I give him this once again, history will repeat itself. Our track record isn't the best, and he's still yet to say the words to me.

"Gracie." He forces me to open my eyes again. "I'm close."

His hand finds my clit again and he starts to rub circles. My body, in all its turmoil, starts to respond. He kisses me, touches me, and I let myself free of everything. I grip his shoulders, digging my nails in as my toes start to curl. "God! Yes! Trent!" I yell as white-hot pleasure tears through me.

His orgasm follows shortly after, leaving us both slick with sweat and breathing heavy. As the pulses of pleasure fade, spikes of panic take their place. Unaware of the war that's waging inside me, Trent shifts his weight and gives me enough room to scoot off the bed. I need space, a door between Trent and me, so I close myself in my bathroom and flip the lock. My heart firing a hail of pain and regret and longing and love.

I stare at myself in the mirror and fight back the tears. What the hell did I just do? How could I sleep with him? I was over him. I was working on it at least, and then I give in? There's seriously something wrong with me. We'll never stop making the same mistakes.

My hands grip the counter, and my head falls. I truly don't know how we went from yelling at each other, his circumventing telling me how he feels, to us having sex.

I'm a stupid idiot.

A weak, stupid idiot.

I slap the counter and sink to the floor.

Well, now what? I can't go back out there. I can't face him because clearly I have no rational thinking when it comes to him.

"Grace?" Trent knocks on the door. "You all right?"

"Yeah, I'm fine." My voice is shaky, and there's no way he'll fall for it.

"What's wrong?" he asks softly from the other side of the door. *Oh, just lost my dignity and sanity. Nothing new.*

"Please go. I'm not feeling so good." I try for the only excuse I have: hangover. "I don't think the wine is agreeing with me."

Trent doesn't say anything and hope blooms that maybe he'll believe me. "You were fine a minute ago."

"I'm feelin' a bit nauseous." *And I can't look you in the eye.*

Trent clears his throat and tries to open the door. "I have to meet my father and brothers for that fishing trip, I don't want to leave you if you're sick. Plus, I think we should talk about what happened."

I put my robe on and tie it tightly around me. He isn't going to leave if I don't face him. Plus, I doubt I'm getting away with anything here. He knows me well enough to tell when I'm lying.

I open the door to see him standing there fully dressed. "Hi," I say sheepishly.

"You okay?"

"I drank a lot last night."

His eyes narrow the slightest bit. "Right." The hurt flashes across his face, but he recovers quickly. If I didn't know him so well, I would've missed it.

I need to get out of this room. Instead of staying here, looking at the crime scene, I head out to the living room.

Trent grasps my arm when I try to move farther away. "Where are you goin'? And don't tell me you not being able to look me in the eye has nothing to do with what just happened."

I close my eyes and muster all the strength I have. There's no going back, I made my choice, and now I have to face it. My chest tightens as all my emotions from the last hour bubble up.

His hand drops and I turn to look at him. "This never should've happened. Nothing is different. Nothing has changed. You still can't give me what I want, and I clearly can't walk away from you."

"Have you heard nothing I've said over the last few weeks?" Trent bellows. "Are you fucking kiddin' me?" My head pounds as he gets louder. "You think nothing has changed? God dammit, Grace!"

I shake my head and take a step back. "Stop yelling at me!"

He moves closer. "So what was that?" He points to the bedroom. "Was that just some slip up?"

"I told you! I told you I was done! This is what we do!" Instead of moving away from him, I get closer. My anger takes hold as I let it all out. "I tell you it's over, and you find a way to break me down. You push me and manipulate me into believing it'll be different each and every time. I love you! I love you so much it hurts, and you keep breaking me! You don't love me. You don't know what that even means!"

"The fuck I don't!" Trent is in my face in an instant, his hands grip my arms, and he pulls me forward. "This isn't the same as before. This is me tellin' you I'm changin'. For you, I'm tryin' to be the man you want."

I shake my head, trying to stay strong, because I don't believe him. I tear my arms out of his grasp and take a step back. "I need you to leave."

"No."

"Please, I need to think. I need to not be hungover when we have this conversation."

"I need to know what I did that was so bad that you're willing to push me away. What did I do that is so fucking awful that you decide to punish me by dating Cooper?"

I stop moving and the blood drains from my face. He thinks I'm purposely trying to hurt him? That's the last thing I would ever do. All I want is for the two of us to find some semblance of happiness.

"I'm not punishing you. None of this is about you. It's about me and tryin' to find someone who will love me, Trent. Don't you get it? Don't you see that I'm dyin' inside because you won't love me?" I move so we're standing face to face. Tears fill my eyes as I pour my heart and soul out to him. "I miss you every single day. Each day I wake up, roll over, and you're not there. It hurts me so much more than you'll ever know." A tear falls from my face. "But the thing is, I've been missing you for a long time. I've been alone even when you were here. You build this wall and shut me out. I wish I could pinpoint when it happened. I wish I could fix it, but I *can't* do it anymore."

Trent's hand ascends and touches my cheek. "I can tell you exactly when it happened. It was the day the deputy the next town over was shot. I responded to that call, and all I saw was us. Nick was only thirty years old. He had a wife and a child. He had a whole life in front of him one second, and it was gone the next. When I closed my eyes, it was you crying over that casket."

I think back to how upset he was about it. Nick was his friend, I could tell it was affecting him, but he refused to talk about it. Trent grew distant during the statewide manhunt for the shooter. I assumed it was because of the hours he was spending on the case, not that he saw himself in Nick. If I had known, I could've at least been there to reassure him.

"Why didn't you tell me?" I ask.

"I don't know."

"You could've talked to me."

Trent sighs and grips his neck. "Because you'd want to talk. You'd make me think I was being crazy, but that could've been me, Grace!" Trent pounds his chest. "I could've been the guy in the ground and not him!"

I hate that it's been years that he's been struggling with this. I should've known, but I was so focused on helping Nick's widow Penelope that I didn't think it was hurting Trent.

I take a step closer. "That's the risk I knew I was taking when I fell in love with you. I held Penelope's hand. I saw what it did to her, but she said she wouldn't take back all the love they shared. I wanted that with you."

Trent touches my cheek before his hand drops. "If you give me another chance, it'll be different this time. I'll be different."

I wipe my face and try to hold on to my fading resolution. He gave me a glimpse inside himself, a tiny sliver of what I've been begging him to give me. It would have been enough a month ago. I would have fallen back into his arms and forgiven him. Now, though, I'm not sure a glimpse is enough—if it's only one more scrap. There are too many times I've gone back. Too many times I've taken his apology at face value. "I've heard this line before."

He steps closer, but I lift my hand. "Gracie."

"No. No you don't get to do this to me again. You can't promise me things that will never happen."

"I love you, Grace. I've always loved you. I love you, and I promise it'll be different. I need you, sweetheart."

Those words.

Those three words that I've waited forever to hear.

Another scrap.

My body starts to shake and a strangled sob breaks from my chest. Trent's arms wrap around me, and I fall apart. I've had plenty of people tell me he loves me. I think in some convoluted way he believes he's told me, but hearing it come from his mouth is too much.

So long I've hoped that he did love me. But love isn't a weapon to be wielded at another. Love doesn't wound the other person, and right now, I'm in pain.

I need to breathe and think.

I need some space to sort myself out.

Slowly, I get myself under control. I lean back and wipe my

eyes. I look into his blue eyes and shake my head. This is everything I wanted, and yet, I would give anything for him to take it back.

Trent must sense what I'm feeling, and he starts to speak quickly. "I'm telling you what I should've said a long time ago. I've hurt you so much, and I will never forgive myself."

He has hurt me, and he's doing it now without meaning to.

"Please, stop," I plead. "Please give me some time."

"I want to make it up to you. I think we should—"

"Dammit, Trent!" I push against his chest and step back. "I can't do this today. I've had a really confusing night and then all of *this* before noon, and I need some time alone. I've waited so long to hear those words, and I can't process this right now."

Trent takes two strides and lifts my chin to look at him. "Are you going to give me a chance to prove it? Doesn't it change anything?"

"You're not going to pressure me into this. I won't let you."

"And I won't watch you with another man. I can't even think about him touching you like I just did."

Then, I understand why he finally gave me the one thing I've wanted for so long. He doesn't love me. He doesn't want things to change between us. He only cares that I'm not with Cooper. I look at him with hurt and frustration.

"For you to say that to me—"

Knock, knock, knock.

My eyes snap to the door, and Trent stares at me.

"Expectin' someone?" he asks.

"No."

"Grace!" Cooper's deep voice calls from the other side.

"Well." Trent grins. "I guess you should answer that."

chapter NINE

T HERE'S NO WAY THIS IS going to be good. Not one single scenario I've run through will yield a positive outcome, so I'm going to suck it up. I can't change it, might as well face it. I throw on clothes and walk back out to the hall where Trent is leaning against the wall.

"If you want to finish this conversation, you won't be a jerk," I warn as I walk by him, but he just watches me. When I open the door, Cooper stands there wearing a pair of jeans and worn T-shirt.

"Hey." Cooper smiles.

"Hi," I say as regret floods through me. I hate myself for this. I know he'll play it cool, but I ended our date and then slept with my ex-boyfriend. I'm a horrible bitch. I deserve to die a lonely cow. "Listen, Coop," I say as I put my hand on his arm and push us both outside. "Trent is here."

I close the door so Trent won't hear my conversation with Cooper. It's bad enough they're both here. The least I can do is try to make this less uncomfortable.

Cooper nods. "I saw his car."

Right. Okay, and he still stopped by? I'm so confused, and the alcohol fog mixed with regret isn't helping.

Cooper steps forward and puts his hand to my cheek. "You

don't look so good, you feelin' okay? Are you sick?"

Does mentally unstable fall under that category? If so, I'm most definitely sick.

"No, I'm not feelin' okay."

"I can get you some medicine if you need it."

Why does he have to be so sweet? Why can't he call me a slut or worse and tell me he hates me? It would be no less than I deserve. I slept with Trent, and now he's here because he's a good guy. Not because he wants to take advantage of me, but because he cares.

What is wrong with me?

I shake my head and drop my arm. I hate myself right now. I'm so confused, and I don't know what is real anymore. In this moment, I don't trust myself at all.

All I know is that Cooper doesn't deserve this. And I don't deserve him or his friendship.

"I'm not sick—not in the physical way, at least. And you're so sweet to offer to take care of me. I'm . . ." I pause, trying to think of the right words to say, "I'm . . . I'm so sorry, Coop." I touch his arm and pray he hears the sincerity in my voice. "I'm awful. I'm so awful and I'm so sorry. I swear, I never meant for any of this to happen. I hate myself right now."

"Grace." Cooper lets out a heavy sigh and pinches the bridge of his nose. "I don't like it, but I'm not your boyfriend. You don't owe me an explanation. I basically had to twist your arm to get you to go on a date with me. It really wouldn't be fair of me to give you shit about somethin' I have no right to be upset about. It just means I'm going to have to step up my game so you call me the next time you need someone."

I stand completely immobilized by his words.

Did he seriously say that? Any of it? I would be ripping some girl's hair out if the roles were reversed.

The door opens behind me and Trent walks out. "Good

morning, Cooper."

"Trent," Cooper replies and then blows a long breath from his nose, seemingly in an attempt to keep calm.

"Have a good night, Coop? I sure did."

I'm going to kill him.

Cooper shifts his body weight forward, and I intervene. "What time is your fishing thing today? Don't you need to be going?"

"Would you give us minute? We were in the middle of talkin', and I'd like to finish." Trent says to Cooper.

I truly don't know what is happening. There's no way this is my life—but it is.

I turn to Cooper and touch his arm. "If you want to wait for me inside, I won't be long."

Trent huffs. "Or you can leave."

He's freaking dead. Gone. Dead. Killed. I don't feel bad about having to explain to his mama why I killed him either.

Cooper moves around behind me, his hand touches the small of my back, and Trent's eyes don't miss it. "I'll wait." Cooper kisses my cheek before entering the house.

My stomach drops as I watch Trent's face morph from smug to hurt, but he doesn't give me a second to think. "So, you're going to talk to him? After everything that I said?"

"I'm not doin' this now."

"If you don't tell me to stay right now, you're making your choice."

"Don't threaten me." I glare at him. "I need time. I think you can give me that."

Trent shakes his head. "Time is the only thing we've ever had, and we've wasted enough of it. I need to know if you love me. I need to know if everything we had is gone. I need to know if you're going to go back in there with him or if you're going to choose me."

He has no right to stand here today and make demands. He's the one who threw me away time and time again. He's sweet to me one time and he thinks that it erases decades of suffering—as if I was the one at fault for wasting all those years?

"If you want an answer today, then you won't like it. You had twenty years to make this right. Twenty *years* to tell me everything you dumped on me in a single morning." I throw my hands in the air. "It's too much. It's not fair. You can't expect to say all the right things and then"—I snap my fingers—"I forgive you, just like that. I'm asking for space. I'm asking for a chance to get a grip on what I'm feeling."

Trent's hands shake as he touches my cheek. "I love you! I fucking love you."

I close my eyes and try to find my lungs. It hurts to breathe. "I've waited so long to hear that." I release a heavy sigh. "But that doesn't mean you can use that as a way to make me stay. I need time, and if you can't give that to me, then you don't love me."

"So, you're askin' me to go?"

"I guess I am."

I'm not asking him to leave. I'm asking him for time, but he doesn't seem to hear that. I owe Cooper an explanation. I owe myself a chance to wrap my mind around everything. I have a pattern of falling back into the same situation when it comes to Trent. I don't think I'm asking for too much.

"You made your choice, Gracie. It's clear that even after laying it all out there, you're going to choose him."

"I'm choosing me!"

Trent's phone rings and he groans. "I have to go."

"I'll call you in a few days."

He steps forward and grabs my face. "Don't choose him. Just don't choose him."

He crushes his lips to mine swift, hard, and desperate before turning and walking away, leaving me a dumbfounded mess.

I know he's angry, but so am I. I didn't mean for that to happen. I didn't intend to ever sleep with him again, yet I did. I can try to blame the alcohol and what not. I can form a million excuses as to why it happened, and all of them will be bullshit. I did it because I love him. I did it because I need him. I did it because I'm a fool.

"Grace?" Cooper's voice breaks the silence as I step back in the house.

I turn to face him, unsure of exactly what I'm feeling. "I don't know what to say, Coop. I feel awful, and I really don't know why you're still here. You should be yellin' at me or tellin' me how much you hate me. You should make this hard on me."

He shifts his weight and runs his hand down his face. "I don't want to make this hard for you. I can see you're already broken up about it." Cooper starts to pace. "I'm not happy that he was here. I know you and Trent have history. But I like you, Grace." He stops in front of me and takes my hands. "I like you, and I have for a while. I'd like us to go on a date, a real date, so I can show you there's more than Trent. There's more than what he's given you all these years."

My mouth falls slightly agape. "Even after this?"

It's hard to believe he isn't angry. Instead, Cooper is fighting for another chance. Why does this have to be so damn hard? It would be different if Cooper was like Trent, but he isn't. He is everything I want in a man.

Cooper wiggles my hands and grins. "I've waited a really long time. I'm asking for you to give me one night to show you that what you had with him, isn't what you need."

Cooper is the kind of man you throw it all away for.

"I don't know." I look around at everything but Cooper. "This is crazy. You're perfect and I'm broken."

He pulls me on the couch and leans back. "You're not broken.

You're confused, and I get that. I'm not trying to make things worse for you."

"Then why are you asking me out? Clearly, I'm not as strong as I thought I was."

If he knows I'm confused, then why try? It doesn't make sense to me. He's good-looking, owns his own business, and has everything a girl could want, but he keeps pushing for something with me. It seems nuts.

Cooper smiles and grazes his thumb across the top of my hand. "Have you ever wanted something and couldn't have it? And then it's so close, just within your grasp but not quite there. Either you can surrender or keep reaching. I'm not a man who gives up."

"And when you grasp this, and it's cracked or not as shiny as you thought it would be, then what?"

My house phone rings, and I hear the machine answer. "Grace, it's your mother. Listen, I need you to come over here and help your daddy out today. His hip is givin' him trouble and he's a stubborn mule who thinks he can work through the pain." My mom lets out an annoyed huff. "If you can get here quickly that would be great. I tried you on your cell phone, but you didn't answer. Call me back."

I look to Cooper and quickly explain. "I'm sorry, but I really do need to help them. My father doesn't understand he shouldn't be workin' on the farm like this."

"I'm free for the day. Let me come help."

"What?" I ask with surprise.

"I do know my way around a farm." Cooper stands and puts his hand out. "I'm sure you could use some extra help. There's never a short list of things to be done."

He's right. I do what I can when I'm over, but there's a lot that I can't. My father taught me to ride horses, not woodwork. If he's willing, it would be a lifesaver. "Are you sure?"

"Hurry your cute butt up before I change my mind. We've got

work to do." Cooper grins, and I place my hand in his.

"All right."

I stand and pull him in for a hug. It's sweet that he's willing to go over there with me, especially after the morning we've had. I don't know what I've done to deserve his friendship, but I'm so thankful.

We ride over to my parents' house and find my father in the barn. "Hi, Daddy."

"Gracie Lou!" Daddy calls out from the other side of the barn. "There's my beautiful girl."

"Mr. Rooney." Cooper steps forward and shakes his hand. "Good to see you, sir."

My dad chuckles, "Cooper Townsend, what brings you here to our home?"

My father looks at me and then Cooper. Oh, Jesus. If my father has to pick a side in this, he will be team Trent. It isn't that my dad doesn't like Cooper, but he loves Trent. I mean *loves* Trent.

They've gone fishing, hunting, shooting, and God knows what else together. I don't know what it is that bonds them, but they've always gotten along. My father has never been quiet about wanting the two of us to be married and refers to Trent as the son he always wanted.

I hope bringing Cooper here wasn't a mistake.

"Daddy, Cooper's here to help out with some of the things you need done. We were talkin' when Mama called, and he offered to come out here to get more accomplished than I can do on my own."

"Well," he pats Cooper on the shoulder, "that's awful kind of you helpin' my little girl. I appreciate the assistance, son."

"Sure thing, Mr. Rooney. I'm happy to help."

Daddy gives a very long list of things that he's trying to tackle, and I try to keep my composure. He prattles on about broken engines, a fence falling down, and the siding he needs to replace.

There's no way he could've gotten half of this done. Between the mess at the store and the disaster on the farm, I'm going to have to talk about this with them sooner rather than later. They can't keep letting things get this bad without any help.

"I'll get started on some of the fence issues if you want to work with your dad," Cooper offers.

"You're so sweet. Thank you. I'll come find you in a bit."

Cooper heads off with tools and a plan while I try to supervise Daddy a little. He climbs the ladder and inspects one of the loose boards.

"Hand me that hammer, would you?"

"Sure thing." I grab the tool, place it in his hand, and observe him for a moment. The last few years have aged him. His once jet-black hair is now mostly gray, his gait is a little slower, and he looks tired. Not that I can blame him. Running a farm is hard work. It's long days, unforgiving weather, and a lot of headaches. We've sold off acres of land over time, which allowed Daddy to scale back, but I know he wishes he had a son to pass it on to.

"So, now you and the Townsend boy are dating?" Daddy says as he bangs the nail.

I knew this was coming. "We're friends, Daddy."

"That's not what I hear."

My mother and her big mouth. My father lives in a world of working on the farm and watching golf. He has no time for gossip. If this is what he's hearing, then there's only one source.

"I think you heard wrong."

"There's nothing wrong with my hearing darlin'. As much as I wish that had gone first," he mumbles, "then maybe your mama wouldn't nag me so much."

I giggle. "I think she'd find a way."

"Probably right. That woman would hire one of those planes

that writes messages in the sky if it meant me doin' what she wanted."

It's cute how happily they irritate each other. "You know you'd be lost without her."

He grunts. "Don't ever tell her that."

"It'll be our secret."

My dad continues to fix the board, and I breathe a sigh of relief.

"Cooper, huh?" he asks as he climbs off the ladder.

I guess I'm not out of the woods.

"It's not like that. I don't know if we'll be more, but he's a good man. He came out here to help you on his day off."

"Uh-huh. So, you gonna fix things with Trent?"

He walks over to the tool bench and sits. This can't be good. He's hunkering down for a real conversation.

"He doesn't love me. How do you fix something like that?"

He jerks his head. "You know, it's not always easy, but you have to fight, baby girl."

"It's not that simple. I can't force him to become an adult."

My father took it the hardest when Scarlett died. He felt like he failed his little girl, and he became extra protective of me. I think he also likes that Trent is a protector. Daddy respects the law and knows that Trent upholds it, not breaks it.

My father leans forward and touches my cheek. "I reckon you can't. You're a smart girl, and you'll know who's right for you."

Therein lies the issue, I don't know what's right. My heart and my head don't ever agree when it comes to men.

I smile and touch his hand. "I get my smarts from you."

He winks. "I know it. You get your fight from your mama. That woman can argue herself in or out of anything. Enough talkin', let's get back to work."

"I'm going to check on Cooper and help him with mending

the fence. You all right in here?"

Daddy scoffs and waves his hand. "Don't you worry about me. I'm as strong as an ox."

He's a mess.

I start to walk out toward the field where Cooper is working—with his shirt off—and let out heavy sigh. Why can't the man keep a shirt on? I think about how he didn't hesitate to come out here. He actually offered to spend the day working on our farm. Not many men would spend their day off doing hard labor, let alone have it be their idea.

My father was right. I do know who is the right man. I don't know if I can let go of the other one. My mind drifts to last night and this morning. How I felt being in Trent's arms. How he said things I've been longing to hear.

I take my phone out of my pocket and send a text to Trent.

Me: I know you're with your family, but we should talk about what happened today.

They do this trip every year, and one of the rules is no phones unless it's an emergency. This doesn't qualify as one.

"Hey!" Cooper calls out when he sees me.

I wave and start moving in his direction. "Hey, how's it goin'?" I ask as he wipes sweat from his brow.

"Good. I'm about done here. I wanted to help your dad on gettin' his tractor workin'. I think it might cut down on some of the other things he's let slide. If we have some time, maybe we can get the horses some exercise?"

"You really don't have to do that."

Cooper tosses his shirt over his shoulder and laughs. "It's either that or we're workin' here a few days a week."

That is the last thing I want to be doing. I'm sure I can rope Wyatt and Zach into helping out once in a while. They both owe me for saving their sorry butts a time or two.

"That won't be happening. I think Daddy and I are going to have a come to Jesus moment about needing to hire someone."

Cooper grabs the bottle of water and chugs it. I watch in rapt fascination at how his throat moves as he swallows. The way his skin is bronzed from being out here for an hour. I try not to think about how good his body looks, but I fail.

He's the total package.

He finishes his drink and hands me what's left. "Here, you don't want to get dehydrated. It's hot as hell today."

"Yes. Yes it is," I mutter and take a drink. I shake my head, trying to rattle the thoughts of Cooper from my mind and clear my throat. "So, can I help you with the fence?"

"Sure." Cooper lifts his chin and hands me the hammer. "I'll pull the line tight if you can secure it."

"No problem."

We work alongside each other, poking fun at my inability to be able to hit the nail, and then at almost hitting Cooper's hand. Sweat drips from my forehead as we move to the few poles that are left. I had forgotten how much I disliked hard labor.

After ten more minutes, we're done with mending the fence. There's a lot more that needs to be done so we go to the next task, my most hated chore ever, hay bales.

"I think we should leave this for another day," I suggest.

"You would rather haul them on your own?"

"I would rather they catch on fire."

He lifts an eyebrow. "What is with girls and hay bales?"

"What does that mean?" I ask with my arms across my chest.

His hands raise in surrender. "I'm just sayin' all you girls complain when it's time to move them."

I'll be more than happy to explain why.

"Because they're heavy, the hay gets all in your hair no matter how careful you are, your back aches for days after, and it freaking itches."

"Would you rather chop wood? Fish? Hunt? Or clean the stalls?" he questions with a grin.

"I would rather sleep."

Cooper bursts out laughing and wraps his arm around my waist, pulling me against him. "You're a mess."

"And you're gross and sweaty."

He crouches low, grips my legs, tosses me over his shoulder, and starts running.

"Cooper!" I squeal. "Put me down!" He doesn't though. He keeps moving as if I'm not speaking until we reach the creek. He better not. "Do not do it!" I say as I hear the water.

"Do what?" His voice is full of innocence.

I hang upside down as the creek comes into view. I start flailing around, slapping him on his butt, hoping to deter him from what I know is coming.

Cold. Ass. Water.

Sure enough, Cooper kicks his boots off and throws mine over on the side of the creek as well. Then he starts stomping in the water causing it to splash all around us.

"Dammit!" I yell as the freezing water pelts my skin while he spins.

He puts me right side up and the water rushes around my legs.

Well, I don't think so. I squat low and start to paddle water at him like crazy. I'm not going to be the only one who gets soaked. "Take that!" I holler as I get him good.

"Oh yeah?" he taunts and then jumps in front of me, causing water to hit all the way up to my belly.

"You're a dead man!" I giggle and charge forward.

Cooper doesn't relent as he continues to go back at me. After a few minutes, that end with both of us being drenched and cooled off, we're standing with big smiles on our faces. He moves closer and my teeth chatter.

"You cold?"

I nod. "Y-Yes. I'm-m f-freezing."

Cooper helps me out onto the grass and wraps his arms around me. I lean into his big body and let him warm me. I nestle my head under his chin and he rubs his hands against my arms, creating friction.

It's still ridiculously hot, so it doesn't take long for my body temperature to rise back to normal. But I hold on for a little longer. Being in Cooper's arms is different. It isn't familiar, but it's comfortable. Cooper would never let anything or anyone hurt me. I don't worry if he's going to break my heart. I can relax and close my eyes because he'll protect me.

"Why don't we get out of here and check on your pop, see if he needs a hand?" Cooper says without moving his arms from around me.

I lean back and tuck my wet hair behind my ear. "Sure. I bet he's looking for us anyway."

We head toward the barn to get the other tools we might need. My father is standing by his workbench, tinkering with something.

I can't recall how many times I would sit on the stool next to him and watch him work. He was always this big, strong, and tough man. I thought there was no one who could ever hurt me. As long as my daddy was around, I was safe. He set the bar pretty high.

He turns around, and his eyes grow warm. "Hi, baby girl. You guys all done?"

Cooper clears his throat and walks toward him. "I've got a few more things on your list I'd like to get done, Mr. Rooney."

My father smiles appreciatively. "You're a good man. Comin' over and workin' on a day like today. This is a good man here, Grace."

I look at Cooper and grin. "Yeah, he is."

He drops the thing he was tinkering with and leans back. "I need to take a load off. My hip is givin' me a hell of a time. If you need me, I'll be in my chair. Thanks for all your help today, son."

Cooper clasps his shoulder. "Nowhere else I'd rather be."

Daddy walks over and kisses my forehead. "Be good, darlin'."

"Have a good nap!" I call out as he grumbles under his breath.

"If you need to go home and change or run errands, I can finish," I offer.

Cooper steps closer, his dark hair shines in the sunlight streaming through the windows. "How about this . . . I'll finish helping your pop out for a bit and you promise to make me dinner."

"Dinner?"

"Yeah, you know that meal after lunch." He nudges me. "I figure you can at least eat a meal with me since I'm bustin' my ass all day in the hot sun, and you splashed me in the face."

My muscles clench as I try to think of a way out of it. I'm not sure this is the best idea with everything that's happened in the last twenty-four hours.

"I don't know, Coop. Today has been . . . intense?"

"Doesn't mean dinner will be."

He's right, and I'm being crazy, but I feel like I need to be completely transparent with him. Regardless of what kind of romantic possibilities there may or may not be between us, he's still my friend.

Being honest is the only way this will ever work.

"No, but what about what happened this morning? How can you be so cool about it?"

He releases a heavy sigh. "I feel like you want me to be angry about you and Trent."

I pause and think about that for a second. My first instinct is to tell him he's crazy. Why would I want that? But maybe he's right.

I do keep bringing it up, pushing it back in his face, and reminding him after we spent the day relaxed and happy.

I step closer to Cooper and place my hand on his arm. "I'm sorry if I'm makin' you feel that way. I don't think I want you to be angry. I know that if I found someone in your house after the date like we had . . . I'd be pissed."

He tugs me closer, wrapping his arm around my waist. "I'm not happy, but I'm not pissed. I'm the one pursuing you, Grace. I'm the one who's tryin' to get you to see me as more than just a friend. I also know you. You're not the girl who would purposely set out to hurt my feelings. You're confused, sad, and still tryin' to see past the last two decades of Trent. My bein' angry with you won't do anything. Yes, he was with you last night, and I don't want to know what happened. I'm sure I can guess, but I'd rather not have it confirmed. Now," he pauses, and his eyes turn hard, "if we decide that we're goin' to make a real go at this, I'm not willin' to share you. If you pick me, then you'll have to *pick* me."

And there is the part of me that wants to run away. Having to pick him. Because I don't know that if I had to choose right now, it would be him. My eyes close, and I shake my head as I grapple with what to say.

"Before you freak out, I want to be clear that we're not in a rush here. I can be very patient."

"Honestly?" I touch his chest and stare at the freckle on his pec. "I'm scared."

"Scared of what?"

Here it goes. I lift my head and gaze into his eyes. I need to say it and be completely honest with myself. "You. *Us.* The idea of us!" I push back, but Cooper is stronger and holds me against him. "You're my best friend's brother. You're Cooper!"

"And you're Grace," he smirks.

I roll my eyes. "Funny."

"I thought so."

"Don't you get it?" I ask. "You've always been a part of my life. I don't want us to screw that up!"

I look in his deep green eyes and see the fear that floats over the surface. He's scared, too. It may not be for the same reasons, but it's there.

"You're actin' like I think we should get married. We're friends, we'll always be friends, and maybe we can be more."

"I'm not sayin' that. I worry that I'm going to lose something that means a lot to me."

"Which is?" Cooper asks.

"Our friendship."

Cooper gets closer and shakes his head. "You're not going to. Trust me."

I do trust him, it's me I don't trust.

"So, I'll keep workin', and you can decide about dinner."

The least I can do to show my gratitude is have dinner with him. Cooper has been here, busting his butt, and I am eternally grateful for it. Plus, after being with him all day, I want to keep hanging out with him. He makes me feel different. I don't worry about pissing him off and him disappearing. It's easy and light. Not everything is this big deal, and he's sweet.

"All right. I'll have dinner with you."

"How about we avoid driving?" Cooper suggests and gives me a grin. "Lessens the chance that we'll blow a tire again."

"As friends?"

"As friends, just dinner. I can cook if you want," Cooper offers.

There is no way out of this, and if I don't really have a choice, I might as well make sure the food is edible. "I'll cook. Lord knows we don't want to eat whatever you make. Come over to my place tonight, we can talk, eat, and see about a second chance at a date."

"Then I get to pick the movie," he tacks on. "If you're cookin' then I'm providing the entertainment."

I know Cooper's taste in movies. "I'm not watching some John Wayne movie. You're going to have to pick a movie made from this millennium." I point my finger at him, and he laughs.

"They all suck."

"No, they don't. You're stuck on the same five movies. It's time to broaden your horizons."

Cooper leans in, kisses my cheek, and then walks toward the door. "I've got a lot of work to do on that tractor. You've got some food to make." He grins. "Get to it, woman."

My hands brace the edge of the barn door and my temple rests against my knuckles as I watch him walk toward the tractor. I almost think he's going to leave without looking back, but then he turns and smiles.

"Hey, Grace?" Cooper questions. "This may not be a date, but don't be surprised if I bring flowers again."

He seems persistent about doing this, and honestly, I've warned him all I can. Emily is right, he's a big boy and isn't going into this blind.

I lift my head and muster my courage. "Be there by eight."

"I have the perfect movie," he yells back.

"Which is?"

"Not tellin'. I'll see you tonight!"

Cooper waves once before he disappears. Dinner at my house, no chance of tires exploding, and just two old friends sharing a meal.

What could possibly go wrong?

chapter
TEN

Trent

"DAD, STOP." I SWAT AT his hand as he tries to fix the line on my rod. I've been fishing since I was three, and he still treats me like an idiot. Today is not the day to fuck with me. I'm in no mood. We've been out here for hours, and I still haven't caught a damn thing.

"Does Daddy need to fix your line again?" Wyatt tries to piss me off, which happens often.

I flip him off and go back to adjusting the fly.

"Trent has always been a little special," Zach starts in. "Has he ever won?"

"I won twice, thanks . . . asshole."

Not that it's all that much of a competition to catch fish in this lake since we stock it every year specifically for the Hennington fish off. It doesn't mean I don't absolutely dread this day, though. Sure, Zach and Wyatt have won at least ten times each, but that's because they're losers who fish every day. I would much rather be shooting or working out. I'd love to see one of them try to compete in a shoot off. They'd both lose.

"Ohhh," Wyatt says while laughing. "Twice."

"Enough!" My father puts a stop to our bickering. "You three are still as annoying as when you were teenagers."

All three of us look at each other and shrug. We're all close in age, stubborn, a little dense, and yet there's nothing I wouldn't do for them. My brothers are everything to me. When Wyatt lost his shit last year, I was at his house every day. When Zach got hurt, I flew out to California to get him home. Being back in town together is all I could ask for.

Family is the only thing that matters. And Grace, but she let me know where I stand.

"How's work, son?" My father asks.

"I'm hiring another deputy. This way I can work a little less." I finally got the approval last week.

"And how are things goin' with gettin' Grace back?"

"It's not. It's done."

"He got his head out of his ass a little too late," Zach tosses another insult.

Dad clears his throat. "Don't waste time, Trent. If you don't cherish every second with that woman, you'll regret it. Trust me on this, if you want her, you need to prove that to her."

My father loves my mother more than any rational person cares for another. It's a relationship my brothers and I always envied and, in our own ways, tried to find for ourselves. My mother and father can have a complete conversation without words, which probably came in handy when raising us.

"I've told her what I want."

"Then win her back," he retorts.

"It's not that simple."

He snorts. "The hell it isn't. You can't expect her to believe what you tell her. She needs to see that you're changin'."

Dad has always been pushing all of us to find a love like that. I'm surprised he hasn't brought Grace up before now.

"I did show her, and she chose someone else."

He nods. "I guess she wasn't the one then."

What the fuck does that mean? Of course, she's the one. "Yeah, well, I guess I just didn't know until it was too late."

He casts his line and exhales. "A man always knows. It's a matter of being smart enough to act on it."

I don't say anything to that. I've known for a long time that Grace is the one, but I was too stubborn to change. I liked our arrangement. It worked for me. We'd have dinner, go out dancing, have mind-blowing sex, and then go on our way. I didn't have to answer to her and she didn't need to tell me what she was doing.

"Why are you always so wise and vague at the same time?" I grumble. "It's really annoying."

Dad shrugs and turns to Wyatt. "How's my daughter-in-law doin'?"

"I'm doing great, Pop. Work is good, I'm still debating going in with Cooper and becomin' part owner."

My hand clenches the rod as he says his name. Right now, he could be at her house. I have no idea what they're talking about or if he's convinced her that he's the better choice. I'm stuck here, trying to keep myself from going back over there.

She can say that she didn't feel the love between us this morning, but she's lying. I know I'm not perfect, but I'm not playing around anymore. I didn't want to go there last night, but because she needed me, I did. Never did I think we'd have sex, but I couldn't resist her.

The way she moaned my name. The sounds she made and how she nestled against me while she slept. It was everything I could do to keep from ripping her clothes off in the middle of the night. Now, all I can think about is that she's with Cooper.

"I didn't ask about you, I asked about Angie," he retorts.

Wyatt scoffs, and I choke back my laughter. "She's doin' all right. It's different this pregnancy than the last."

"And you both are talkin'?" My father looks at the hill, which is his subtle way of remembering the baby they lost last year.

"Faith is always somethin' we talk about."

"And when am I going to get another grandbaby from you, Zachary?"

Sometimes being the only one not married has its perks, like now. Though, I got my fair share of flak for not being married with kids. When I hit forty, he gave up completely and let it go.

Zach grumbles and casts his line. "Oh, look, a fish!"

"Here fishy, fishy, fishy!" Wyatt calls.

All of us turn to look at him as if he's lost his fucking mind. "What the hell?" I ask.

"What? It's my and Angie's thing. You had to be there."

"Are you drunk?" Zach questions.

He shakes his head. "Why don't we drink when we do this?"

Dad clears his throat. "Because when you three drink someone gets a damn black eye and I end up listenin' to your mama for two hours about corralling you idiots."

He has a point. "Still, it would make this a little more fun. We could make a drinking game out of it."

"Yes!" Wyatt agrees.

My father starts to sway a little, and I grab his arm. "You all right, old man?"

He yanks his arm away. "I'm fine. Focus on fishing and maybe we'll actually catch something."

I go back to my line after casting a look at both my brothers. He suffered a stroke a few years back, which is what caused Zach to stay after his injury and run the ranch. I debate questioning him, but think better of it. He does not do well with us worrying about him.

At all.

"I'm getting the boys quads," Zach pipes up.

"Oh, that's a great idea. We never got in trouble on ours." Wyatt adds.

Dad shakes his head and starts to pull in his line. "I got something." Like the lifelong fisherman he is, he reels the trout in with finesse.

I still haven't caught anything.

I hate fishing.

He walks out to the edge of the dock and puts it in his bucket. My brothers and I turn back to our conversation and joke about the lack of sex Wyatt must be having. Angie has been sicker than usual and will barely let him near her. I swear her child has turned her into the devil. She threw something at my head when I stopped by a few days ago, and all I did was say she looked pretty.

She told me I was a liar and to get out of her house.

"She's crazy!" Wyatt complains. "Presley came over yesterday and told me to call a priest to come extract the demon from her."

"Pres said she's never seen her so miserable."

"I don't know what to do with her," he admits. "I love her, but I don't like her much right now."

"She's scared," I tell him. "She went through hell the last time she was pregnant. The last thing she wants is to be happy."

"When did you become all in-tune with women and their thoughts?" Zach looks over with a smirk.

"It's not rocket science! I get fear. Fear can make you do some stupid shit."

Wyatt smiles. "Like letting the girl you love date someone else?"

"Yes, asshole. Like that."

"Keep talking like that and Dad will have your ass," Zach warns.

Where is he? He usually can't get back here quick enough so he has a chance at winning. "Dad, I could use some backup."

"Pop?" Zach calls, but he doesn't respond.

I look over by the buckets, but he isn't there. I start scanning the shoreline, trying to see where he went, but when I find him, adrenaline rushes through my veins. I drop my rod and rush toward him. "Dad!"

My brothers are on my heels as we rush to where he's lying on the ground. "Dad!" I call again, but he doesn't respond. "Call 911!" I scream to Wyatt who already has his phone out.

I roll him onto his back and check for a pulse. "Trent?" Zach asks as I search for any sign of life.

"He's not breathing, I'm starting CPR. Call Mom!"

I push on his chest and blow air in his mouth. Wyatt and Zach get the Gator out of the way for the emergency crews on their way, and I keep going. I check for a pulse and still can't find it. I don't know how long it will take, but I don't relent.

"Come on, Dad!" I yell as I do another round of compressions. "Come on, don't give up!" I blow another breath and start right back.

My arms begin to cramp. My chest hurts, and I'm out of breath, but there's no way I'm letting him die.

"How long has it been?" I ask Wyatt.

"Four minutes. I hear the sirens, they're almost here."

"Let me," Zach tries to get me to move, seeing the sweat dripping down my face.

"I got it!"

My brothers stand ready to step in, but the trees are now filled with emergency lights. The two EMTs, Beau and Thom, rush over, and I start rattling off what I can remember about my father's medical history. Both of them worked on Angie last year. I pray to God that we have a better outcome.

"Ride with them," Zach yells to me. "We'll be right behind you!"

I run toward the ambulance, hop in the back, and watch as they try to revive my father.

"WHERE IS HE?" MAMA RUSHES through the doors with Mrs. Kannan.

"He's with the doctors." Zach grabs her arm. "They haven't said anything."

Mama hurries to the counter and starts yelling about needing to see the doctor right now. "You need to call Dr. Halpern here! Right now!"

"Mama." I touch her shoulder.

"Now! Go get him!" She scolds the nurse and turns to me. "Boys." Her eyes fill with tears. "I-I—"

Wyatt rushes forward, wrapping his arms around her. "It's going to be okay. He's going to be all right."

"No." She cries in his arms. "It's not going to be all right."

"He's strong." I rub her back. "He'll pull through."

Her head lifts and she cries harder. "He won't, honey. He won't, and I can't . . ."

"What do you mean?" Zach questions her. "Why do you think he won't pull through, Mama?"

She steps out of Wyatt's arm and starts to shake a little. "I'm so sorry. I shouldn't've listened to him, but your daddy was very firm on what he wanted."

My stomach drops as she starts talking in circles. "Ma?"

The three of us stand in line as her tears spill down her face. "This isn't how I planned to tell you, but I don't have a choice." Mama shakes her head and straightens her back. "Six months ago, he was diagnosed with Leukemia. It's incurable, and he begged me . . ." She grabs my hand and Wyatt's, forming us into a huddle. "He made me promise not to tell you. He told me that he didn't want you boys to know, and he was goin' to spend his time the way he wanted. I fought him, but you know your daddy."

I take a step back. "No." I shake my head. "No way. He's young! He's not even sixty-five yet. There's no way he's dyin'. You can't believe this is true."

"When they explained the possible side effects and risks of treatment, he refused it. It's stage four, and there's very little chance that anything would work."

"So, he's going to just die?" Wyatt's voice rises in anger. "No second opinions? We're just takin' what he heard as Gospel? Are you serious?"

"Baby." She tries to comfort him. "It wasn't an easy choice, but Dr. Halpern explained his options, and he wanted to live his life without bein' sick from the treatment."

Zach remains quiet as Wyatt and I keep going back and forth. "There are other doctors. There are other options, and if you'd told us, we could've helped!" I grow angrier by the second.

"Mrs. Hennington," the doctor calls to her, and she wipes the tears away before turning to my father's primary care physician.

"Thank you for coming, Dr. Halpern. My sons didn't know, and I wanted to be sure that you were called right away. Is it the cancer?" She walks away with him.

I sink in the chair with my head in my hands. How the hell could this be happening? My father is the strong one. He wouldn't just lie down and let his life slip away. Not when he has a grandchild on the way, my mother, and his sons.

He wouldn't do this.

He can't.

There has to be a way to save him.

chapter
ELEVEN

Grace

A FTER I LEFT COOPER AT my parent's house, I was filled with nervous energy. I stopped at the store, grabbed everything I needed for my dinner, and tried to convince myself this was still a good idea. When I got home, I was a woman on a mission. I stripped my bed, getting rid of the evidence of last night, and started cleaning. Not a light clean, either. I'm talking hands and knees scrubbing of every inch of this place. Hours later, I finally got everything in its proper place.

I'm not too proud to admit that I called and texted Trent, too, but both went without response.

I guess he really did make his choice.

I wasn't sure what to do, so I called Emily and told her the story as she went from hysterical to stunned silence. She encouraged me to have dinner with Cooper and see what happens, but she also said I needed to figure things out with Trent.

However, he's apparently not talking to me. It's ironic that when I don't want him around, he's everywhere, but when I do need to talk, he's ignoring me.

I push my wayward thoughts aside. Cooper is due here in about two hours. I'm going to fix his favorite dish, which my mama happens to also be famous for making. Her pork chops are a town favorite, and I know Cooper loves them along with her potato salad and green beans. For desert, I'm going to bake an apple pie.

I love cooking, and I know this meal is filled with all the things he enjoys. I'm grateful for everything he did today, and I'm hoping he appreciates this.

I get everything prepped, the pork chops are marinating in the whiskey, and the pie is assembled. I grab my phone and see a text from Cooper.

Cooper: I'm grabbing a bottle of wine. Do you like red or white?

Me: I think skipping the wine is a good idea.

Last night wine and I were best friends. This morning, not so much. Wine makes me a foolish girl.

Cooper: Beer?

Me: Perfect.

Cooper: My kind of girl.

Me: Well, I sure hope so. You've been quite persistent.

I smile as I picture him laughing.

Cooper: Tonight I'll prove why you should choose me.

My teeth grip my lip as I debate how to respond. I can be cute and coy or go with a much more forward response. I completely understand why people stay in crappy relationships, because this dating shit sucks.

I stare at the phone and another text appears.

Cooper: I didn't mean it like that. I just meant that I'm planning to win you over.

> *Me: I hope you're hungry.*

I hope you're hungry? Really, Grace? Could I be anymore awkward?

> *Cooper: Starving.*

I thank my stars that he let me off on that one. I could've said a million different things, but my bumbling mind went with that.

> *Me: See you in a few hours!*

I toss my phone and start to get ready.

Since Cooper and I are only hanging out tonight, I want to be comfortable. I grab a pair of jeans and a cute top that makes my boobs look a little bigger. I'm the only one in my family who wasn't blessed with a chest. Instead, I'm best friends with any kind of push-up or cleavage-enhancing product.

My alarm on the phone goes off, alerting me I need to start cooking. I toss the meat in the oven, check on the potato salad, and mix the green beans. I say a prayer the food tastes great.

Right on time, Cooper knocks on the door.

"Hey," I open the screen, and he enters.

"You look beautiful, as always." Cooper notes as he looks me up and down.

Two friends. We're two old friends sharing a meal. One where I'm not planning to be the entrée or any other course.

Keep it neutral.

"Thank you."

"You okay?" he asks.

"I'm great. I've got dinner in the oven, it should be ready in about fifteen minutes. Do you want a beer?" I look at the case in his hand.

"I'd love one." Coop follows me into the kitchen and runs his hand down my arm. "Grace?" he says after a few seconds.

"Yeah?"

"Relax, there are no expectations, okay?"

I let out a deep sigh. "I know. I'm just nervous."

"Nervous of me?" he questions.

It baffles me how he still doesn't get it. Maybe guys don't see all the complications that can happen when you start dating, but considering what I'm going through on the breakup side . . . it's a lot. We'll be around each other, like I'm around Trent all the damn time. There's no avoidance in this town.

"More of what it means for us," I explain as I pop the tops off two beers. I hand him one and take a long draw from my bottle. "You see what it's like with . . . him."

"I'm not anything like Trent. If this doesn't work out, then it doesn't. You'll still be Grace, and I'll still be Cooper. We'll act like adults."

Well, that's a concept I clearly have no experience with.

"Okay, no more talking about this. We're on our friend date." I lift my bottle.

"Deal, but it's a date, date, remember?" Cooper clinks his bottle to mine.

"Sure. Whatever you say, Coop."

We both chuckle. "It smells great. Is that your mama's whiskey pork?" His face brightens, and the familiar scent fills the air.

I nod with a grin. "Yup!"

"They say the way to a man's heart is through his stomach." He raises a brow. "Are you tryin' to seduce me, Grace Rooney?"

I shrug and let my playful side out. "Maybe, or maybe I'm hopin' you think I'm a shitty cook and run for a better woman."

Cooper's head falls back as he laughs. His arms wrap around my waist, and he pulls me close. "You're out of your mind. I know you can cook."

"What if I forgot?"

"Then I'm sure your mama could give you a few lessons," he suggests with mischief in his voice. "Just don't ask Presley. I can remember Mama tryin' to teach her and Pa and I gagging after we tried to eat. I pray, for Zach's sake, she's improved."

He isn't lying. Presley and I were always in the kitchen and half the time we'd toss whatever she made because it burned so bad. If it didn't burn, we'd wished it had. It was the little of this and little of that part she couldn't do. Baking was always her niche.

We would spend hours imagining we were old married women, making things for our husbands. Some kids might have played house with dolls, but we did it with our houses. We would put our mama's aprons on and pretend to be the Hennington wives. Presley would pretend Zach was coming home after a long day of baseball. She and I would clean the house, make dinner, and have big plans for a night of television with the boys. At least it worked out for one of us.

"He seems to be okay, unless he's going to his parents' house to eat."

Cooper's eyes shimmer as he smiles at me. "Well, I would eat your crappy food because that's what a man does for a woman he likes."

"Good answer."

He leans down, kisses my cheek, and releases me. "How was the rest of your day?"

I groan. It was fine other than when I returned to the store, which was still a mess.

"That good?" Coop questions.

I fill him in on what is going on at the store as he leans against the counter. He listens as I tell him my fear with my mother and father. I know that Cooper can empathize because he took over when his dad couldn't do it anymore. But that was what Forrest wanted, and I know I'm going to have to force my mom's hand. She still thinks she's thirty. "I don't know if I should hire someone behind her back or talk to her about selling the store . . ."

Cooper looks at the bottle and then back at me. "I think it's a tough call. You definitely should talk to her. It's hard because it was my dad's idea. He was the one who was tired, and I think he wanted me to take over everything before I could leave town."

"Would you have?" I've always wondered if Cooper had bigger dreams than this.

I was always content to stay in Bell Buckle. As much as I hate it at times, I love this place. It's full of heritage and landmarks. It's a place where your kids can run outside from sunup to sundown and you don't have to worry.

We didn't have cell phones when we were kids; we had neighbors. That mentality is still strong here. I always hoped I would have kids that could experience a childhood even half as fun as mine.

Cooper takes a second to think and then shrugs. "I don't know. When Presley left, it wasn't a choice anymore. Someone had to take over on the farm, and that someone was me. I was angry about it for a while, but this is my life. Whatever choices I made, I don't regret. I work hard and have a good life. I'm just hopin' for the rest of things to fall in line."

"Yeah," I say on a sigh. "Hey, I meant to ask you, has Wyatt said anything about Angie? I called over there today, but she didn't answer."

"He's at that family fishing thing so I haven't heard anything. I know this pregnancy has been tough on her." Cooper takes a swig of his beer. "I told him to take some time off to stay home, but he knows we're shorthanded since one of the ranch hands left. I keep pushin' him to take care of his family."

"You know Wyatt . . ."

Family is everything to us here, but so is honesty and integrity. Wyatt is stuck between the two things he deems the most important. And to an extent, the Townsend's are family. All our families are very deeply intertwined.

The timer dings, and I shoo Cooper out of the kitchen. I need to get the pie in while we're eating so that it will be done in time. I open two more beers, put the pie in, drain the remnants in my first bottle, and plate our dinner.

"Here we go." I sit the plate and beer on the table.

"This looks amazing, Gracie." My heart sputters. Cooper never calls me Gracie. Trent is the one who started it, and he's the only person that ever says it. I freeze and try to get myself under control, but Cooper grabs my hand. "Did I say something?"

I shake my head and I try not to let my nerves ruin tonight. "No, you didn't do anything. Let's eat."

Cooper doesn't release my hand, and my eyes go back to him. "Don't lie. If I said or did something you need to tell me."

He deserves to know why I became an ice sculpture. This is the stuff he mentioned and I need to be open. "No one else calls me Gracie but Trent."

He leans back, clearly a little uncomfortable. We've done so well for the last thirty minutes, but once again, Trent manages to wiggle his way in. Thankfully, it isn't literal this time.

"I'm sorry. It just came out."

"Please, don't apologize." I take his hand. "It's just that no one ever says that, and it took me by surprise. I've been having a lot of fun tonight, and I would like us to finish our dinner and then the God awful movie you picked."

Cooper's body relaxes a little. He shifts, rests his other hand on mine, and nods. "All right, but you're going to choke on those words when you see the movie."

"I doubt that," I tease.

"You'll see."

I shake my head and pull my hands back. Cooper grabs his fork and knife, and we dig in. Dinner is nice, we talk a little about the farm and how he wants to change a few things. There's a lot more to Cooper than I ever knew. I always knew that he was smart, but he has some ideas that are inspiring. He explains a little about the project Presley's working on, and I go into some of my plans for next year. We talk long after our plates are empty and beers have run dry.

"Ready for the movie?" he asks in one of the very few lulls in conversation. I glance at the clock, realizing we've been talking for well over an hour. Time flew by, and we didn't have any time where it was weird or we didn't have something to talk about.

"I should clean up." I start to grab the plates, but he grips my wrist.

"Leave it. Live a little. Let's watch the movie and then we can take care of the dishes."

He releases my hand, and I put the plate down. "Okay."

It's so not in me to do this, but different is good sometimes.

Cooper pops in the DVD before turning with a grin. "You excited?"

"Curious."

He chuckles and sits on the couch. Both of us sit on each end, I'm not sure what the hell is supposed to happen, so I'm going with better safe than sorry mentality. "I won't bite," he says as he drapes his arm over the couch.

Jesus. Here I go.

I scoot closer as Cooper watches me with an open arm. My butt hits his leg, and he adjusts himself so we're even closer. My throat goes dry as my body rests very much against his. I can't tell if I'm uncomfortable or the nerves are because of how attracted I am to him right now. I've never been blind to Cooper, but he's always been—brotherly. Between today and now dinner, things shifted a little. He never once made me feel small or as if I was just Presley's friend. He talked to me like a woman.

Tonight has felt good, and this feels good, too.

The movie comes on screen, and I can't hold in the laugh as I tilt my head so I can look at him. "You did not!"

"I thought we could use a repeat."

"Goonies never say die!"

Cooper's other arm rests on my knees, and he holds me tight. When we were kids, Presley and I were so obsessed that we wore the VHS out. We would run around the house, searching for the gold and pirate ship we believed were hidden somewhere. Cooper would tell us we were naive, but it didn't stop him from looking with us.

I nestle in, not thinking about the fact that he's Cooper. He's a man that I'm on a date with, one who I also find attractive. The movie plays on as we stay cuddled together. We both laugh at our favorite parts, and I jump a little when Ma talks about cutting out their tongues, which makes him laugh against my ear. The heat from his breath sends a shiver through me.

I try to cover it over by playing with my hair, but Cooper doesn't miss it and tightens his arm a bit.

My head lifts a little and our eyes meet, causing a knot to twist in my stomach.

There's no mistaking what's burning in his green eyes. The heat is clear, and he wants to kiss me.

I should move my head and stop it.

I could clear my throat and leave the room.

I could, and probably should do all that, but I don't think I want to.

I don't want to look back and wonder.

Instead, I turn into him a little more, resting my hand on his chest. "Do you want me to move?" I ask, staring and waiting for something to change.

"Not at all." Cooper's head drops a little, giving me another chance out. He moves slowly, measuring each shift in my body.

I lift my lips just a smidge. "Okay," I say as we grow closer.

His mouth is right there. He could kiss me, but neither of us moves.

Fuck it.

I push myself up and plant my lips on his. His arms go around me instantly, and he drags me closer. I kiss him without restraint and let my mind go so I can feel.

Cooper's hands glide up my back and tangle in my hair.

I wait for the fluttering in my stomach to start.

I try to find the passion where I'd want to leap into his arms. I search for a smidge of feelings I feel when I'm in Trent's, but there isn't one.

Well, okay . . . this isn't what I was expecting, but I keep holding on and waiting for something to happen. Instead of passion, it feels like friendship. The only thing I feel right now is that . . . I'm cheating on Trent.

I break the kiss and look at him.

Cooper releases me, and I hold on to his shoulders. "Was that?" he asks.

"Weird?"

"Maybe we were caught off guard? We should try again," Cooper suggests. He pulls me back to his chest, and I focus on how it feels against his body. He slowly brings his lips to mine.

I close my eyes and hold on to his strong arms as he kisses me. My mind starts to wander a little, it feels nice, but this isn't a first kiss that anyone talks about. I make a mental note to add milk to my grocery list.

Groceries? That's what I'm thinking about? This is so not

going well.

It's nothing he's doing wrong, it's . . . it's . . . bland.

Cooper tilts back and looks at me. "So?" I ask, and he laughs. "I'm not really sure."

"It wasn't bad," I say quickly.

Cooper gives me a disbelieving look. "It was . . . nice."

"But . . ." I say.

Out of all the vivid, what-if situations that played in my head, this definitely wasn't one. I thought maybe the stars and fireworks would explode and we'd be naked, or Cooper would make me forget my name, Trent's name, or a hundred other amazing experiences. Never did I conjure the idea that the kiss would be awkward or feel as if I were lip locked with a friend in spin the bottle.

Cooper groans and I sit back against the couch. "Unreal. I've waited a long time to kiss you like that. I didn't think it would suck so bad."

I slap his chest and giggle. "Hey! I've been known to be a great kisser."

"Well, I've never had any complaints, either."

"Yeah, Betsy loved tellin' all the girls how you stuck your tongue down her throat in seven minutes in heaven."

"She was a prude." I lean into his side and let out a little sigh. "How are we so bad at this together? It's like there's been something keepin' us apart from the beginning."

I drop my head to his shoulder and let out a slow breath. "We shouldn't've had to work so hard at this." I sit up and tuck my leg under me. "And there has been somethin' between us, Coop. And even if he's not here right now—he's here," I say as I touch my heart.

"You told me all of that, but I thought I could win you over somehow."

"I really wish you could've."

I close my eyes and lay my head on his shoulder a split second before a loud screaming noise echoes through the house. The fire alarm blares loudly, and a second later, the house alarm joins it.

Both of us jump, covering our ears against the deafening sound. I look around and see the smoke billowing out from under the kitchen door.

"Shit!" I scream. "The pie!"

It's been hours, and I completely forgot about the damn pie. Now, my house is on fire.

chapter
TWELVE

I RUSH TOWARD THE KITCHEN, hoping I can save my house. Unreal. Absolutely unreal.

"Don't go in there!" Cooper's arms wrap around my waist as he moves me over to the side. "Where's the fire extinguisher?" Cooper yells.

"In the damn kitchen!" I scream and follow him in there, moving to open the window as Cooper grabs the completely destroyed pie from the oven.

After a few minutes, we get the alarm to silence by fanning the hell out of the kitchen. The smoke is cleared out, and I call the alarm company to cancel the fire department, but they explain they've already been dispatched.

"Well," he lifts the charred pie, "I'd say our desert is done."

I attempt to smile so I don't burst out in tears. "I've never, not once in my entire life, burned a pie!" My hands cover my face to hide the fact that I could no longer stop myself from crying. I'm sure Cooper will think it's about the damn pie, but really it's about so much more. This pie is just one more thing I've failed to do right.

"Don't cry." Cooper grabs me and pulls me against his chest.

"You don't get it," I cry into his shirt. "I burnt the pie. I slept with Trent. He told me he loves me, and then I kissed you. I'm a mess. I don't even know who I am!"

Cooper rubs my back and kisses the top of my head. "I promise, it's going to be fine."

"Grace!" Voices yell from outside the house, and I hear the sirens, faint but growing louder with every passing second. "Grace, are you in there?"

"Oh my god!" I grumble against Cooper's chest. "This can't be happening!"

"Grace!" A familiar voice yells louder as they continue banging on the door. "I'm busting the door down!"

I lean back and wipe my eyes. I'm not about to have a broken door on top of all this. Our volunteer firemen will do it without question. They're a little overzealous when it comes to fire safety since we haven't had a fire in . . . ever.

"No!" I yell as I rush toward the front door. "I'm fine! We're all fine!"

I throw the door open as I see Beau's foot in the air. "You're really okay?" he asks quickly and drops his foot.

"Everyone is fine," Cooper says from behind me. "Some food spilled over in the oven and created a lot of smoke."

Beau looks disappointed. "I still need to check things out to be sure."

I give him a pointed stare. "No hoses in my house. There's no fire. We're not on some episode of *Chicago Fire*."

"Killjoy."

Cooper jerks his head to the side and puts his hand on my shoulder. "Yes, sorry that we didn't set the place on fire so you had something to do."

I watch him walk off and turn back toward Cooper. "I'm sorry about tonight. Hell, I'm sure we can go back a month and still not cover all the things I should apologize for."

Cooper grabs his jacket and walks toward me. "It's me who

should be apologizin', Grace. I never should've pushed you. I knew you weren't feeling anything, but I needed to know for sure."

Beau walks back out and shakes his head. "No Southern woman burns a pie like that. It's unheard of."

I ignore his jab. I'll be sure to send his wife a text about his new hunting bow he's been hiding in my store, thinking she isn't going to find out.

Cooper punches Beau in the arm and chuckles. "He's an idiot. I had a good time tonight."

"I did, too."

"Until you set the kitchen on fire," he jokes, making my lips tilt in a smile.

"Shut up."

He comes in close and holds me tight. I wrap my arms around him and squeeze. Cooper kisses the side of my head.

"Well, at least we didn't have Trent show up this time. Come to think of it . . ." There's no way Trent wouldn't be here. Angry or not, if he heard my address and a fire, I can't imagine him ignoring it. He may not always do the right thing when it comes to our relationship, but he's extremely protective of me. This wouldn't be a call he'd ignore.

I step outside and search for the police cruiser I know is somewhere close. "Hank?" I yell, and he turns to me with a smile. "Isn't Trent workin' tonight?"

"You didn't hear?" His grin falls as he walks toward me. "Rhett collapsed this afternoon. We rushed him to the hospital, but he was still unconscious when I left. It's been a busy day for us."

"Oh my God!" I clutch my chest. "Is he all right?"

Hank shrugs. "I haven't heard much. The whole family is there. Trent worked on him until they got him to the hospital."

"I have to go! I need to be there!"

I run back inside, and start searching for my things. I can't find my purse. Where did I put my purse? My heart races as I think about Trent and his family. His father means everything to them. I don't know what is wrong or why he didn't call, but I have to go.

"Grace, calm down." Cooper's hand is on my shoulder.

"I can't find my keys! I don't have my phone. Why didn't anyone call me? I should be there! I didn't know and no one told me. Where the hell are my damn keys?"

"Okay, okay. Where did you put them?" Cooper asks.

"I don't know! I just . . ."

"Listen, you're not in any state to drive. I have my keys right here, grab your phone and bag, and I'll drive you there."

I cover my mouth with my hand and nod. "All right."

Cooper helps me locate the items I need and we climb in his truck. I've been a part of that family for a long time. Rhett and Macie are like a second set of parents to me. My leg bounces as he drives. I think about Trent working, whatever that means, on his father. I envision them all gathered around and how alone Trent must feel.

"I'm sure it'll be okay, Grace," Cooper tries to reassure me.

"Thank you for drivin' me."

Cooper smiles with sadness in his eyes. "I told you we'd always be friends."

He did, and it's clear he keeps his promises.

"Coop?" I pull his attention back. I want to ask him something, but don't know how it'll go. "Are you upset? About . . . you know . . . this?"

"You mean me driving you to the man you truly love?" he asks, and I nod. "Before I came over tonight, I talked to Presley," he admits. "I told her about what happened this morning and on our date, and she of course laughed, but she tried to explain what it's like to love someone the way she loves Zach. I think the way she feels about him is how you are with Trent. I could never compete with that."

"Coop," I try to stop him, but he takes my hand in his.

"I've known you my whole life, and you've never looked at anyone like you look at him. I may wish it was different, but it's the truth."

"I never wanted to hurt you."

He shakes his head and chuckles. "You didn't. We're friends who tried to see if there was anything there. I told you that I had no expectations. We both deserve to be crazy about each other. Shit, I want a girl to come runnin' into my arms and not get enough of kissing me."

"I'm sorry I'm not her. You deserve that, you really do."

And he does. Cooper is a textbook perfect man. He's like my daddy. He works hard, loves harder, and is a good man. He's going to make some woman very lucky someday. I hope he finds her fast because he deserves everything he wants.

"Thanks." He gives me a rueful smile. "In another life, I think we would've been perfect. In another time, we would've been happy. More than anything, I want that for you."

"Cooper Townsend, walkin' away from you is going to be my greatest regret."

He smirks. "I can live with that. Just make him treat you right."

I don't say anything because my knee-jerk reaction is to defend Trent, but that isn't right. Cooper has a right to say what he needs to, and he isn't wrong. Trent hasn't been great, which hasn't been a secret.

"Thank you for being such a good guy."

"I guess all the clichés are comin' true. Nice guys do finish last."

"That's not true." Cooper doesn't see the flip side. "Settling with me would've been you comin' in last. Now, you can find the girl that deserves your love."

We enter the hospital's parking lot, and my nerves start to rise.

I don't know how he's doing or if he's okay, and I want nothing more than to run into that building and find him. Yet, when I reach for the door handle, I pause, turning back to Cooper.

He shakes his head and gives me an encouraging smile. "Go to him," he instructs.

I lean over, kiss his cheek, and rush out of the truck.

The hospital isn't hard to navigate, but with how many times I get lost, you'd think I've never been here. The white walls all look the same. I called Presley and Trent again, but got no answer. I decide to ask a nurse where Rhett is, when she refuses to release the information, I lie and tell her I'm his daughter.

Now knowing where to head, I follow the red line to the intensive care wing. My heart is heavy with worry. The Henningtons are a strong unit, with Rhett being the head of them all. I can't imagine what the boys or Mrs. Hennington are going through.

I round the corner and stop dead in my tracks when I see Cooper standing there.

"Hey. What are you doing here?"

"You forgot your purse," he explains as he holds out my bag.

"Thank you! I didn't even realize. I've been walkin' around this place for what feels like forever and I still haven't seen any of them. I don't know if he's all right or . . ." I say as my eyes mist over. "I can't get ahold of anyone either."

"If something happened we'd know. My mama and yours would've called." Cooper's hand touches my shoulder in a comforting way.

He's right. I can't imagine our parents wouldn't let us know. Okay. I feel a little better.

I look up and Cooper's entire body goes still. When I turn to see what has him on edge, relief fills me before flickering away, causing my heart to plummet.

Trent is standing there with a murderous expression on his

face. His hands clench into fists and he stomps forward. I've seen him like this two times in my life. The first was when he found William after he killed Scarlett and the second was when he heard someone beat their infant to death a town over.

He wanted to tear them both limb from limb.

And it looks like Cooper is the object of his rage right now.

Cooper's arm drops, and I rush toward Trent, hoping to diffuse a situation before it happens. "Trent, I came as soon as I heard. Is your dad okay?" He doesn't look at me. He keeps moving toward Cooper. "Trent!"

His gait halts, and he turns to me. His face is hard and his jaw clenched. His deep blue eyes lock on mine, allowing me to see the emotions playing out: confusion, surprise, anger, and lastly, resentment. "Why the hell are either of you here?"

"What?" I ask with shock. "Why would you ask me that? Why wouldn't I be here?"

"I'll let you two handle this." Cooper puts his hands in the air and retreats.

Trent turns his head toward Cooper and the vein in his neck pops. "How noble of you."

Cooper bristles and shakes his head. "Look, I didn't come to start anything."

"Then maybe you shouldn't have come here." His voice is hard as his eyes slice to mine and he adds, "Either of you."

I thought coming here was the right thing to do. I wanted to offer him support, but he's being an ass.

I take a step back and try to hide my hurt. "I wanted to be here. I wanted to be here for you."

Trent laughs. "You and your boyfriend? How nice of you. So, not only do I have to deal with the fact that my father is dying but also I get the added benefit of seeing you with another man."

Cooper jumps in before I can. "You need to calm down and

listen to what she's sayin'. All I did was I drive her here."

"Sure you did. You couldn't help but be her knight in shining armor. Here comes perfect Cooper and his white horse."

"This is your problem, Trent," Cooper says. "You act like this. She heard about your dad and couldn't get here fast enough. She was too upset to drive, so I gave her a ride. So, if anyone should be pissed off, it's me. I drove her to you."

"Was that after you worked on her farm all day? Or after dinner?" Trent sneers and then looks at me. "Your house okay? I would hate to see you without a place to live. But then again, maybe you can move in with Cooper."

Tears flood my eyes and start to fall. He has this all wrong. I'm not here *with* Cooper. I'm here because Cooper was kind enough to drive me. I'm here for Trent, and he's treating me as if I'm a heartless bitch who wants to rub Cooper in his face.

"Stop it." I put my hand on his arm and he tears it back. "Cooper and I had dinner, but I'm here for you because I wanted to make sure you were all right and your dad was okay. You would know that if you would just listen." I wipe my face and try again. "We're not . . ."

He puts his hand up. "I don't want to fucking hear it. I'm dealin' with enough right now. My father is lying in a hospital bed, dyin' of cancer, and I don't need to add this on top of it."

Cooper scoffs and shakes his head. "I'm going to check on Presley and Wyatt. If you need me, Grace, you know where to find me."

I nod and watch him walk away.

"You can go with him," Trent says with hostility. "I'm sure he wouldn't mind."

"If you'd—"

"Just go, Grace."

I get that he's hurting. I understand completely that he's in pain and angry at the situation he's dealing with, but if he'd stop lashing out at me, I could explain.

"No." I shake my head, digging my heels in. "I'm not leavin'."

"I don't want you here."

I hear the slight tremor in his voice. He may say he doesn't want me here, but I think he's scared. This family has been through a lot in the last two years. Losing his father is going to be a major blow.

When I step closer to him, my voice is low and comforting. "I think you do."

Trent's eyes go hard and his voice is ice. "I tell you I love you. I lay it all out, and you fucking ask me to leave and then spend the day with him. What do I get to do? I get to spend the entire day thinkin' about you. I have to wonder if he's touchin' you, kissin' you, or makin' you smile, and then you come here with him. I don't fucking care what you think you know, because you're wrong. I don't want you here. I don't want to see you or him anywhere."

Too damn bad. I am not leaving. I need to stand my ground. He isn't pushing me away anymore, and I'm not running either. It's time that we fight for each other rather than against each other.

I lean forward and push onto my tiptoes so we are chest to chest before I grab his face between my palms. When I open myself completely to him, two things can happen. Either he'll hear what I say and see the truth in my words or he'll push me away. Our lives' course will be determined on how he steers the horse, he can throw us off or ride steady.

"I'm here because I love you, you thick-headed, unwilling-to-listen, lovable idiot! I'm here because I choose you. I've always chosen you because I can't imagine my life without you. I'm here because I love you so much my insides hurt no matter how many times I tell you that I shouldn't keep runnin' back." He tenses, and I watch the shift in his gaze. "So, if you want to keep arguin' about this, I'm happy to, but you said you love me, and I'm standin' before you askin' you to let me do the same."

Trent searches my eyes and his breathing stops as he touches my cheek. "What?"

"I said I love you."

His thumb grazes my lip. "Say it again."

"I love you."

"No." He shakes his head. "The other part."

My breathing is shallow, and I know what he needs. "I choose you. I didn't choose Cooper. There really never was a choice. It's been you since I was sixteen."

Not a second later, Trent's mouth crushes against mine. His lips are soft, but the kiss is not as he holds my head to his and pours all his emotions into me. His fear is palpable as his fingers slide into my hair, holding me closer, breathing my air, and taking what I'm offering him. It's as if I can feel him telling me I'm his reason for breathing.

He pulls back, and I run my fingers through his hair. We stand here together with his forehead against mine. My heart rate starts to slow as the seconds pass.

"I need to check on my family, but I just want to stay here," he murmurs.

I lift my head, remembering why I'm here in the first place. "Is he okay?"

He shakes his head.

Trent takes my hand in his, and we start to walk toward the waiting room. He doesn't say anything as we move through the hall. I can tell he's on the edge of falling apart.

"What happened?" I urge.

Trent replays the scene at the pond. His voice cracks when he gets to the part about doing CPR on his father. I can't imagine what that was like for him. He's had to do all kinds of life saving measures as a police officer. There have been calls where he's lost someone and times he's saved them, but from the pain laced in his voice, this time will never leave him.

Knowing the choice that you make in a single moment will dictate if someone will live has to be scary, but knowing it could be your decision that could end the life of someone you love is terrifying.

"So, what are the doctors sayin'?" I ask, watching closely as his face falls.

"I don't know. All Mama said is that he has stage four cancer."

"What? When?"

"Apparently, he was diagnosed six months ago. I don't know how the hell they could keep this from my brothers and me. It's such bullshit!" Trent stops in front of the doors. "Everyone is tryin' to wrap their minds around it. Zach isn't handling it at all, and Wyatt is just Wyatt."

"How are you handlin' it?"

He moves closer and pulls me back in his arms. "I'm not sure. I've been so messed up today between him and you." Trent lets out a heavy sigh. "I didn't lose you, and I'm damn sure not going to lose him. I'm going to have to convince him to fight."

We enter the waiting room hand in hand, and I hope there's a way he gets what he wants.

THIRTEEN

Trent

EVERY MINUTE FEELS LIKE DAYS. We all sit quietly and
wait for any news from the doctors. They're still running some
tests, so it's a waiting game.

Grace's mother arrives, looking frantic as she rushes over to
Mrs. Kannan and Mrs. Townsend.

"Is it the cancer?" she asks and they all nod, but Grace's head
snaps in their direction, her eyes narrowing.

"Mama, you knew?"

"It wasn't my story to tell, sugar."

"You *all* knew?" I yell. "Y'all knew that he was dyin' and didn't
tell us? You let us go to Zach's wedding without knowin' it could've
been his last? You let us skip Sunday dinners with them, and all
the other things we could've been doin', all the things we *should*
have been doing!"

These women are like family. They've been to every event
in our lives. They're my mother's best friends, and none of them
thought we should know. Not one thought it would be important
for us. The time I could've spent with him . . . gone.

Mrs. Kannan steps forward. "We begged them to tell you,
honey. Y'all had a right to know, but we weren't going to be the

ones to tell you."

I start to pace as my mind spins. "There has to be something we can do."

Someone coughs, and I turn to look at the doctor now standing there. "Trent," he says, dropping a nod in my direction.

"Dr. Halpern, is he all right?" I move closer.

"He's resting. His anemia is affecting his heart. The lack of oxygen and red blood cells in his body have started to cause other organs to struggle. We warned him this would be possible, but I think he pushed himself too hard today. He needs some other tests, and I'm recommending a blood transfusion immediately. If we can get the anemia under control we can assess what to do next."

"What about the cancer?" Zach asks. "Is there a chance he can beat it?"

Dr. Halpern shakes his head. "Your father would need to undergo a great amount of chemo and then most likely would need a bone marrow transplant. Considering the fact that he's allowed the cancer to grow for the last six months, I'm not sure that treatment is even an option at this point. It's up to him now."

Rage starts to boil in my blood. Wasted time we can't get back. Things we can't fix because we didn't know about them. I can't understand what he was thinking.

"All of this can be discussed later, right now, we need to focus on getting him stable. He needs a blood transfusion to control his anemia. I want to warn you all, this is when things start to move quickly. He's going to need regular transfusions."

"I want to see him," I say quickly.

The doctor nods. "He's exhausted and can't handle much excitement. Just go in one at a time."

I turn to my brothers, who both nod when I take the step closer. "I won't be long. If you want to go get your blood drawn . . ."

Wyatt clasps my shoulder. "I'll see you in a few."

I nod. Zach looks away despondently and follows Wyatt. Zach is by far the closest to my father. He's always been the most like him, and I hope Presley gets here soon. She was out by Knoxville delivering a horse for Zach and is on her way back. I hate seeing him so broken, you can tell he needs her.

Grace takes my hand and squeezes. "I'll be right here."

I pull her against my chest and kiss the top of her head.

With each step toward his room, my heart breaks. I don't know what to say to him, but I know that I can't let this be the end.

"DAD," I SAY AS I enter the room.

"Would you give us a few minutes?" he asks my mother.

"I'll be back in five minutes." Mama points to me. "Don't make him upset or so help me God."

There's little chance of that. I try to remember he's in the hospital and that I was performing CPR on him hours ago. I hate seeing the man I've admired my whole life looking weak and sick. He's the one who always stood on this side of the bed when my brothers and I did some foolish stunt, now I'm the one hoping to talk some sense into him.

I need to stay calm and convince him why he's going to do this. Why he *has* to do this.

"We'll be fine, Mama."

"I'll go give everyone an update."

When she steps out, I move around to the side of his bed. My legs tremble as I stand here. My father is sick. My father is dying, and I don't know what to do.

"Thank you, son," Dad says as I get close.

"For what?"

"We wouldn't be talkin' right now if it weren't for you."

And if I don't get him to turn the boat around about treatment,

I may not be able to save him next time. I need my father. I need him in ways I probably don't understand. He's the one who keeps me on track. He calls me on my shit, which there's a lot of, and makes me see reason. If it weren't for him, I wouldn't be who I am today.

I need him to fight.

I need him to win.

More than that, I need him to stay alive.

"Dad." I step closer.

He puts his hand up. "I know what you're goin' to say, and I'm not changin' my mind."

Unacceptable.

"You have to try."

"I know all of what the doctors told me, and I'm not doin' it. I won't become a man who can't get out of bed, can't eat, doesn't function. That's what'll happen. I watched my father die like that, and I won't do it."

"You're not even willing to give it a shot? That goes against everything you've told us our whole lives."

My father scoots up in his bed. "I know you think that, but for what end? So, your mama is forced to watch me be sick? She can't go through that, and I don't want to be that man. I won't do that to her." He draws in a deep breath, which sounds too much like a struggle, and points to the door. "That woman can barely see me with a cold, you want her to suffer through that?"

"And you think her burying you is gonna be better?" I cry out.

My father's face pales, and I know I struck a chord. This is my opening and as much as I hate doing it, I'm going to use it. "You can't do that to her. You can't, Dad. You have to try. At least give it a shot. She won't be able to survive you dying. None of us will."

The man who doesn't cry wipes his eyes. "I don't think it's an option anymore."

I grab his hand. "We'll find out. Because if you don't try, I'm not sure any of us will be able to live with ourselves."

Wyatt filters in, and I look at my father again.

"Pop?" I say the word but beg with my voice.

"All right."

"All right," I pat his arm before looking at my brother. "I'll let you visit with Wyatt."

"Trent?" he calls out. "Don't tell your mama anything yet."

I nod with understanding. He doesn't want to give my mother false hope. None of us do, but at least I could get him to even contemplate fighting it. However, I know my father and it's going to take a lot more to convince him. Once he makes up his mind, it's almost impossible to change it.

I head back to the waiting room where Presley sits with Zach. "Hey," she says as she gets to her feet.

"Pres." I give her a hug and she sniffs back her tears.

"How's he doin'?"

I look over at Zach, who still doesn't move. "Are you goin' in?"

"Nah," he says, looking at the ground. "I'm letting Wyatt and Mom in for now."

"Are you kidding? You know he wants to see you."

"Trent," Grace whispers, putting her hand on my arm and drawing my attention. "I'm sure your brother will go." I glance over at her, and she shakes her head slightly. Grace's eyes are soft and she bites her bottom lip. The way she looks at me, so open and loving, makes me pause. "Why don't we sit?" Her small hand wraps around mine, and I nod.

Zach can be pissed, but not going to see Dad is unacceptable. He needs to man up and be there. I don't have a problem reminding him if he needs it. This isn't about him. This is about Dad.

Time passes with each of us taking turns going in an out. Zach, however, remains in the waiting room. It's taking everything inside me not to punch him.

He's acting like a selfish prick.

After another hour passes, I finally reach the tipping point. "Go in there!" I get to my feet and he glares at me.

"Don't tell me how to act," he fires back as he gets toe to toe with me. "I'm doin' what I can. You don't get to dictate how we all handle things. You're not exactly the authority on doin' what's right."

"Trent." Wyatt steps between us and puts his hand on my chest. "Not like this. Not today."

"He's sitting out here! Dad is dyin', and he's fucking sitting there."

"Dad understands," Wyatt says, trying to get me to relax. "Don't do this."

I stare at my brothers as I push the air out of my nose. I'm fuming. We're stronger in numbers and Zach needs to go in. "He's the one he'd listen to the most." I choke on the words. "He'll listen to him." I point at Zach, and his face pales. "If he tells him to fight—" My throat starts to close and my chest aches. "He'll listen to him."

"You don't know that," Wyatt tries again to reason with me.

I do know it. Zach has always been the one Dad hears. When we were younger, if Zach told Dad it was his fault, none of us got in trouble. I don't think he had a favorite, but if he did, Zach would be it. Sure, he's listening to Wyatt and me, but he's waiting for him.

Mama walks through the doors and looks at the three of us ready to fight. "Not happenin' here, boys. You three are goin' to get along and that's that."

I see the fear in her eyes. She's right. We don't need to be doing this here. "Yes, ma'am."

"Sorry, Mama," Zach says and moves back to Presley.

"Good. Now, they started the first transfusion. He'll be here a few days. I want you all to head home and get some rest. I promise I'll call you if anything changes."

"Mama," I start to protest.

"No," she refutes. "This isn't a suggestion. Go home, shower, and come back in the mornin' when we know more. This is comin' from your father, and you don't want to go against his wishes, do you?"

"No," Wyatt says and gives us each a look that says we're to do as she asks. Dad listens to Zach, where as Wyatt is the one Mom trusts to get us to listen to her. She doesn't leave room for a discussion and arguing will upset her.

"I love you all," Mama says and kisses each of us on the cheek. "I'm sorry we lied to you. I hope you'll forgive me."

I pull her into my arms and kiss the top of her head. "We'll do whatever we can."

She pats my back and looks in my eyes. "I don't know what I'll do if I lose him."

Her eyes fill with tears, and I squeeze her again. "Then convince him to fight, Mama."

FOURTEEN

Grace

I T'S BEEN THREE DAYS SINCE Rhett collapsed. Trent has been at the hospital or working, and we haven't had a chance to see each other or talk about anything. He texts me every day, telling me he can't wait to see me, but our communication has been minimal. Presley told me that the blood transfusion worked well, and they're now talking about chemo options. The last thing I want to do is add stress to Trent's plate about where we stand.

His focus is where it should be, but he asked me to come over when he gets off work in an hour. I decide to head over early because I can't handle just sitting here. I've talked myself into and out of a million things that he could say.

It wouldn't be crazy to think he's changed his mind, but God I hope he hasn't.

I pull up to his house and look around. I haven't been here in a while, but everything is still the same. His car isn't outside, but I still have my key, so I can let myself in.

His house sits on the southern edge of his family's land. It's not big, but it's perfect for him. The house is decorated with deep mahogany wood, leather furniture, and all very masculine art on the wall. He's a simple man, and doesn't need much, but he let me do some small things to make the house more homey.

I walk in and set my purse down, but then he emerges from the back room, scaring me half to death. "You're here?"

"I came home to grab something," he explains. "What are you doin' here already?"

My heart races as he approaches. "I didn't want to wait."

"I'm glad you didn't. I've been goin' out of my mind."

Trent's body moves with such assurance. His sandy-blond hair is in disarray. His dark blue eyes shine with wonder. Everything inside me clenches when he stops in front of me. My breathing grows shallow, and I fight the urge to jump him. This is what has never been an issue for me. Trent makes my blood pump, and I come to life around him.

"Why?" I ask.

"Because I don't know what we're doin', sweetheart. I don't know what you want or what this means for us." His hand rises to caress my cheek, but he drops it and blows out a deep breath. "I've pushed you away and messed with your head, and I'll never forgive myself. I don't want to do that anymore. I love you." Trent, who seems to have run out of restraint, hooks his finger in mine. "If you want to be with me, you're going to have to be the one to decide."

I'm terrified to say what I'm feeling. Years of the back and forth between Trent and me are playing tug-of-war inside me. No matter how much I want to dive in and embrace his love for me, a tiny voice is telling me I'm a fool and that he said all of that as a way to keep me away from Cooper. He doesn't know about the disastrous kiss between Cooper and me, but now is definitely not the time to tell him.

"I'm scared," I admit, offering a safe answer.

"You think I'm not?"

I look up at him. "What do you have to be scared of?"

"I have no idea what you're thinkin' right now. For the most part, I've always been able to tell where your head is, but I don't right now. It's killin' me. The only thing I know is what I feel and that there's nothing in this world I want more than you."

I stand before this man that I've spent my entire life loving. A man who, no matter what I do, I can't eradicate from my heart. Our love may not be perfect, but nothing in life is. I want him by my side. He's who I'll always need.

"I don't know how to live without you. I don't want to try to learn, either."

His arms are around me in an instant. "Say it," he commands.

"You have to promise me things. You have to let me in. I need a man who's going to give me his whole heart. I need you to love me and not just because we were separated. If we do this again, I can't have you half in."

"I'll do whatever you want."

My hands touch the stubble on his face, and I study his dark blue eyes. "It's not just about what I want. I need to know you want this, too. I want to get married. I want a baby if we can. I want a life. I want it all. I can't do this alone, and I don't want to do it with anyone but you. What do you want?"

"I only want you. All of you—always," Trent says before his mouth is on mine.

His arms tighten, and I lose it. Our lips move together in perfect harmony. His tongue seeks entrance, and I gladly give it over. Every part of my body is humming when he presses against me. I kiss him with everything I have. All the weeks I went without his touch were agonizing. The hours I spent crying for him. The way we could've kissed when he told me he loved me. All the emotions I've held on to . . . I let go.

Trent moves us backward until we fall onto the couch and then braces himself over me without breaking the connection. Our hands roam each other's bodies, my fingers tracing each ridge and valley on his perfect body. The last time he kissed me, we were yelling at each other, it was passion and anger, this time it's coming together. He's the other half of my heart, and right now, I'm beating in perfect sync with him.

Trent pulls back. "I love you," he says before finding my mouth again.

I break the kiss and look him in the eyes. "Show me how much."

His grin spreads and he adjusts me so I'm on top of him. "I'm going to do much more than that, sweetheart." The mirth dances in his eyes. "However, I'm on shift for another hour, so if I get a call, I can't say I was busy makin' love to my girl." He kisses my nose. "So, you stay right here, and I'll be back to make good on that promise."

I know what that means. Fun time for Grace.

It takes Trent another twenty minutes to actually get out the door, and as soon as he leaves, I start to get excited about when he'll return. I'm sure the next half hour is going to go by extremely slowly for both of us. With nothing to do but pace Trent's house and drive myself nuts while I wait, I grab my phone and text Presley.

Me: You home?

Presley: Yes! Please tell me you're stopping over!

Me: I'll be there in five.

I leave a note on the table for Trent in case he comes back early and head to her house.

"Grace!" she says, standing from her seat on her front porch and rushing toward me. "I've missed you!"

"I've missed you, too," I say as I embrace her. Even though we saw each other a few days ago, it was hardly time for us to catch up.

"Come sit. I have coffee or wine. Zach's at the hospital finally visiting with this dad."

We head back to the big couches that sit out on the porch. She and Zach built this house, and it's truly amazing. It's brand new yet feels like it's always been here. The inside is modern rustic and the way they positioned the house they have a front row view to one of the ponds on the property.

"Where are the boys?" I look around and wait for the noise, but it's quiet. Her twin boys are always running around and then there's her man-child . . .

"They're out camping with my brother and father. Since Rhett is still in the hospital, my parents figured they could take them so we're freed up a little."

"That's really nice of them." I smile.

She laughs and shakes her head slightly. "I think Daddy was a little ambitious and realized two teenage boys are a handful and called Cooper in for reinforcements."

"I'm sure they'll be fine."

"Cayden is such a prankster, though. I can't even imagine what they have planned for this trip."

I fold my legs under me and listen as she fills me in on the boys. They're such great kids, and it's been wonderful seeing them with Zach. He loves them as if they were his own. Logan is the quieter of the two, but he's blossomed being on the farm. Between Cooper, Wyatt, Zach, and Trent, he's surrounded by strong and outspoken men, they've all been influential. From the conversations that Presley's had about their father, he wasn't that way. Todd was soft-spoken and much more reserved.

You won't find much of that around here.

It's a death match for who can be louder and more outrageous. At least that's how it was when we were growing up, and most of the aforementioned have yet to become adults.

"How's Zach handling everything with Rhett?" I ask as we sip our coffee.

"You know Zach." Presley purses her lips as she leans her head back against the couch tilting it in my direction. "He's close with his dad and this is killin' him. I think he feels responsible in some way. As if he should've known. How's Trent handling it?" She gives a sly grin. "I saw you two at the hospital."

I shake my head and let my smile stretch over my lips. "Can I ask you somethin'?"

"Of course."

"Do you ever wish things had turned out differently?" I've wondered how she truly felt after her life settled. She always knew Zach was the one for her, but that dream wasn't set in Bell Buckle. She spent our childhood talking about seeing the world and with Zach playing baseball, it meant a life outside of here.

Presley looks out at the water. "I think life works in mysterious ways. I believe I was meant to leave here, find Todd, have the boys, and then come back. It sounds nuts, but I truly believe my life is exactly how it should be. The boys love it here, I'm with the man I love, and I'm happy. Do I wish the boys had their father? Absolutely." She gives a small, sad smile. "Todd loved them, but now they get to know a different kind of dad. Zach is active and crazy. Todd was structured and academic." She shrugs. "But back to your question. No, I don't ever wish things had turned out differently."

I don't know why, but I feel like crying. She gives me hope that I can have it all. I look away and fight back the tears.

I love that Presley's happy. She's been through hell and then found her heaven.

"Grace? Are you okay, honey?"

"Sorry." I laugh and sniffle. "I'm just bein' a girl."

"Why don't you tell me about what happened." Presley leans over and takes my hand.

"I . . ." I don't know what to tell her. "It's . . ."

Presley's eyes are filled with concern. "Cooper and I talked. I told him I thought he should step back and let you find your way back to Trent," she admits. "I don't know if he told you, but I think we both know what it's like to love a Hennington. It doesn't go away. It doesn't ebb. It takes over your entire heart and soul. Trent is your forever love, honey. Even if you and Cooper were to have really given it a go, I'm talkin' full out dates, doin' the things I won't say, and all that . . . can you image what it would've been like to see Trent?"

I shake my head and clutch my throat.

"Your heart hurts just thinking about it. Am I right?"

"Yes."

"Yeah, that'll never go away. Believe me, I know."

My chest tightens, and then I feel a sense of relief. I was so worried I'd lose Presley in some way. She was in a no-win situation with Cooper being her brother and Trent being her brother-in-law. And even though I didn't actually date Cooper, it was hard not talking to Presley about what was going on in my life.

I nod. "I love his stupid ass."

"And he loves you." She squeezes my hand. "Trent was over here the day before your date with Coop. In all my time around him, I've never seen him cry. Not one time, and when he realized you were seriously movin' on, he lost it. He tried to hide it, but I saw his tears."

I shake my head and look away. "Why did it take for me to think about dating another man for him to see me?"

"Oh, honey. Because all men, especially Hennington men, are idiots." We both laugh a little. "Look, I love my brother, but I never saw you guys as a real match. I hoped I was wrong, but I don't know," she rubs her hand against her arm. "Maybe because Cooper hasn't had a serious relationship since high school, but he wasn't going to be the one. He works too much, he's stubborn as all hell, and I think after a few months, you guys would've killed one another."

"He is sweet, though," I defend him a little.

"Of course he is. He's Cooper. But he's also . . . Cooper." She squishes her face, and we both laugh, and I know exactly what she means.

"Since I'm pryin' into your life and all . . . I wonder because we're the same age, do you think you'll have another kid?" I ask.

"Hell no!" Presley almost chokes on her coffee. "Dear Lord, I think my uterus just died a little."

"Why not?"

She puts her cup down. "I'm not saying that if it happened I wouldn't be happy, but Zach and I have talked about it at great length. We've only been married a few months, we spent seventeen years apart, and we don't want to add more into the mix. To him, Logan and Cayden are his sons. He doesn't see them as just mine. He jokes that he's glad he missed the diaper stage, but we're content with it being just the four of us."

"I can understand that. We're not all that young, either." I grab my coffee and try to chase away the thought with caffeine, but it is useless. I'm close to forty, and with as much as I want a baby, I'm not sure if Trent even wants kids. Sometimes I hate that I let him drag me around this long and I might have missed my chance.

"You're only thirty-six, Grace. Plus, Angie's doin' it."

"And look how miserable she is," I retort.

She shrugs. "Her first pregnancy was nothing like this one. It depends. But it's not too late for you to have a baby if you want one. Look at where you are right now. You always have the ability to change. I think that's the best part of life, you can make somethin' happen if you want it bad enough. Trent thought all hope was lost, and look where you two are."

"I hope so, Pres. I don't want to lose him."

She shifts forward and takes my hand in hers. "Then don't let him go."

I smile and nod. That's exactly what I intend to solidify tonight.

chapter FIFTEEN

"GRACIE?" TRENT CALLS OUT FROM the living room. "In here," I yell to him.

After my talk with Presley, I had a good idea of what I needed to do. The first is to set some ground rules for this to work. I plan to be clear about what will fly this time around. I think with his very logical mind, this will be the best approach. I just have to resist his attempts at seduction. I've never thought about how much he uses sex against me. But when I sat back and looked at it with a bit of perspective, it was all there.

I'm unable to resist him. He knows how to please me, and he uses that to get out of these conversations.

Not this time.

Trent walks into the kitchen where I'm sitting at the table with my hands in front of me.

"Sorry that took longer than I expected. I thought you'd be in the bedroom," he says with a grin as he strips out of his shirt.

"Sit," I command. The smile he had fades. "Please."

"Did something change while I was gone?"

"Not like that." I try to be reassuring. "If this is going to work this time around, we have to talk first."

"We can talk in the bedroom." He raises a brow.

And here's the flirting I'm susceptible to. I squash the tingling in my belly and focus on my task. Trent will not get me naked in his bed before we finish this talk. That is my goal. I must resist the five o'clock shadow, the way his blond hair is falling in his eyes, and the blue smoldering look he's giving. I need to stop focusing on his arms and how the muscles are much bigger than I remember. I can't think about that.

I have to stay on task.

"No bedroom, honey. We'll talk right here." I attempt to maintain my composure. But then he removes his undershirt and walks around to the seat next to me.

"Sure. What do you want to talk about?"

"Us."

"What about us?" Trent's voice drops. "Because I'd like to do a lot more than talk, sweetheart. I went far too long without touching your skin when we were apart. And I'd like to fulfill the promise I made. I'm going to enjoy hearing you scream my name."

I melt. My entire body becomes liquid, and I can't help the shudder that wracks through me. Damn him and his mouth. That mouth that I know can do some pretty incredible things.

No, shut it down, Grace. Stay strong.

"Trent." I shift in my seat. "We had sex the other day, and it led to a lot of issues. I'd like to avoid that this time, so no sex or anything close until we talk."

"We'll see." There's no mistaking the challenge we've both made. He's going to make this talk incredibly difficult, and I'm going to end up naked on the table.

"I want us to move in together by the end of the month."

"Done."

He doesn't blink. He just agreed? Is this a joke?

"I'm sorry," I say in disbelief. "Are you agreeing?"

"Yes, we'll move in together by the end of the month. What's next?"

"Okay." I bat my eyes in confusion. That was much easier than I thought. The last time we talked about moving in together, it ended with him storming out.

"Can we live in my house? I like your place, but mine is a little bigger."

I know this will be where we'll have the most resistance. He loves his house, and I love mine. However, I have three bedrooms, and he has only one. I would eventually like to have kids . . . maybe.

"Sure. I like your place just fine. How about we start moving there now?"

"Trent!" I glare at him. "Agreeing to agree isn't going to get to the sex any faster."

He leans back and rubs his chin. "I'm not doin' that, sweetheart. I'm telling you we're going to move in together this week, to your house, and now, I'd like to take you back to my bed and spend the next few hours enjoying you . . . thoroughly."

I'm dead. He's going to kill me with words. Trent's hand moves to my knee and slowly creeps up my leg. "Stop."

"Stop what, sweetheart? I'm just familiarizing myself with the lay of the land while we talk. Bein' efficient and all."

I need to talk faster. Much faster.

"Do you love me?" I ask.

His hand stops moving, and his eyes lock with mine. "I love you."

"I need to hear it. I need you to mean it. I'm going to be needy. I'm going to question you. I've had almost twenty years of doubting us, can you handle that?"

Trent's hands move to my face. His eyes are sad and full of regret. "I did this to you. I hate that I did. I hate that I put any doubt in your head. You're going to have to forgive me and I'm going to have to earn that. I know this, and it isn't anything less than I deserve. I won't do that to you again, Gracie. I won't hurt you like that. I plan to tell you that I love you every day, because I do."

A tear slides down my face. Who knew that he could be so damn sweet?

"Can I kiss you?" Trent asks.

I can't speak, so I nod. Slowly, his face moves toward mine. It's a sweet kiss filled with promise and a chance at redemption. I hold his hands as he cups my cheeks. Another tear falls as I give my heart back to him. Each piece of it is his. I wish it could've always been like this, but I try to let that go. He's here now, loving me like I always wanted.

He leans back and rubs the tear away with his thumb. "What else do you need, sweetheart?"

I shake my head. "I only need you."

Trent's hands don't move as his jaw tightens. The air around us shifts and fills with tension. "Say I'm yours," he demands.

I don't hesitate. "You're mine."

"Say you're mine."

"I've only ever been yours."

Trent stands and pulls me to my feet, his arms hook under my knees, and he lifts me. "You'll only ever be mine."

I touch his cheek. "And you?"

He smiles as he starts to move toward the bedroom. "I don't see anyone else but you, Gracie. I'll fix this. I'll fix us."

"I know you will." I smile.

He kicks the door open and lays me down. My hands glide across his bare chest, and his eyes stay trained on mine. Trent's body has always been firm, but now I'm takin' the time to appreciate it all. His arms are big and strong and his stomach is toned and hard. I like it. My fingers make their way to his face, and his eyes close.

I run the pads of my fingertips across his lips, feeling his breath as he sighs. *"I've missed you."*

"I've missed you, too," I confess.

He moves quickly, flipping me on top. My hair falls between us, and he pushes it back. "I want to see you. I want to see your face the entire time."

I drop down and kiss him. Our tongues dance without restraint, giving and taking. He's unforgiving as he nips at my lip. This is everything we are. The need I feel for him is insurmountable. I want him to remind me of what we were and all we can be.

"Don't make me wait," I say as my mouth moves to his ear. "I need you."

Trent's hands move up my back as I lean back, allowing him to remove my shirt. He stares at me, muttering, "So damn gorgeous," before pushing me to my back, sliding off the bed, and taking off the remainder of his clothing.

I smile. He's always made me feel beautiful, especially when we're in bed.

Trent pushes me back and I watch as his body moves, loving every second.

"You've been workin' out," I note.

"It was either that or I beat the shit out of someone. I didn't think that would earn me any brownie points." He smirks.

"Good choice."

He climbs back on the bed and stares at me. "Get naked, sweetheart. I'm done talkin'."

I remove my pants and climb under the covers with him. His mouth finds mine, and our limbs tangle together. My body responds to his touch without a thought. His hands cup my breasts, his thumbs brushing across my nipples and making me groan.

When he takes one in his mouth, I buck under him. "Trent!" I cry out as my desire spikes.

He doesn't stop. He sucks, nibbles, and massages each breast. My fingers fist the sheets as he continues to extract pleasure from my body.

When Trent's fingers find my clit, I almost lose it. I'm so primed from his words and just being with him again that it isn't going to take much to get me there. Thank God, because I'm going crazy as it is.

He slides down my body and hooks my legs over his shoulders. My head falls back as he swipes his tongue up and down. I can't breathe as he starts to work me over. I grip his hair with my fingers as I shudder and squirm beneath him. It's too much. His tongue circles, and when he presses against my clit, I'm gone.

I writhe beneath him as he refuses to yield, driving my orgasm on and on. When he's content that I can't take anymore, he climbs back up so we're face to face. "Look at me," he requests.

My eyes open, and I see it all reflected in his gaze. The love he has for me. The promises he intends to keep. The pain he endured from losing me. And the determination rolls off him in waves.

"I love you," he says as he lines himself against my entrance. "I want you to keep your eyes here, understand?"

"Yes," I say on a moan as he pushes into me slowly.

Trent has always felt good, but here . . . right now . . . he's giving me more. He's giving me the piece of himself I've been missing, and it's overwhelming. I want to close my eyes and bask in it. The need to imprint the feeling to a permanent place inside me flutters my eyelids, but I hold them open, trying to focus on his face. Watching the way his jaw tightens as he pushes deeper inside me. I relish in the fact that his control slips with every inch and how he's the first to break eye contact when he's fully seated.

"Trent," I whisper. "Love me."

"I'm going to, hold on, sweetheart."

And he does.

He loves me with everything inside himself. He loves me enough for the two of us. He loves me like he's never done before.

After my second orgasm, I think I'm going to pass out, but he keeps me going. We make love for a long time, both of us are sweaty and out of breath but completely sated when we finally collapse. We lie here with our legs intertwined, and my head on his chest as I listen to the sound of his heart.

Neither of us speak for some time. I'm in my own head thinking about how different that was for me. We've made love countless times, but this was like coming home. It was the same, yet it wasn't.

Trent's hand plays with my hair, and I gaze at him. "That was . . ."

He grins with self-satisfaction. "Yeah it was."

"Who knew that all we needed was a break."

Trent pulls me on top of him and kisses me before sighing. "I don't think we should try it again."

"You missed me that much?" I say playfully. His look doesn't have any humor, though. He looks sad and forlorn. "Honey?"

"I don't know how I lived through these last few weeks." His eyes harden. "Seein' you with him, it killed me, Gracie. You have no idea what it did to me."

I roll off him and turn so we're face to face. "It wasn't easy for me, either. I was wrestling with tryin' to move on while still lovin' you. I don't want you to think it was a cake walk for me."

Trent shifts a little and runs his fingers against my lips. "I don't think that. I just don't think you can imagine what it would be like if I were datin' Charlotte or anyone else. You want to beat the shit out of anyone who talks to you. You want to beat the shit out of yourself. It's not easy, and it sure as hell isn't fun."

"Why didn't you ever try to give me more?"

He rests his hand on my hip and gazes into my eyes. "Because I believed you'd always be there. I never thought you'd leave me. I was wrong and took you for granted. When I realized you weren't mine anymore, that you'd given up on us and it was my fault, I woke up. I knew I had to find a way to prove what you've always meant to me."

My fingers make patterns on his chest. "I hadn't given up, I had to move on. I thought if I could date someone else, I could finally be happy. But it was you I wanted. I wanted this," my hand presses against his heart. "I want your heart. I want you to trust me."

His hand covers mine. "I'll do everything I can to prove it."

"Just don't pull away. Don't go back to shutting me out."

While Trent has never been this open before, he was somewhat like this when Scarlett was killed. He was sweet, unguarded, and took care of me. I thought that was the turning point for us, but after a few weeks, he was back to not returning calls and disappearing. I don't want that to happen this time.

"If I start to drift, pull me back."

"I will."

His eyes drop as he starts to succumb to the exhaustion. I tuck myself against his body, and he cocoons me with his limbs. My heart feels light as I start to fall asleep in his arms.

"Don't let me fail you, Gracie," he mutters against my hair. I turn back, but he looks completely out. I'm not sure if he said it or I imagined it so I turn back and try to calm my beating heart.

I really hope he doesn't this time.

"I'M FINE, MACIE." RHETT SWATS at her as she fixes his pillow again and fusses over him.

"I want you to be comfortable. Your first round of chemo is in the mornin'."

Rhett looks at his wife with an adoring smile. "Okay, darlin', if you need to make me comfortable, go right ahead."

Trent smiles and grabs my hand. "How are you feelin', Dad?"

"According to your mother, I'm uncomfortable."

"You hush," she scolds him.

We've stopped by the hospital the last two days to spend some time with his parents. The boys have devised a schedule that works for everyone so they can always have someone around just in case.

The doctor was very honest and told us chemo is a long shot, but it would hopefully give him more time. The fact that we don't know how much, is making everyone tense. It doesn't help that Rhett is having problems with his red blood cells and had to have another transfusion before he was cleared for his first chemo treatment.

Wyatt will relieve us tonight and take the next two days. With Angie finally feeling better, he's able to be here more often. I think all the boys are trying to find their way of handling this, some better than others.

Zach is still struggling. He and Trent were fighting on the phone last night, and he had to walk out of the house to get a grip.

I tried to explain that some people pull back because they think it'll ease their suffering, he didn't care, which I understand as well. Trent is trying to get Zach to realize it isn't about what he wants. That it's about their dad and what he *needs*, but emotions are irrational things.

"So," Rhett clears his throat, "I see you got your girl back."

Trent smirks. "I sure did, Pop. You'd be proud."

"That's my boy. I always knew we'd done something right with him." He takes Macie's hand. "I was a little worried there for a while, with him bein' so hardheaded, but he smartened up. You make sure you keep him on the right track, Grace."

"Hey," Trent complains. "I'm your son, shouldn't you be on my side?"

His father laughs. "I think because you're my son I should

sympathize with her."

It's great seeing his father in good spirits. It's weighed heavily on Trent. He doesn't always say anything, but I can see the gravity of the situation in his overall mood. I love my father so much, and I know I would be broken if I knew I was on borrowed time with him.

"I wanted to tell you something," Trent garners our attention. "Gracie and I are going to move in together. I'm going to start bringin' my things over to her place and we should be fully done this week."

Macie's face illuminates. "Oh! Finally!"

"Ma!"

"Don't 'Ma' me." She slaps his shoulder. "We've been hopin' you two would move forward. You can't say it hasn't been a long time comin'. I'm so happy I could cry."

"I know that was my first thought." I shrug.

Trent incoherently grumbles under his breath. "Women."

Macie asks a million questions about how we got to this point. She almost falls out of her chair when I tell her how easy it came together. Her eyes brighten by talking about how happy we are. Rhett's spirits lift as well.

After a few hours, Trent explains we have a lot to do and need to get going. We say our goodbyes and promise to come back tomorrow.

I already love being back around this family.

"You all right?" Trent asks as we drive back to his place.

I've been in my head since we left. Thinking about how Trent will be moving off their land. I'm not sure it's the right thing with everything going on.

"Are you okay with movin' in to my place?"

"Of course I am. Why would you ask that?"

"Because your mom might need you now more than ever. Zach is on the other side of the property, and Wyatt is so busy with

Angie, which will only get worse after the baby is born. It makes sense we're around to help more."

Trent's face brightens, and I can't figure out what he's happy about. His father is sick and we should be around if they need us, especially since he's the firstborn. His mama is going to be dealing with Rhett's treatments and then whatever complications might arise.

"What are you smilin' for?" I ask.

"Because you said *we* should be around to help," he replies unapologetically.

"You're a mess."

"Never said any different, sweetheart."

I laugh to myself and get back to the issue at hand. "You still want to move?"

Trent places his hand on my leg. "I'm not letting you get away, Grace Rooney. If you don't want me movin' in, you're going to have to find a better excuse than this. My father wants nothing more than for us to be happy. In fact, I promised him I would do everything in my power to make you smile."

"Okay, so you want to do this?"

"Yes, of course I do. It's not like your house is an hour away. Look, I want to live with you. I want to wake up beside you every day. I want to make you very happy, sweetheart."

I touch the side of his face as he pulls in to his drive. "Well, I can't wait for all of those things. Maybe you should make good on that promise. I can think of a few ways . . ."

chapter
SIXTEEN

TRENT HAS BEEN MOVING HIS things over without me saying a word, helping Macie get Rhett settled at home, and spending as much time as he can with me. Today though, is full on moving in day.

He said he was done bringing things in drabs, he wants to build our life together and is tired of pussy footing around.

After his first wave of belongings, I realized I would actually have to make room for his stuff. I don't think I fully understood that part. Thankfully, Presley came over to help me downsize. She and I spent hours going through clothes, boxes of memories, and a bottle—or two—of wine. There's now room in the closet for at least some of his clothes, and I cleared four drawers, which was a miracle.

"Where should we put this?" Trent holds the deer's head that he had mounted.

"In the garbage?" I offer.

He chuckles, but I'm not joking. There's no way that ugly ass thing is hanging in my very well-decorated home. He can use his house as a man cave for all I care. He can smoke, drink, play cards, and hang his kills there because it ain't happening here.

"Oh, come on. It's a great coat rack."

"No way." I point outside. "It's not comin' in here."

Trent grumbles and carries it back outside. I've already agreed to the ugliest chair known to man. I don't know where he was storing it, because I've never seen it in his house, but he marched in and said it had to stay or he was leaving with it. It's made of the scratchiest wool I've ever felt, and we won't even talk about the plaid pattern. Whoever made it took whatever colors of wool they had and went for it. It doesn't match anything.

And yet, here it sits in my living room.

Aside from the ugly chair incident, we've migrated his things in pretty seamlessly. However, that dead deer head isn't going anywhere in this house.

I manage to help him unpack a few more boxes before he grabs me by the waist and throws me to the bed, saying we needed to christen the house now that he lives there. Who am I to protest?

"You think we're goin' to regret this?" I ask as we're lying in bed with only the sheet covering us.

"What? Movin' in?"

"Well, yeah."

He moves in close and pushes the hair off my face. "Nope. There will be zero regrets from me. I wasted a lot of years and for the dumbest reasons. I don't see a downside to us livin' together. Besides, I get to see you naked a whole lot more this way. Just think of all the sex we'll have now."

I smack his arm. "And think of all the things we'll have to adjust to."

"We'll figure it out day by day. If Angie has found a way to deal with Wyatt, we should be fine."

"I'm pretty sure your brother would say the same about you."

Zach and Wyatt are the closest of the Hennington brothers. Trent's always been on his own. When they wanted to ride horses, Trent was out shooting. He didn't have much interest in working on his family's farm. I never understood it, but even in high school, he was looking at other vocations.

Even after his daddy had a stroke and Trent had to help run things, he hated it and eventually chose to walk away. He explained that he knew what he wanted to be and didn't want his family to waste their time. It was strange to me, but then again, Trent has always been a mystery to me.

We get out of bed, toss clothes on—well, I do—and head in to the kitchen.

"Friday is the Fourth of July celebration," Trent mentions as he leans against the counter with just a pair of basketball shorts on. I think just knowing he lives here somehow makes him sexier.

He snaps his fingers. "Earth to Grace."

"Oh! Sorry, yeah, Fourth of July. What are you workin'?"

He always does. I'm used to it by now, I don't think we've ever gone together. When you're dating the sheriff, you get used to spending holidays alone, which is something I resigned myself to a long time ago.

"I took off."

"What?" I ask with shock. Well, that never happens.

"I figured we could go out on the horses and watch the fireworks away from the crowd, if you want to . . ." I rush forward and kiss him. His hands wrap around me, and he laughs as I assault him. "I take that as a yes?" he asks between my kisses.

"You're full of surprises." I smile and press my lips to his again. "I would love to. You know that this is my favorite holiday."

"Okay, I want to help Mama a bit in the mornin', but I'll be back early enough to get to the spot I want to go."

"Keep this up, and you may get all that sex you're hopin' for."

His deep, throaty laugh echoes in the room. "All part of my plan, sweetheart. I can grab you here or meet you at your parents' house. We need to ride to get where I want to go."

My horses are still at my parents' house. I have a small paddock on my property, but it isn't great. Plus, it gives my daddy something to do when he's pretending to tinker in the barn.

"I'll meet you there." I try to contain my excitement, but I fail. I can't stop jumping around.

"All right. I better get ready for work. You got any plans?"

"I'm going to the store."

"Okay, I'll see you later." He leans in for another kiss. One that I'm all too happy to give him.

I don't remember ever feeling this happy. It's been a long time coming, and I'm on top of the world. Everything feels so right. We're living together, we're happy, we're in love, and there is nothing hanging over my head.

Trent leaves for work, and I head off to the store. Today is always a busy day for us since it's delivery day, and I cringe thinking about it. I have no idea what state I'll find the place in when I get there.

When I push through the glass door and the tiny bell sounds, Mama is arranging some things on the shelf.

"Mornin', Mama!" I beam as I get close.

"Mornin', baby." Her eyes study me. "You look different."

"Different?" I don't know what she could be seeing. I haven't changed a thing.

"Yeah." Her lips purse, and she tilts her head. "You look happy."

"I am happy. I told you the other day that Trent was movin' in."

Something she was not happy about. She doesn't think "kids these days" should be living together before they're married. I think she's convinced herself I'm still a virgin. I sure as hell haven't told her otherwise. A few years ago, she gave me another version of "the talk" regarding the marriage bed. No matter how many times I've tried to forget the things that we said that night, my mind won't erase it.

"I'm glad to see that boy is finally movin' toward a future, but he's a little dense on the order of how this goes."

"Sure, Mama."

"Don't you 'sure Mama' me," she chides. "There's a way we do things, and it ain't like this."

"Presley and Zach lived together and so did Angie and Wyatt," I remind her. She never had a word to say about that.

"Well, Macie and Rhett may allow that in their children's lives, but your daddy and I do not." She huffs before tacking on, "I know for a fact that Macie laid into those boys about gettin' married. Sometimes we raise our babies the best we can and they still screw it all up."

I can't believe she's still this old fashioned and judgy. Usually, their old lady clan complains about other people's choices, not choices their own kids make. Lord knows they all thought Wyatt was acting like an idiot last year, but no one said a word about it. Now suddenly because I'm moving in with Trent, she has something to say?

"No one is screwin' anything up, Mama. We're all adults."

"Actin' like children."

I learned early on not to argue with her when she gets like this. She's set in her ways, and there's no telling her any different. I also know that she and my father were pregnant with Scarlett before they got married. The whole nine-pound baby that was two months premature didn't fool anyone, but I let her have that secret.

"I'm going to finish cleaning the back room," I tell her as I kiss her cheek.

"Finish what?"

Please tell me she didn't touch anything. "Organizing the stock . . ."

"Sugar, you're going to be done awfully fast, there's no stock to be put away." She comes around and points. "It's all done. It was done four days ago."

"But?"

"I came in to check on things so I could get the stock room cleaned before you go back to school, but . . ." Mama looks around the store with a smile. "It was already done."

For the first time since I got here, I actually look around, and my mouth drops. Everything is done. It's all put away, there are bins holding the overflow with it all in order. I go over each row in the back room with so many things racing in my head.

Only Wyatt knew how bad things were. Surely, he wouldn't . . . Would he have told his brother?

I don't even know what to say.

Trent is the only one who would've done all this. It would've taken him hours to figure out all the boxes. This would've taken me a week, and he did it without me askin'.

"Trent?" I breathe as a smile stretched over my lips.

"He was here the other day and asked me not to say anything. He did good," Mama remarks.

"Yeah, he did."

Mama pats my back. "I think we should talk, sugar."

This might be the time to tell her about my concerns with the store. She's just so stubborn, and I know this won't go well.

"Sure, Mama. I wanted to talk to you about somethin', too."

"Go on and sit, honey."

We move around to the two chairs, and she takes my hand in hers, which is something she has always done. She used to say it was so she felt connected. It's probably why I do it as well. Her dark blue eyes that mirror mine are filled with worry.

Fear starts to build as she doesn't say anything. She's usually very forthright, so her hesitation starts my mind reeling with what could be wrong. Considering what the Henningtons are dealing with, I start to worry and bite my bottom lip. "Are you okay?"

"Oh, I'm just fine," she says, laughing. "It's nothing like that, I'll be around for a long time. I've been thinkin', and you see, Macie, Becca, and Vivienne are all retired now . . ." A rush of relief courses through me, this is even better. It's her idea, and now I don't have to be the bad guy. "And I just would like to be able to do coffee dates and card games with them. With Rhett's treatments startin', we're all going to help during the day. I know you work, but maybe you can take over the store and hire people to manage it?"

I do my best to hide my emotions and look a little disappointed. "Well, it would be an undertakin'." Her grip tightens a little. "But you and Daddy need to enjoy your time."

She scoffs. "Who said I wanted to spend time with him? I see him so much now that I'm surprised I haven't beaten him with a rollin' pin."

I burst out laughing. "Oh, Mama."

"You wait, Grace Louise. You just wait. Spend fifty years with the same man and then come back to me. I'm a damn saint, and that man is the devil some days."

A saint? Oh, dear Lord.

"Whatever you say, Mama. I'll take over the store. Don't you worry."

Her eyes tighten a little as she tilts her head. "Hmmm."

"What?" I ask.

She leans back and taps her chin. "What was it you wanted to talk to me about?"

"You know, I can't remember."

Crap. She's on to me.

"Right."

"Well, let me know how you want to handle all this. I'll start lookin' for a manager and some workers."

There are a lot of kids who are trying to save, and this would be the perfect job for them. I hop up, knowing she's about to pry into what I wanted to talk to her about when we sat. "I love you, Mama."

"I love you, too, sugar."

Phew, that was close.

I spend the rest of the day preparing the store before I have to start back at school. I put a few flyers outside to advertise that we are hiring and call the local paper so I can put an ad in tomorrow's edition. Mama may drag her feet a little, but knowing her best friends are all pushing her, she won't doddle too much and I can rest easier about the future.

IT'S FINALLY FRIDAY. TRENT HAS been messing with me all week about what we're doing today. He's been at his parents' all morning, and I'm on pins and needles.

"Hi, darlin'." My father says as I saddle Lightning.

"Hi, Daddy."

I walk over and kiss his cheek before watching him shuffle over to his workbench and take a seat.

"You're goin' out on a ride?"

"Trent is supposed to be meeting me," I explain.

He smiles. "I heard somethin' about that. You women are more confusin' than that confounded cube thing we used to try to make line up. Remember that?" I nod. "Damn thing made me so mad I peeled the stickers off and won. Anyway, so Trent is who you chose?"

"I think you knew I was going to choose him, didn't you?"

"Did I ever tell you the story about how I decided I loved your Mama?"

"I've heard Mama's version." I abandon the leather straps I'm trying to tighten and move to where my dad sits.

"She don't tell it right." He waves his hand dismissively. "It wasn't like one of those books she likes to read."

My mother has always been creative in her storytelling. Daddy is always more realistic, but as a kid, I loved her version. It was filled with undeniable love and magic. Who the hell wouldn't want that?

Maybe that's my damn problem.

"We were only seventeen when we met, two weeks before my eighteenth. I just enlisted and was leaving in a month for basic. All I wanted to do was serve my country. Your granddaddy was a Marine, his daddy was a Marine, and by God, I was going to be, too. She was the prettiest thing I'd ever seen, and she was dating some idiot from another town."

Here's where my mother would tell me that he fell head over heels in love with her the second their eyes met. And he walked over to her, told her they were going to get married, and she was going to love him because he loved her already.

"I told her he was a fool, and if she would go on one date with me, I'd show her what a real man was like."

"Daddy, you weren't even a man yet."

"Hush, darlin'. She didn't know that." I giggle and lean back, listening to my father tell his story. "Anyway, I couldn't afford much, but I knew I needed to put my money where my mouth was. So, I worked a few extra hours for your grandpa and scraped together just enough for dinner and one rose."

Trent exits from the shadows of the barn with a single rose. I stare with surprise as he steps in front of me and extends the flower. He doesn't say a word as I watch him.

"Our dinner wasn't much," Daddy continues as if my boyfriend didn't materialize out of thin air. "I found a basket in my kitchen and filled it with two sandwiches, a bottle of wine I stole from our liquor cabinet, and one piece of cake."

Trent removes his other hand from behind his back and places the basket in front of me. Everything inside me tingles as I realize that Trent's heard this story before and he planned this. All of it. He moves around behind me and pulls my back against his front.

Daddy touches my chin, forcing me to look back at him. "I saddled my horse and picked her up. I told her it would only take one night for her to see why I was worth the chance. Sure, I had no money, I was leavin' in two weeks, and she didn't know me. There was nothing I could offer her except my heart. That night, I decided I was going to love her. I was going to give her the best life I could." His voice cracks on that last part. "I left her two weeks later, and I hurt her. I didn't write like I promised. I didn't go see her when I came home on leave like I told her I would. But she came to me, darlin'. She found me and forced me to see the mistake I was makin'. The right woman will always make her man see sense." My father looks over at Trent and then back to me. "But it takes the right man to hold on to her once he finds her."

Trent's arms tighten around me, and he bends close to my ear, whispering, "I won't always see sense. I won't always do right, but I know you're who I love, and I won't be such an idiot again."

I look at him over my shoulder with more tears falling. "I'll make you see sense."

He leans in and touches his lips to mine. "I'm countin' on it."

Daddy stands, shakes Trent's hand, and then touches my cheek. "Love isn't always easy, baby girl. It takes a lot of work. Sometimes it fails, and sometimes you have to let it go to get it back."

"I love you, Daddy."

He smiles at me. "I love you more." Daddy turns to Trent, and his face grows serious. "I'm trustin' you, son. Break her heart, and I don't care what side of the law you're on."

"Yes, sir."

"All right now, you two go off on your ride, but let's plan to go shootin' this week."

I watch the man I've admired my whole life walk away before

I turn to Trent. "You planned all of this?"

He shifts me so we're face to face, he wraps his arms around my waist, and I lean back. "Your father has told me that story so many times. When we'd go huntin' he would ask me my intentions—a lot. I didn't have any other than I knew I needed you in my life. I was content with how things were, and your father didn't push me. But after Scarlett, he wanted more for you, and then shit changed. Your sister was killed, we lost the deputy a few towns over, and I felt like if I allowed myself to love you, I'd lose you."

I cinch his arms tighter around me, feeling a bit silly for not realizing they would have actually talked while they were on all those hunting and fishing trips. I never knew that they talked like this. Not that Trent or my dad are big sharers about what they do when they hunt. Daddy took me one time, and he told me I could never go again. Apparently, talking while in the deer stand is not a good thing. Neither is eating, having to pee, singing, or any of the other things I did in the two hours we lasted out there.

"But then I lost you. I know we've had breaks before, but this was different. I knew I loved you years ago, but when you didn't say it to me again, I let it go. I thought you knew and sayin' it wasn't going to make a difference."

"You were wrong."

"I know that now." He kisses the top of my head. "My father laid into me after the wedding. He told me that no son of his would let the woman he loved walk away so easily."

"I've always loved your dad. He's a smart man." I smile as I say it, and I know he can hear it in my voice.

"He's raised three idiots."

"I think you Hennington boys aren't half bad," I joke.

Macie and Rhett are the epitome of marriage and strength. They've been together as long as my parents and have had a lot of struggles, but he still looks at her as if she's the sun. When we were kids, we'd walk in and they'd be kissing like teenagers. It was so weird back then, but as an adult, I can appreciate that level of love.

My parents are not too far off, they just bicker a lot more and there's no such thing as public displays of affection. My mother always thought Macie was off her rocker for that.

"You ready?" he asks.

We get the basket secured to Lightning, and Trent grabs his horse from the trailer. "Hi, Montana," I coo as I pet the side of his neck. "You're such a handsome boy."

"Quit makin' him love you."

"Aww are you jealous?" I tease.

"Nope. Not when I know who you'll be ridin' tonight."

"Trent!" I look around, afraid my mother's sonic hearing might have heard.

"Relax." He smirks. "You all set?"

"I'm ready if you are." I mount Lightning and we head off. The ride is nice, although the heat is freaking brutal. It's almost eight, so it should keep cooling down, but it's still sticky and gross. We set a slow pace to the spot we think of as our own, and I turn to him.

"How's your daddy doin'?"

"Not good, the doctors said we need to limit his visitors, Cayden and Logan can't come around, and they may admit him again if this cold doesn't clear up quickly."

"Oh, honey." I pause, trying to find the right words. "I'm sure your mama is watchin' him like a hawk."

He nods. "Let's enjoy tonight and try not to think about this."

I hate this, but at the same time, I understand wanting to distract yourself from the reality of life. So, that's what I do. I distract him by talking about everything and anything I can think of.

We get to the top of the hill, and Trent helps me off Lightning. We set up a small picnic, and I smile when he takes out two sandwiches and a single slice of cake. We don't have to talk. I am perfectly content just being with him.

After a few minutes, he shifts and grabs the wine. "Here you go."

"Did you steal this from my parents?" I smile as I take the glass from his outstretched hand.

"I did." He lets out a deep chuckle and pulls me onto his lap. "Your dad said I needed to be authentic."

"You know my daddy proposed to my mama that night."

"I do."

My mouth goes dry. Oh my god. What if this is his plan? I don't know that I'm ready to say yes. We just got back together, and it feels like we've gone from idle to full speed in the matter of a minute. I love Trent, and I want to spend the rest of my life with him, but I want to be sure this is all real.

"Trent—" I touch his hand.

"Grace, I've been with you for a long time. You've waited. You've been patient and understanding."

"Please." I try to stop him. I don't want to say no, but I don't think I'm ready to say yes. A few weeks ago, I was on a date with Cooper, we weren't together, and my life wasn't any less crazy. This is way too soon.

"Listen to me, sweetheart." Trent takes the glass, shifts me off his lap, and then climbs to his knees in front of me. "I need to finish what I came here to say."

"But . . ."

"Shhh." His hand covers my mouth. "I know you're not sure about us. I've given you pretty much every reason to doubt me. So," he removes his hand, "I'm not going to propose, but I am going to tell you that I don't plan to wait long. Losing you taught me something I won't ever forget. I have every intention of tying you to me—legally."

I let out a deep sigh of relief. "I want to believe all of this is the new you."

"But you don't, yet."

"I'm gettin' there."

"You once said you wanted a love like your parents."

My smile is soft as I lean back to look at him. "I remember."

Trent sits back on his feet. "I can't give you that, Gracie. I'm not your father and you're not your mother, but we are who we are. I can give you me. I won't be perfect. I'll make mistakes, but I won't make the same ones again. What your parents have together is theirs. I want to make something that's ours. The story we tell our kids won't be as sweet as what your dad told us, but it'll still be beautiful."

Kids.

The thought steals my breath and answers the question I never asked him.

I climb to my knees and press my lips against his. He's had times in our years where he said the most beautiful things, but this will forever be my top spot. He's right. I've been trying to have something like his parents or mine, instead of seeing what we share as being good enough.

Trent grips my shoulders, pulling be back before cupping my face. "I love you."

"I love you, too."

"Good. Now, come here."

We both get comfortable again and a few minutes later, the fireworks begin. The bright colors paint the sky with light and warmth.

"I love the fireworks." I remark as the lights flash. "They're so beautiful."

Trent holds me close and he lifts my head to him. "You're what's beautiful, Grace. You make the sky bright. This," he looks back up, "this is nothing compared to you."

"Keep sayin' these sweet things, and I'm gonna keep you."

He smiles and leans in for a kiss. "I'm plannin' on it, sweetheart."

SEVENTEEN

Trent

"THREE WEEKS HE'S BEEN SUFFERING!" Mama yells at the doctor. "And now we're back in the hospital again?"

"Mrs. Hennington, I warned y'all this would be possible. His immune system is weak and the leukemia has spread. I'm sorry, but at this point, we need to do another blood transfusion. We have to treat the symptoms as they arise."

My mother falls in the chair and begins to cry. Instantly, my brothers and I move to her side.

Her red-rimmed eyes look at each of us, and my heart breaks. It's happening so fast. Maybe my father was right to deny treatment. He's barely able to stay awake or eat, and it's been wearing on my mother.

We're back in the hospital after his blood work came back with his red blood cell count lower than when he collapsed. It feels like the chemo accelerated his body's breakdown.

"Do whatever you can. Just give us more time with him." Defeat is clear in Mama's voice. Something I don't think I've ever heard from her. She's a fighter, but she's trying to fight a battle she never had a chance of winning. Cancer is robbing her of everything she loves.

Dr. Halpern clears his throat. "Our blood banks are a little low."

Wyatt steps next to me and huffs. "What do you need?"

Dr. Halpern writes something on the chart he's holding. "We'd like to have a good match donate blood since your father will be needing more frequent blood transfusions. Are you all willing to be tested? Most of the time we can find a match in the family."

"Of course," my brothers and I all agree.

I enter the waiting room where Grace, Presley, and Angie are waiting. I don't know if I could've made it this last month without Grace. She's been at my side each time I've needed her.

"How's he doin'?" Presley asks.

Zach shakes his head.

Wyatt explains what the doctor said, and we head to the lab before breaking off into separate rooms.

Grace holds my hand, offering me her support as I wrap my mind around the last few hours. I can't accept defeat. There has to be a way to get him through this.

The nurse comes around and describes the process. "The doctor explained about the increased need for blood?"

"Yes."

"Good. Most of the time, there's a good match in the family and we could store blood exclusively for your father. We're rushing the results so we should know in a few hours."

"I understand."

After they get the vial done she asks us to stay close for the results in case one of us is a match. I ask a few more questions, and I pray I can be the one to help my father. I need to *do* something, and if giving blood will get him there, I'll give every ounce I have.

"How's the baby doin'?" Grace asks Angie, breaking the silence as we all sit and wait.

"Good." She rubs her stomach. "I'm so glad we're over all the puking and what not. This baby decided to make good on everything that satanic pregnancy book warned about."

"Especially the mood swings," Wyatt pipes in.

Angie silences him with a death stare, which makes everyone around them laugh. I love my sisters-in-law. Both of my brothers found women I enjoy being around. I nestle Grace into my side and kiss the top of her head. I was hoping my father's health would stay stable.

For the last two weeks, I've been planning a big trip for us. She's always talked about wanting to go to the beach. Mama has a friend whose daughter lives in Virginia Beach. Natalie's husband, Liam, is a Navy SEAL and she's visiting her family for a month while he's deployed. She offered us their house instead of staying in some hotel. I haven't seen Lee since she was eight. She and Wyatt used to be close when they were kids, but then they moved out of town and we lost touch. However, I'm not sure if we'll get out there next week if Dad keeps getting worse.

"Take a walk with me?" I ask, needing to get out of this waiting room. She nods and we start down the hall. "I hate it here."

"I don't think anyone likes hospitals." Grace holds on to my bicep as we walk. "Your dad is okay, though. He'll get the blood, and then you guys can figure out a plan. I know it seems like it's a lot, but I know if any family can find a way, it's yours."

"And then what?" I ask. "He goes through another round of chemo and we maybe get another month with him?"

"I know it's not ideal, but you have to have faith."

For the first time since all this came crashing down, I understand why he chose to not tell us. There's no guarantees and what if all of this was for nothing? What if all that fighting only causes him to miss out on living his life because he's too sick to leave the hospital. If he didn't agree to fight it, he could've spent time with his kids and wife.

I think about the calls that I didn't answer or when he asked me to go fishing and I blew him off. I'm so fucking mad at myself. I should've been there checking on him. He's my dad and I can't help but think about the wasted time I can't get back.

We sit on the bench outside the entrance. I feel helpless, and that isn't something I'm used to. "If we lose him . . ."

"You can't think that way, honey. You have to be strong for him because he's going to look to you." Grace's blue eyes fill with emotion. "You're the oldest, Trent. You have to hold this family together."

She's right, but I don't know what to do. If I push him, am I doing it for selfish reasons? No. It's not selfish for me to want my father to live. There are things he has left to do. Like seeing Wyatt's child, watching me finally stop being a pussy and marry Grace, go hunting again and bag the deer, beating up on the three of us when we fight at our annual fish off, and so much more. He's the glue in this family.

He may not be the vocal one, but he's the backbone.

"I can't let him die." My head drops into my hands.

Grace's arms wrap around me and she holds me together. I'm not an emotional person by nature. I think my job has forced me to always keep some barrier between me and my feelings. It isn't as if I work in a big city riddled with violence, but I somehow think that makes it worse. Having to respond to a traffic accident or incident involving someone I know is far worse than one involving a nameless stranger. To do my job, I have to shut it all out. This, though, this is unlike anything I've ever felt.

He's my father.

And I'm going to lose him.

Grace and I head back to the waiting room, and the doctor is there waiting. "Trent, good. I have the lab results." He holds the papers in the air.

"Are any of us a match?" I question.

"Wyatt is the closest match, so we'd like to get him started first. Zach is the next best option." The doctor extends his arm as Wyatt steps forward. "Go ahead with the nurse and she'll get you ready."

Zach goes back to his seat, and I move toward the doctor. "Doc? Was I not a match?" I ask.

"Your blood type isn't a match, so unfortunately you won't be able to donate."

"I see." I hate that I can't contribute in any way. "So, Wyatt will donate and if need be Zach will also? Is that the next step?"

"Yes." He nods. "Your mother is also a possibility, but she doesn't carry the same antibodies as your brothers."

"Well, I'm glad some of us can help."

"Trent?" He pauses and then shakes his head. "Never mind. I'm going to check on your dad, and I'll be back with some answers once we start the transfusion."

"What did you want to say?"

"Nothing, son. I need to get back there." He drops what's supposed to be a reassuring pat on my shoulder and walks away.

I had hoped I could do something. The sitting around and waiting is driving me crazy. I want to help, go get a new doctor, find a treatment plan, donate blood, or anything at this point.

"You okay?" Grace asks as I watch the doctor walk down the hall.

"Yeah, I'm fine. I'm glad you're here." We sit so her head rests on my shoulder and I start to calm a little.

"There's nowhere else I'd be."

"I should go check on my father," I say, trying to keep my shit together.

"Okay, honey."

We walk through the doors, and Grace heads to the waiting room to check if anyone needs anything. Wyatt is still getting his blood drawn, Zach is still in the same fucking chair, and my mother is with Dad.

I'm not sure how it'll go, but I know that time is of the essence, and I'm not wasting anymore.

I walk closer and hear my mother's voice animated and frustrated.

Please don't let this be bad news.

"No, you can't tell him anything."

"I didn't say anything to him because I wanted to talk to you first, Macie, but he has a right to know what the tests came back as," Dr. Halpern's voice is agitated but remains quiet. "If he sees this, he'll know."

"He can't know. Do you understand, John? He can't know, it would destroy him."

I hang back and listen. My mother has kept quite a few secrets lately, and she's not going to do that to my father. If there's something going on, he and my brothers have a right to hear it.

But then I hear my father's voice. "He doesn't need to know. Not now."

"I'm not tryin' to get involved in your family business, but that boy isn't dumb, and he'll figure it out. It should come from you both. Before it's too late. The test results are his to see. I can't hide them from him."

"Only if he asks to see them."

"If he asks, I won't keep them from him."

My mother lets out a heavy sigh, and I shuffle forward a bit more, needing to know what the hell is going on. "I know. I know what you're sayin'," her voice shakes.

"I'm just bein' a friend and tellin' you that if he's not his son, he should know."

Every muscle in my body locks as I hang on every word. Then it hits me. Someone in our family isn't my father's son. Someone who wasn't a match. There's only one someone here who was clearly not a candidate.

This can't be real. There's a mistake.

"Trent is his son in every way that matters," Mama says before falling silent for a beat. "We'd planned to tell him, but—"

"No one tells him I'm not his father."

And the floor drops out from under me.

I'm not my father's son.

I'm not a Hennington.

EIGHTEEN

Grace

"IS TRENT DOIN' OKAY BACK there?" I ask Mrs. Hennington as she returns from where Mr. Hennington is now receiving the transfusion.

I figured he was talking to his parents and getting things in order, but it's been over two hours. He wasn't in the greatest shape when he left the waiting room, and I've been sitting here worried sick about him.

"I haven't seen him, sugar."

"What? He went back there a few hours ago . . ."

Mrs. Hennington looks around. "I've been in the room the entire time, and I never saw him."

I'm confused. I watched him go. "Has anyone seen Trent?" I ask, and everyone says no or shakes their head.

I grab my phone and text him.

Me: Hey. Where are you?

"I'm sure he's in the cafeteria. Maybe go check there?" Zach suggests.

"I'll be back." I walk down the hall with a niggling feeling in my gut. Something's off. Trent wouldn't be in the cafeteria for two hours. Not when he said he was going to check on his dad.

I search the cafeteria, but he isn't here. I check the lab and then the chapel, all with no Trent. There's still no reply from him, and my heart starts to race.

Me: I've been looking for you, are you here?

"Hey." Presley bumps into me on my way back to the waiting area. "Did you find him?

"No. He's not anywhere."

She grabs her phone and raises it to her ear. "Trent, I don't know where you are, but please call me back." Presley disconnects the phone. "I'm sure he's fine. Maybe he went to clear his head."

"For two hours?"

"I don't know . . ."

"Yeah." I sigh. "I don't either."

"I'm sure he'll turn up. He could've gotten called for work?"

That's possible. A call could've come in, and because he's the sheriff, he would have to go. Although, I'm not totally sure that's it. He would've said goodbye. I can't put my finger on it, but my gut is telling me something is off.

We head back to the waiting room where everyone is sitting around. Everyone except him. "Did he come back?"

"No." Wyatt shakes his head and looks around. "Anyone else see him?"

No one has, which makes the knots in my stomach twist tighter. "I'm going to head to the house and check the station." I grab my purse and turn to the door, but Zach stops me.

"Let us know when you find him."

I nod and shoot off another text.

Me: I'm getting worried. Please tell me you're okay.

He doesn't respond, and now I'm running to the car trying to figure out where Trent would have gone on foot since he didn't drive here in his own car.

I call him three times, and all of them go straight to voice mail. No text messages back, nothing. This isn't like him. Even when he would pull away, it was never radio silence. And if it were a work thing, he'd have texted me back.

I pass the station, and his squad car sits in the lot, but he is not there. The deputy on duty hasn't seen him but promised to let me know if he hears from him, which isn't very helpful.

This is crazy.

My mind reels as fear starts to take hold. I don't know where he is or if something is wrong. After the way he was in the hospital, I can't imagine him taking off like this.

I go to his house, and his truck isn't there either.

Shit.

I check inside, just in case, and nothing is missing or moved. Where the hell did he go?

There's no telling why he left like that. I call Presley, giving her the rundown of all the places Trent isn't. Before I hang up, I let her know to tell everyone I'm headed home to wait for him and I'll call if I find him.

All I can do now is hope for the best.

IT'S BEEN FIFTEEN HOURS AND no sign of Trent. I've lost track of how many times I've called him. He must've shut his phone off because it doesn't even ring anymore.

I try to keep calm, but nothing makes sense. He's changed so much over the last few months. He's been steadfast, strong, and even with his father being sick, he's been happy. He wouldn't leave like this. He promised me he wouldn't just leave like this.

I head back to the hospital, hoping maybe he'll materialize there.

Angie walks over and embraces me. "I'm sure he'll show up. He couldn't go far without someone seeing him."

"It's been hours." My voice trembles. "No one has heard from him?"

She shakes her head.

Mrs. Hennington comes out from the back and heads right to me. "Where's Trent?"

I look to everyone, but Zach steps forward. "We're not sure. He's been gone for a while now."

"What do you mean he's gone?" Mrs. Hennington asks with worry laced in her voice. "Gone where?"

"I don't know. I haven't seen him since yesterday when he said he was goin' to see you and Rhett," I explain. "I've checked his house, the station, our place, the ranch, but I can't find him."

"Do you think he left?" She looks to Wyatt. "With Dad in the hospital?"

I feel hollow inside. I don't want to believe he took off without a word. His family, me, and his friends are all mystified. I know he's in pain, I can accept that, but this isn't the way to handle things.

Presley puts her hand on my back while Zach starts cursing and pacing. He's had plenty to say about what he thinks.

Wyatt grabs his phone and dials. "Listen, you selfish son of a bitch. You got two hours to get your shit straight and then I better see your ass at this hospital."

Wyatt doesn't run away from issues, for the most part. He's always been the one who forces us to deal with our issues. If he finds Trent first, I have a feeling someone will have a few bruises.

"I can't believe he'd do this with his father in the hospital. I mean, I know he can do senseless things, but this seems out of character, even for him."

Wyatt moves forward. His hands are balled into fists and his jaw is clenched. "He's an asshole. Always an asshole. Dad's sick, and he's bein' a selfish prick."

Angie steps over to Wyatt. "Listen, until someone talks to him, I think we should all hold our opinions to ourselves. We have no idea what's going on. For all we know, he's handling something we don't know about. Did anyone talk to Hank?"

"Hank hasn't heard from Trent, but he promises he'll call if he shows up."

Mrs. Hennington sits and puts her head in her hands. "What if something is wrong? What if he's hurt? Why wouldn't he call his family?"

Angie shrugs. "I don't know . . . I'm just hoping for the best."

Wyatt leans in, kisses her lips, and shakes his head. "I love you, baby, but my brother has some explaining to do. He's not at the farm. He's run off because shit got hard. It's what he does."

"Those in glass houses . . ." Angie trails off and takes his hand. "I love you, too. I would really love you more if you could get me some fries."

He laughs and crouches in front of her belly. "You're hungry again, little one?"

"He or she has their daddy's appetite," she grumbles.

"It's a boy," Wyatt says proudly. "I can feel it."

Angie rolls her eyes.

"I can't believe y'all won't find out." Presley shakes her head. "Mama H. and I are goin' crazy!"

"I'm sure—" Angie grabs her belly and winces. "Damn Braxton Hicks." She breathes through a few seconds, and Wyatt helps her to a seat.

"You need to get my daughter-in-law to her bed," Mrs. Hennington urges. "She's been on her feet all day . . ."

"I'm fine." She waves her off. "I'm in the hospital so if anything happens, we're in the best place."

"Angie, honey." Mrs. Hennington takes her face in her hands. "You need to take care of that baby in there." She turns to the rest of us. "Dad has a few hours before anyone can see him. Dr. Halpern said he needs his rest. Tomorrow, we're going to talk to the doctor again, but we've all been here a while, and nothing is changin'."

"If anything changes, you'll call, right?" Zach asks.

She gives a sad smile. "Yes, honey, no more secrets. I promise I'll call if anything happens."

Everyone starts to hug and say goodbye. Mrs. Hennington heads back to her husband. Zach and Presley leave. Then Wyatt and Angie are the next to go, but I just sit here. I'm not family, but I don't want to go home.

I start to rack my brain even more about where he could be.

My phone dings with a text, and I scramble to find the small device buried in my purse.

> *Hank: Trent called and said he's going to be out of work for a while. Didn't say why or for how long, but I thought you might want to know.*

> *Me: Thanks.*

If I thought I was confused before, it's nothing like now. I vary from hurt to anger. He's taking time off? He called Hank but not any of his family who are all worried sick? I can't believe he would be so heartless. Not after all his promises not to pull away from me again and all the talk about wanting to marry me. He has roots here. He wouldn't rip them out when he needs them most.

I drop my head and let out a loud cry of frustration. "Just talk to me, I would be here for you," I mutter as my heart aches.

"Grace?" I lift my head and wipe my tears away, not wanting to face him but knowing I have no choice.

"Cooper, hi."

"Is he? Is everything—with Rhett?"

I stand and shake my head. "Oh, he's fine. I mean, not fine, but he's okay. He's stable."

"Then why are you out here crying?" Cooper asks.

I'm not sure what to say. My heart is broken on one end and I'm angry at myself on the other. I knew this would happen. I would go back to Trent, and he'd do the same shit like he always does. Now, Cooper stands in front of me, and I remember how dumb I am. I fooled myself into thinking this time would be different.

"Hey," he says, and his freaking kindness is the last straw. It breaks me, and I double over, wracked with sobs. He drops to his knees in front of me and wraps his strong arms around my shoulders, holding me while I fall apart. "It's okay, Grace."

"No. It's not."

"Did something happen? Are you okay?" he asks like the good man he is.

Cooper wouldn't do this. He wouldn't run out without a word.

I shake my head back and forth as the tears soak his shirt. "Trent left."

"Left?"

"He's gone." I pull back and try to collect myself. "He was here, then he disappeared, took time off work, but no one knows why. I don't know . . ."

Cooper looks at me as if I'm crazy. "Seriously? I heard you guys have been great and moved in together."

This is what has me thinking there has to be more to this. "I didn't want to leave in case he came here . . . but I got a text from Hank, and all I know is he's not sure when Trent will be back."

I start to wonder if I shouldn't have stayed home. What if he packed his shit while I was here?

Cooper sits beside me and rests his elbows on his knees. "You and I both know that Trent doesn't handle personal shit well. He's not good at reactin' to things when it comes to anything serious. You knew this when you chose to go back to him."

That doesn't excuse his behavior.

"I can't keep doing this." Cooper doesn't say anything, and I instantly feel like shit. "God," I sigh. "I'm such a bitch. I'm sittin' here tellin' *you* about this. I'm so sorry. I'm such a stupid girl."

Cooper laughs and then takes my hand. "We're friends. And we are much better friends now that we both know that's all it's going to be." He nudges me. "But as your friend, I'm going to say something you're not going to like."

"Coop."

"No, Grace, I think you need to hear it. You know this is what he does when he's scared. He runs because emotion scares the fuck out of him. Something must've spooked him, and he cut tail. I don't agree with it, but that's who he is. For better or worse, this is how he deals with life. So, now you've got a choice."

"Me?"

He nods. "Yeah, Grace. You chose him. You love him, but you have to love all of him. You have to accept him for who is, and that means knowin' when he gets like this . . . he's going to shut down. But you're the only one who can reach him. I think you know that, which is what's eatin' you up inside."

I suck in a deep breath. "No, I'm hurt. I'm angry that he hasn't called me back or anything. I left him close to a hundred messages."

"Yeah, you're angry. Yeah, it sucks and it's wrong, but he's your guy. We're dumb. We screw up like it's our job. So, you can sit here waitin' for him to come back when we both know that ain't happenin', or you can go find him."

I lean back in the seat and let what Cooper says penetrate. Trent has told me time and time again he needs me to not let him fail. He's asked me to step in and help. I just don't know how.

"He needs you, Grace. If you love him, then do what he needs you to do."

"I don't even know where he is," I say frustrated.

"I can't believe I'm helpin' his dumb ass," Cooper complains. "Think about where you'd go to get away from life."

Where would he go? My mind reels with the possibilities. I've already checked most, but . . . maybe I just missed him. Cooper is right, though, I need to find a place he'd go to escape.

"Thank you, Coop."

I give him a hug and make my way out the door.

"I saw you guys a week ago," Cooper calls out.

I stop and turn around. "You did?"

I haven't seen Cooper since the night I almost set my house on fire. I thought about dropping by, but I wasn't sure what to say or how he'd feel about it. Presley told me he's fine and to stop being an idiot, but I didn't want to make him uncomfortable.

"You looked happy." Just a day ago, I was extremely happy. "He makes you smile, Grace. You don't see other people when you're with him. I see that now. Go get him before he regrets this more than he already will," he moves close to me.

"You're a good friend, to me and to him."

He chuckles. "Until I tried to steal his girl."

I smile and touch his arm. "I'll remind him of this moment."

"Go."

I turn and rush out of the hospital. I need to do what I promised to do and pull him back. He isn't drifting, he's floating away. I hope I'm strong enough to carry him back to shore.

NINETEEN

THERE ARE ONLY SO MANY places he can go without his truck. I check the lake where his father collapsed, his farm again, and my family's store. I didn't think he'd be at the last one, but I'm trying not to leave any stone unturned.

I sit in my car and drum my thumbs against the steering wheel, talking to myself. "Where would you go?"

A smile forms across my face as it hits me, and I berate myself for not thinking of it sooner. I throw the car in reverse and head off to get my horse.

He better have the excuse of a lifetime when I find him. He can run, and turn off his phone, and try to shut the world out, but there's no way I'm going to quit on him.

Not this time.

I get to my parents' house and head to the barn.

When I get inside, I'm so focused on what I need to do to get to my and Trent's spot, that I almost miss the amber light shining from the stable where my old horse used to sleep. I never could let Lightning in there. It felt wrong.

I open the door, confused about who was in here and why they left a light on, but then I see his body on the ground. Anger boils over as I realize he's been here the whole time. Hiding at my parents' house instead of coming home.

"Trent?" I ask as he gets to his feet.

The disappointment I was feeling fades away the second his eyes find mine. This isn't Trent. This isn't an angry man who ran away because he was afraid of losing his father.

This man is shattered.

His eyes are red rimmed from crying, he reeks of alcohol, and he's destroyed. I can see the pain and hurt splayed across his face.

"Trent," I say softly as I step closer. "What are you doin' here?" My need to comfort him is instant.

"How? How the hell did you find me? Just go home."

"This is my home. Why are *you* here?"

He steps back and grips the side of his head. "Fuck! This is why I didn't want to be found."

"Do you know how worried I've been? How sick your mama is over this?"

The skin around his eyes tightens. He goes from broken to irate in a second. "Good."

"Good?" I ask incredulously. "Good? How is this good? Your daddy is sick, and he's havin' a hard time with the transfusion and you're hidin' at my barn?"

"I can't . . ." He looks away.

"Why are you here? Why did you leave?"

When his gaze meets mine, the pain is so clear I can feel it. It billows off him in waves.

"Because I was far enough away from you that you wouldn't push me, but close enough I could feel you."

My chest tightens and tears fill my eyes. He's always pulled away, but this time he tried not to. However, something has him on the verge.

What I have to do is rein him in. He's going to push me hard. I know this. "Why did you leave?"

He drops his eyes before turning away from me, but I don't back off. "Let me in, Trent. I'm not going to let you drift away, not now, not ever. I love you. Talk to me. Tell me what happened. Please." My words are soft as I step toward him and touch my fingertips against his back.

He shakes his head but doesn't pull away from me. "I'm too fucking tired to fight you, but I'm not doin' this."

I watch him head to the other side of the stable. My lips part as I take in everything scattered around the floor—the lantern, beer cans, the shirt he was wearing yesterday. What stops my eyes are the pillows and blankets that are in the same spot he held me the night my horse died.

"Trent, tell me what's going on."

"Not a damn thing," he spits out.

It seems this is going to be harder than I thought. "Honey, what are you doin' here?"

He grabs another beer and cracks it open. "Where should I be?"

I walk toward him and rip the can from his hand. "With your father! Remember? The man who is in the hospital, sick, and needs his family. The man you were so worried about not even twenty-four hours ago!"

"Oh, you mean the guy who is *not* my fucking father!" he screams in my face and takes his drink back.

He's drunk and ridiculous. "Are you insane?" I slap his chest with both hands, shoving him back. "Your father is dyin', Trent, and you're out here, in my barn, gettin' drunk!"

"He's not my fucking father!" Trent screams again, and his eyes fill with tears. "He's a liar and so is my mother!"

"What?"

"Jesus Christ! Are you deaf?" Trent's eyes flame and then his head falls. "Leave, Grace! Let me be alone. You don't get it. No one gets it, and I'm not going to explain it."

My heart races as I watch this man fall apart. I don't leave, but I do have to hold my own emotions at bay because I have never seen him this distraught. "You're not makin' any sense."

He turns his back on me. "I don't know how to be any clearer. I'm fucking done. I'm done with everyone in this fucking town and all their lies. I'm leaving as soon as I'm sober enough to get the fuck out of here."

"So, you're done with me?" I ask. Trent spins back around but doesn't say a word. We stand here, neither of us blinking, and a tear leaks from my eye. "Is that what you're saying? You're done with everyone in this town, which includes me? Huh? Have I lied to you? I don't even know what happened!"

"I don't know, Grace, have you lied? Did you know that I'm a bastard? Did you keep the secret just like everyone else?"

"The secret that you're not Rhett's? Do you hear yourself?"

A tear falls down his face and his body sinks to the ground. "Go the fuck home, Grace."

"No." He's going to have to drag me out and drive me if he wants me gone.

I try to think about what could've caused this. He was upset, but not like this before going back to talk to Rhett. It has to be because of something when he was there.

"What happened in the hospital?"

"I can't deal with this!"

"What happened in the hospital?" I repeat. "Why do you think he's not your dad?"

"I don't think . . . I fucking know!"

I've known his family my entire life, and this is crazy talk. Whatever he thinks he knows . . . he's wrong. Rhett needs him, and he's being crazy.

"How?"

"God! It's like no one listens."

"I'll listen when you explain yourself!"

"I overheard my mother talkin' to the doctor and my father. He said somethin' about the blood test and that I wasn't a match."

"Okay." I sit beside him and gather one of his big hands in both of mine. "But that doesn't mean you're not his son."

Trent shakes his head and another tear drops. He clearly believes this crazy talk. "I heard them say it. I heard my mother say I wasn't his son and that they weren't going to tell me. It's not a fucking lie or me bein' stupid. I heard her say that I wasn't his son. I heard with my own ears them say I wasn't supposed to find out. Well, too fucking late! I found out, so yeah, I'm right where I belong. Alone."

My mouth opens a little as he crumbles. "You don't mean that."

He releases a sarcastic laugh. "Oh, but I do. Don't you see it now? It all makes sense. I've never been a Hennington. I don't look like my brothers. I have blond hair and they have brown. I'm the only one with blue eyes. I hate fishin'. I hated the horse farm. It's crystal clear, and I don't know why I never saw it before . . . I'm not his son!"

"Honey, listen to me." I shift and his eyes lock on mine. "There's a mistake somewhere."

Trent leans over, grabs a stack of papers, and shoves them in my face. "Tell me, Grace. Tell me how this is a goddamn mistake! Look at the papers! I'm B positive. My blood type is B positive. My father is A positive and so is my mother. There's no fucking way I could be his kid."

"But . . ." I look at the papers that prove Trent's blood type is different from the rest of his family's. "I don't know what to say."

He looks at the ceiling and wipes his face. "I don't know who I am! I've always been a Hennington. Now, who the fuck am I? I don't know who my father is. And my mother! She kept this from me. She lied to me for forty years. Both of them did."

"Listen to me." I get to my knees and hold his face in my hands. "You know who you are. And some blood test doesn't tell you who your father is. A life does. A family does."

"Don't give me that shit. They've lied to me! My whole life. His name is on my fucking birth certificate. If he's not my father, who is? Why lie? Why not tell me at some point?" Trent goes on, clearly upset. "They never planned to tell me. They got unlucky, and that's how I found out. Everything, Grace . . . I don't even know who I am."

Hearing the words from his lips, destroys me. I don't blame him for being so distraught. If I found out my father wasn't my actual dad, I would be the same way. He loves Rhett, and I'm sure he feels as if this is a huge betrayal. And it is. I honestly can't believe that his parents would lie to him. Family is everything to them. That being the case, it doesn't change who he is. His parentage doesn't affect the man Trent has become.

"I know this is impossible. I can't begin to imagine what you're feeling." I drop my hands.

"You have no idea. You have no fucking clue what I feel. I need you to go. I need to be alone. I don't want to listen to your reasons or any of that shit. I'm not going back to that hospital."

I try to recall what Cooper said about how Trent was going to push. When he feels scared, he lashes out at those around him. He's going to push me away because that's what he does. He's hurting, though. Like my mama always says, anger is the outward cry of fear.

"Well, I'm not leavin'."

Trent yanks his hands back. "Then I'll leave."

I shrug my shoulder. "Fine. I'll follow you."

"Grace—"

"No, you're upset. I get it. But you're not going to walk away from this. Not from me. If you want to be angry, then I'll sit here and let you be angry. If you want to scream and rant, I'll listen. I'll help you in any way I can, but I'm not leavin' you. We fight together, because I love you."

Trent shifts forward, his hands are on my face and he crushes his lips to mine. He kisses me as if I'm the only thing in the world. It's hard and brutal. I hold on to his arms as he moves me closer. It's like he's inhaling me, and I take it all. Trent pushes me onto my back.

His body covers me as he devours my mouth. Our tongues dance and passion fills the air around us. Trent's hands drift down my side and behind my thigh so he can hook my leg around him. His tongue glides from my neck and then across my shoulder. I close my eyes and arch my back when he heads toward my ear.

"Make me forget," he pleads. "Make me forget like only you can. I don't know who I am, and I need you to remind me."

His hands drift lower and grip my ass. He kisses me harder than the last one, but I don't care. If he needs me, I'll be here.

I touch his face, breaking the kiss, and bring his eyes to mine. "I love you. I love who you are," I say ardently as I kiss his nose. "I love everything about you." I bring my lips to his eyelids and touch each one. "I know who you are." I kiss his mouth before looking him straight in the eyes. "You're mine and I'm yours. Nothing changes that."

His blue eyes fill with pain. "I can't—"

I bring his lips back to mine and try to make him forget. I kiss him as if he's everything. I kiss him with every fiber in my being. He's the same man he's always been, and I'll show him that. He's lost, and I want to help him find his way. If this is all I can do, I'll be the balm to his pain.

I'll save him by loving him.

"I'm lost," he admits before his lips touch mine again.

His hands are everywhere, and I let him lead. His touch is

rough but never painful. I moan when he removes my pants hastily, tossing them across the stable, and then promptly finding his way to my clit. He kisses my neck and ear as he continues to rub in tiny circles. I buck when he inserts a finger, curling it to hit the spot that drives me crazy.

Before I know it, my shirt and bra are off before my breast is in his mouth. Trent continues to draw pleasure from my body as I whisper, "I love you."

I wait for him to say something. I can feel him pulling back, it's time to take over. Using my hips, I flip myself so I'm on top. I move down his body, kissing my way to his navel.

The low hiss comes from his lips when I keep going lower. I discard his pants, and then free his cock. Slowly, I lick his length, loving the sounds he makes. "Fuck, Grace. I can't . . ."

"You can. You can feel. This is us." I use my tongue again as he groans louder. My hand drifts up his chest, feeling his muscles tense beneath my fingers. He fights but loses it completely when I wrap my mouth around him.

I take him in my mouth and start to bob. His fingers tangle in my hair and he grunts as I suck him hard. I go up and down, taking him deep and loving every sound that falls from his mouth.

"Now, baby. Now," he says as he pulls me off. I climb his body, and he tugs my mouth to his. "I need you," he moans against my skin. "I need you, Gracie."

"I'm yours. Take me," I say, but I'm already climbing on top of him and sinking down onto his length.

"Don't give up on me," he says as I rock back.

"Never. I'll never give up on us."

I start to move, trying to remind him of what we are and who he is. His hands grip my hips and he helps me keep the pace. We don't say much, but we never break eye contact. I try to show him everything he is. I don't hold anything back as I give him my body, my heart, and my soul.

We continue to make love. Our connection is stronger than ever, and I don't need words to see what he's feeling. He needs me and this as much as I do. The sounds of love and ecstasy fill the air as I give myself to him. I take all of him. I love all of him. Every broken and damaged part is mine because he is.

I lean down, touch his face, and tell him again how much I love him. I want the words to be etched into his soul. I want him to not just hear them but to feel them.

He drags me higher so we're nose to nose. "You're the only thing I know that's real."

"I'm real. I'm yours, and I love you, Trent."

I'll say it until he believes it, until he knows that even if everything else we know in the world is taken away, I'll always be his.

TWENTY

Trent

WE LIE HERE ON THE blankets with her arms wrapped around me. Just like all those years ago, we're here, alone but together, and one of us is hurting. My mind replays the conversation in the hospital on repeat.

"Trent is his son in every way that matters," Mama says and then sighs. "We'd planned to tell him, but . . ."

"No one tells him I'm not his father."

Not my father.

A part of my entire being slipped away in that second. He's my father, but he's not. The lies and deception eat away at me. They could've told me, but they chose to keep their secrets.

All those times I was told I was a Hennington.

Lies.

Tons of lies.

Grace props her head on my chest, and I try to calm my heart. "Talk to me," she urges.

"There's nothing to say."

"Trent, don't pull away from me, please."

Her blue eyes beg me more than her words. I'm fighting it. I wish she knew how hard I'm trying to stop myself. When she showed up, I wanted to toss her out. Not because I didn't want to see her but because I knew she'd fight me. She'd use every trick she could to get to me, and I would let her.

Grace has a way of breaking through the steel wall I erect. She always does, and most times, I'm grateful for it.

I look in her blue eyes and rake my fingers down her spine. "I'm glad you found me. I think I wanted you to all along."

A phone rings, but neither of us moves. I don't feel like talking to anyone but her right now. Grace is all I have that makes sense in my life.

She smiles and shakes her head. "Is that why you came here?"

"This is the first place we spent the night together. You slept in my arms, and I remember thinking I was a lucky bastard."

"And you came back here to be alone with your beer?"

I chuckle and squeeze her tight. "I don't think you get it, I needed you and you came. I didn't want anyone, but I needed you."

"You could've just went home and waited for me. You didn't have to run away."

I hate that I disappointed her again. I wasn't thinking. I knew that I couldn't stand to be around anyone. I had to go where no one would find me. I thought about going out to the cabin, but my brothers would look there. I thought about taking a hike into the woods, but didn't feel like packing for a campout.

So, I came here.

I wish I would've stayed home, because once again, I caused pain to the person who has never betrayed me.

She deserves an explanation. "I didn't want to hurt you, sweetheart. I just couldn't look at any of them."

Grace tilts her head and looks at me with sadness in her eyes. "You can't stay here, honey. Your daddy needs you."

Here we go.

I knew it was coming. I start to get agitated because I wanted to avoid all this shit. Talking to my parents isn't going to help anything. Plus, she keeps forgetting that he already has his sons.

"Did you miss the part where I said he's not my father?" My voice is terse, and I know she hears the anger. Her eyes close, which makes me feel like shit again. How is it that with one look from her, she can make me feel as if I kicked her dog?

"I heard you loud and clear, honey."

Grace gets up, grabs the blanket we were using, and wraps herself tight.

"I much preferred you naked." I try to joke, but she isn't budging. She gives me a quick look before sitting beside me.

"I need you to hear what I say and not stare at my boobs."

Smart girl, but since she said it, I'm picturing them just fine.

She snaps her fingers in my face. "Hello, Trent."

"Sorry." I shrug and rest my hands behind my head. "I'm listenin' to all the reasons you think I should go talk to them."

Grace gives me a pointed glare, and I sit quiet. "When I left, your dad wasn't responding well to the transfusion. He's sick, and you and I both know he's dyin'. You're not going to get answers about who you are and why they've been lying by hiding out here."

"What if I don't want the answers?"

She shifts a little and sighs. "I don't think that's the case."

When did she get so damn knowledgeable about me? I do want answers, but I'm too pissed. They lied, they hid things, and now I feel like everything I thought I knew—vanished. Just like that.

I lived in a house of cards that was built on a crumbling foundation.

"It's better if I get my head straight first."

Grace curls herself back into my side with her head on my shoulder. "There has to be a reason why they never told you. I don't think your parents ever wanted to intentionally hurt you?"

"I don't know what they were trying to do."

"No, I don't believe you think that. Your parents are good people. They love you and sure, you're hurt, I get it, but they would never intentionally set out to destroy you."

But that's exactly what happened. If it weren't for the blood test, I never would've found out. I would've gone through my entire life believing that I was the firstborn son of Rhett and Macie Hennington. Instead, I'm the bastard son of another man.

"My mom was seventeen when she had me," I say, tangling my fingers in her long brown hair. "I always assumed my dad knocked her up when they were kids and then they got married. Turns out that I have no idea what happened. Did she have an affair? Did he think I was his until I broke a bone and they found out? Does my real father know I exist? Hell, is he even alive?"

So many fucking questions. I'm losing my mind.

"There's only one person who has those answers," Grace reminds me.

The phone rings again and Grace goes to move. I hold her in place, not wanting anyone to break this moment.

"I should check that," she says, but I shake my head.

"I don't give a shit right now. Let them call—"

"Listen, I get that you want to avoid all of this, but you can't, Trent."

Grace doesn't give me a chance to say another word. She gets up and grabs her phone.

"Hello?" She walks around the stable, cleaning the mess I made. "I'm here with him now. Yes, he's okay, but . . ." Her eyes shoot to mine. "He should tell you why. Because it's not my place to say." There is a stretch of silence before she speaks again. "Okay, is everything?" Her eyes fill with tears, and she grabs her chest. "We're on our way!"

"What's wrong?" I ask, already knowing the answer.

"We have to get back."

"He isn't gonna make it?" Fear takes away my ability to talk. She nods. "We should move fast."

For the first time since I left, there's no anger toward anyone but myself. Yes, I have a right to be pissed they never told me, but I was still selfish, just like she said. I throw on my clothes, and take Grace's hand. All I want to do is get there.

I pray I can make it before it's too late.

chapter
TWENTY-ONE

I'M SITTING IN THE PASSENGER seat since Grace refuses to let me drive. She claims I drank enough beer to put a horse to sleep, although I feel completely sober.

It's one of those moments when whatever buzz you were feeling disappears instantly.

The guilt and remorse I'm drowning in washed away all the alcohol. I hate myself for thinking I could hide away. The thought of what would have happened if Grace hadn't found me, and I didn't have the chance to get here, is like a punch to my gut.

Grace was right, he's the only father I have. The only man in my life that has been there, and I abandoned him.

"Too bad we don't have your squad car." The hospital is about thirty minutes away. "I'll drive as fast as we can." She tries to reassure me.

I lean back in the seat and close my eyes.

My mind goes through memory after memory. My father showing me how to fish for the first time. I remember the pride in his eyes when I shot my first deer. He clapped me on the back and told me I'd done well.

I remember the first time my brothers and I got in a fistfight. Dad put boxing gloves on us and told us if we wanted to fight, we did it like men. Zach always had quick hands, and he clocked me good, Dad showed me how to block the next punch and had me go back until I learned how to fight.

"What are you thinkin' about?" Grace asks.

I glance over at her and touch her leg. "Memories of my dad from when I was a kid."

She peeks over at me and attempts to smile. "Like what?"

"I was remembering goin' hunting with him, and him teachin' us how to fight."

"I remember that makeshift boxing ring you had." She laughs. "Wyatt tried to convince Presley and me to fight in it. He told us that all the kids did it, and if we wanted to do it in a bikini, he was all for it."

"I would've watched that." I squeeze her leg, and she slaps my chest.

"What else do you remember?"

"There's no memory stronger than being a teenager and watching him sit on the porch at night, waiting for us to come home. Our curfew was strict."

"Oh, I remember that. Wyatt and Zach didn't mess around on curfew."

Those two were always late. I learned early on how to get around it.

"Well, for every minute we were late, it was ten minutes shoveling the stables. Three minutes was a half hour of hard labor. I realized after the second time of bein' late, it wasn't worth it. But those two idiots were always late. If you were ten minutes late, it was almost two hours worth of chores."

"If I'd known that, I would've made Wyatt late every day!"

"The trick was so show your face early, hang out with Dad for a bit, and then head to bed. He'd check on you before he passed out, and then you could go back out after."

I was always skating around the rules. It also helped that Dad slept like the dead and Mom used earplugs to drown out his snoring. I'm pretty sure he figured it out, but he never said a word.

"Imagine if you'd thought I wasn't your brother's annoying friend when we were kids," Grace jokes. "We could've had so many nights together."

"I always thought you were pretty."

"No you didn't! You told Wyatt I was ugly and to stop bringin' me around. I was in love with you at sixteen, but you were too cool for me. I had a bad boy complex."

She's so wrong. I was five years older, and the last thing I wanted to do was date her before she was legal. I knew I was going to be sheriff from the time I was in sixth grade. I loved everything police. Dad pushed me for about two years to start learning more on the farm, but I wanted no part. I had a plan . . . go to the academy, graduate, start dating Grace, get married, and be happy.

Funny only half that list got accomplished.

"I liked you, but I wasn't too excited about going to jail."

"Jail?"

"Sixteen will get you twenty," I remind her.

"No one said we had to have sex!"

"You tell my eighteen-year-old boy hormones that. Darlin', I was not waiting until you became legal if we were dating."

Grace shakes her head as she drives. "You're a mess. Tell me more about when you were just a young and horny teenager."

We spend the rest of the drive talking about our childhoods. I sometimes forget because she's been my girl for so long that she has most of her younger memories with Wyatt and Zach. Zach was always around Presley and Wyatt was always wherever she was as well. But I wasn't with them. I had my own life with friends in my own age group.

I go quiet when I start to think about how the dynamic will

change. Knowing that I'm not their full brother could shift things. My brothers are good guys, I don't know if they'll care, but I do. I've prided myself on being Trent Hennington. There's been an honor in being Rhett's son. He's respected in the community, and I grew up not wanting to disappoint him.

My chest gets tighter with each mile that passes by. I pray we're not too late. I have so much to say to him. Questions I need answers to that only he can answer. They aren't so much about who I am, those answers will come from my mother. They are more about who I am to him.

I'll never forgive myself if I don't make it to him.

We get to the hospital in record time. I take her hand as we walk through the doors. I have no idea what's waiting for me on the other side. Grace told me a little about Wyatt's reaction to my leaving, which I expected. However, if the tables were turned, he'd have lost his shit, too.

When we open the doors, everyone turns and looks. Some show relief, while my brothers are clearly pissed.

"Trent! You made it." My mother rushes forward and draws me in her arms. "God, where have you been? You smell like dirt."

I lock up and try to keep myself under control. This isn't the time to say anything to her. "I'm here now."

"Yeah, the prodigal son returns," Wyatt mutters. "Nice of you to join us."

Grace squeezes my hand, keeping me from saying something I'll regret. "What happened?" I ask my mother.

Tears fall from her eyes, and she touches my cheek. "The transfusion didn't work as well as they hoped. He also has developed what we think is pneumonia. They've tried, but his heart is failin' and . . . it's too late to try anything more." A sob breaks free, and I pull her into my arms as she loses it. "It's about m-makin' him c-comfortable now."

I hate this for her. I hate all of it. If this was Grace, I'd be lost. She's spent her entire adult life married to him. I'm not sure how she'll survive. I'm not sure how any of us will.

As angry as I am, it's nothing compared to the pain I feel. "I'm sorry." I'm sorry for so much more than just her impending grief. I'm sorry I left. I'm sorry I wasn't strong enough for her. I'm sorry for the pain that'll come when she finds out I know her precious secret.

She nods against my chest. "I don't know what to do, Trent. I'm gonna lose him."

My brother envelops his arms around Presley as everyone watches her fall apart. Mama is the one who held us together when Wyatt had his tragedy last year. She's the one who knows what to say when we're struggling. Seeing her like this, as upset as I am, breaks me.

"We're all here, Mama. We're here for you."

She leans back before clutching me close. "He wants to see you, honey. He asked for you a few times."

Zach walks over and takes my mother in his arms. "Go," he says curtly.

I'll deal with his shit later.

Grace steps in front of me and holds my hands. "Stay here with her?" I request.

"Are you sure?" she asks.

"Yeah, I need to do this alone."

"Okay." She gives me a sad smile. "I love you."

"I love you, too." I pull her in my arms and hold her close. "Thank you, Grace," I say against her hair. "Thank you for makin' me see sense."

She leans back and kisses me. "I'll always be here for you."

"I know."

I turn and head through the door to where he's waiting.

Each step I take, I feel the despair growing. I'm not sure what I'll say. I don't know if I'll tell him I know, but I know I need to see him.

I pause when I get to the door. This is where I stood when I heard their discussion and everything changed. Once again, I'm going to have a life altering conversation.

I close my eyes, release a deep breath, and step through the door.

When I see him lying there, I fall apart.

Everything inside me splinters, and my chest aches.

My father opens his eyes and attempts to smile. "Son." His voice is raspy and weak.

This isn't the same man I saw yesterday. It's hard to believe how pale and fragile he looks. "Dad."

He takes a haggard breath and raises his hand. I move over to the bed and take his hand in mine. "You left?" he asks.

I've never been one to lie to my father. "I heard something I didn't want to know." I give him half the answer.

Dad nods and covers my hand with his other. His eyes fill with tears, and his lip quivers. "I figured it out this mornin'." He coughs and then clears his throat. "You overheard what was said in my room about you not being my son."

He's always seen too much.

"I did."

"I need you to know somethin'," he says quickly. "You *are* my son. You've always been my son. I've never loved you any differently."

Tears fill my vision as they stream down his face. "Pop."

"No. I need to say it. I've thought about this moment your whole life, and I need to get it out."

I don't interrupt him again. The strongest man I know falls apart as he tells me answers to the questions I've grappled with the last day. "Your biological father got your mama pregnant when she was sixteen. I knew him, always thought he was bad news, but she loved him for whatever reason. He was mean, and I told her to leave him several times. She was young and thought she could love him through it, but when he found out she was pregnant, he lost it. He accused her of cheatin' on him and then beat her. He left her bleedin' in an alley, and I was the one who found her. I lifted her in my arms and rushed to get her help. I stayed with her in the hospital when they weren't sure if you or her were gonna make it."

Pop stops talking for a minute as he recalls some far off memory. I can't imagine what he saw. My mother is the kindest person, and for any man to put his hands on her makes me want to scream and murder someone. Then to find out it was my own father, I can't put into words the hatred I'm feeling.

"I'd always had feelings for her. I think I fell in love with her almost instantly. She would pass me in the hallway and smile, and it would make my heart stop. She was so strong and sure that you'd make it through, though. After about a month, I knew I couldn't live without her. I asked her to marry me, because I knew if I didn't, she might realize I wasn't worth the trouble. I told her we'd raise you and build a family. We worried he'd come back, but I swore I'd protect her. I would never let him touch her or you. We got married right away, with her bein' pregnant, it was what would be done immediately anyway. And we started preparin' for *our* baby. I knew you'd be my child in every way that mattered. The day you were born, I signed the birth certificate, we were already married, so no one questioned it, and then you were mine, Trent. From that day forward, you were my son, and I was your father."

"Why didn't you just tell me?"

He shakes his head. "I don't know. In the beginning, it was fear that if he found out you'd survived, he'd try to take you, but we've never seen him since. After a while, it was selfish on some level. I needed you to always be my son in every way. I never wanted you to look for him. I never wanted you to ask about him. More than that, I was afraid if you knew, I'd lose you, son."

I shake my head as my own tears make it hard to see. "You never would've."

"Look at what happened when you heard," he reminds me. "You took off."

"I took off because you lied to me," I explain. "It was like someone told me the sky wasn't blue. I never questioned you being my father."

"You're my son, Trent. You're my first son no matter what a blood test says. I need you to always know that. I need you to know I never loved you any differently. Not one minute."

I can't hold back. I tried as much as I could, but this is quite possibly my last conversation with my father. And it's him trying to comfort me. My emotions overwhelm me, and I let out a strangled sob. "You can't die now. Not today. Not ever."

My head falls, and his hand moves to the top of my head. "You're so much stronger than you give yourself credit for. One day you'll see it. You've been a fighter since before you were born. Nothin' came easy for you, but you have to open your eyes and let yourself be happy. Marry that girl, start a family, and live your life. It goes fast." I look at him, and he smiles with tear-filled eyes. "You have been my greatest gift. I didn't create you, but I got to keep you."

chapter
TWENTY-TWO

Grace

THE LAST FOUR DAYS HAVE been devastating. We stay at the hospital all day and most of the night. The doctor attempted another blood transfusion, but Rhett hasn't gotten any better. It's the pneumonia that will take his life.

He's on heavy antibiotics to attempt getting it under control, but they explained at this point, there's almost no chance it'll work. The oncologist explained we should prepare, because it will happen very quickly.

Trent spoke with his brothers after he talked with his dad. They forgave him for disappearing, and tried their best to understand. They joked about knowing there was always something off with him.

Idiots.

I don't know that any of us can understand the turmoil he's struggling with. I can empathize with him, but I don't know what he truly feels.

We were at the hospital until around midnight last night. He spent his time by his father's side and tried to focus on every minute they all have with him.

It's hard knowing someone you love is going to die.

It's hard watching people around you struggle and not be able to help.

There's a helplessness that can eat at your soul before the grief has even started.

Neither of us slept much last night, and I try to leave him to his thoughts. I enjoy being in his arms, feeling him close. He's been a pillar of strength since he's had more time with his father.

"Did you and your dad work things out?" I ask. I didn't want to ask him what was said, but the concern is too much to hold back anymore.

"Yeah, I understand him and why they kept it quiet. After knowing how my biological father abused my mother, I can see the want to protect me. I would've gone lookin' for him."

He tells me a little about how his mother was beaten. The fact that Trent could've died at the hand of his own father. A world without him would've been a very bleak place. Trent watches me as tears stream. His mother never deserved that kind of treatment. My thoughts turn to my sister, and I wonder if Scarlett felt the same way. Their stories mirror each other so much. Loving a man who uses his fists.

When Scarlett came home the first time William beat her, Trent was the first one standing in line to keep her safe. He stayed outside our home for two days waiting for Bill to show up. The anger he felt for any man putting his hands on a woman was palpable. Rhett taught him that. He showed him right from wrong and he's the man he is now because of who raised him.

"Don't cry, baby." His thumb wipes under my eye. "It all worked out. I'm here, my mother found Pop, and we're okay."

I nod and try to stop crying. "And your brothers?"

This was the one thing I wondered most about. Wyatt and Zach wouldn't handle this secret any better.

Trent's eyes meet mine as I rest my chin on his chest. "Wyatt was livid. It took a lot to get him to stop yellin'. Zach was quiet and angry that my parents have been lyin' to us. Mom sat there crying and asked them to understand, but it was Dad who finally told them it wasn't their business about how they raised their family. He then asked them if it changed anything."

"And?"

I can imagine Rhett's deep voice and the way a silence would fall around the room. Wyatt would bristle at being told what to do, Zach would brush it off, and Trent would sit, waiting for his brothers to answer. This was probably one of the things that worried him most. His brothers feeling differently about him. I know in my heart it wouldn't, but I also know Trent and the feeling of being thrown away haunting him.

He laughs. "They looked at Dad and snorted, saying the only people they were thinkin' of kicking out of the family were him and Mom."

I smile and lay my head on his chest. Listening to his heartbeat with my eyes closed. I'm content in this moment. Trent runs his fingers through my hair as I rest. This feels incredible. Having no secrets or no worries about our future. It's something I've yearned for. I start to drift, from being both comfortable and sated.

"Marry me?" Trent blurts out as I'm on the brink of falling asleep.

That woke me the hell up.

I freeze. "What?" I ask, thinking maybe I heard him wrong.

"Marry me," Trent repeats.

Okay, so maybe I didn't hear him wrong. I don't say a word as I try to find my lungs. He can't be serious. It's been twenty years of waiting for those words, surely he wouldn't say it on a whim.

"Trent." I shift and look at him as my heart races. "You're going through a lot right now. I'm not sure that this is really what you want."

"I love you. I want you to be my wife."

"Okay, but . . ."

He rolls over, reaches into the drawer on his nightstand, and removes a box. I start to tremble when he puts it in front of me. "I've had this ring since the day before Zach's wedding. I bought it, knowing one day you'd be wearin' it." My hand flies to my mouth as I look at the black box with gold writing. "This isn't some spur-of-the-moment thing. This is me not wanting to waste a single minute. This is me wanting you to be mine. This is me finally listenin' to my heart and needin' to do right by you. I want to marry you. Right now. I want to be your husband. So, I'm asking you Grace Rooney, will you marry me?"

He opens the box and there sits a beautiful pear-shaped diamond solitaire flanked by four diamonds on each side. It's beautiful. "You're sure?" I ask because I want him to be. "If you're not, we can lie back down and forget this ever happened."

He lifts the ring out of the box and glides it onto my finger. "Do you remember what you were eating the first time I kissed you?" he asks as my eyes fill with tears.

"No." I shake my head.

"A pear."

"How could you possibly remember that?" I ask as I stare at my hand with a pear-shaped diamond sitting on it.

"Because every now and then, when I kiss you, I can taste it all over again." His lifts my chin and holds me captive. "You're the best thing that's ever happened to me. You're my heart and soul. I never want to spend a day without you. I'm gonna ask you again . . . marry me?"

I don't have to think about anything. I've loved him forever. I'll only ever love him until the day I die. We've had ups and downs and wins and losses, but we've had them together. He's not perfect, but he's perfect for me.

I throw my arms around him with tears falling freely. "Yes! Yes! Yes! I want nothing more than to be your wife!"

He laughs, and we fall back. I kiss him, hoping he can taste the pear again.

"All right." He holds my face back to stop me from kissing him. "I need to ask you one more thing."

"Ask me anything." I can't stop the smile.

"Marry me today, Grace. I know it's not the wedding you probably imagined, but I want my father to be there."

I sit back and put my hand on his chest. "Honey, are you sure? I'm not saying no, I just don't want you to wake up a week from now and wish we'd waited."

"I think we've waited long enough. My father would want to see this. He loves you, and I will never regret marrying you. Not now, not ever."

It's all happening so fast, but then again, it's really not. I know he wants his father there, and I don't want to deny him that. We love each other, we've been doing good, so why not?

"Okay," I say. "Okay, if you want to get married today, let's do it."

Trent grabs me in his arms and rolls me over. "I love you."

"I love you, too."

We both laugh and he rolls off me. "Go call your family. I'll call mine."

I glance back at my hand and bite my lip. I'm engaged. I'm actually engaged to my boyfriend of . . . forever . . . and we live together. We're going to be married—today.

Holy shit.

I grab my phone and call my mother. "Can you meet us at the hospital in about an hour?"

"Is Rhett okay? I just talked to Macie." Mama sounds worried.

"Mama, Trent proposed, and he wants to get married today."

"Today?"

"Yeah, so Rhett can be there and see it."

"Oh, honey! He's a good man," she says and then yells for my father. "Jim! Trent finally proposed to Grace!" I hear him yell something back, but I can't understand it. "No! She's gettin' married today at the hospital."

"Mama," I try to stop her.

"No! The hospital! So that Rhett can see it." She keeps going as if I'm not on the phone.

"Mama!"

Once again, she carries on. "In an hour, so you need to get off your behind and get dressed!"

"Mother!" I yell louder.

"Well, I don't know about that, James, I found out about it myself not two minutes ago." She huffs before coming back on the line. "Grace, your daddy wants to know if he has to wear his good pants or if you mind him wearin' his jeans."

I shake my head and stare at my ring. "He can wear whatever he wants."

"Well, don't tell him that, Grace. He'll wear his good pants. It is your weddin' after all."

"I need to call a few people, I love you, and I'll see you at the chur—I mean hospital."

I call Emily, and she starts screaming. She's on her way to Bell Buckle as luck would have it. She heard from Presley and was coming to be here for support. I don't know if she'll get there in time, but I hope she does.

I'm in front of my closet just staring. I don't have a wedding dress, and there's no way I'd wear one to the hospital, but I would like something white. I feel Trent's arms wrap around me from behind and his head rests on my shoulder. "You almost ready?"

"I don't know what to wear," I admit.

He leans back, and I turn to face him. "Anything you wear will be perfect. I hate that I'm takin' your white dress and big wedding from you."

"No, no, it's not that." I stop him before he misunderstands. "I don't need all that. Family and friends are what matter to me. I only care about the who, not the where. Plus, we can have a big ole party later on, right?"

"We can do anything you want."

"I've always wanted a barn wedding." I smile.

The barn at my parents' house is rustic and beautiful. It's dark grayish wood and tall ceiling is where I would have my pretend wedding all the time. I pictured Trent standing at the end when the barn doors opened. I can close my eyes and see the lanterns lining the path to him. We wouldn't be dressed up crazy and the ceremony would be small with just the people who truly matter in our lives.

I'm a simple girl. I spent half my life in pageants and wearing big dresses because Mama thought it would make me a lady. I think she liked playing Barbie and I was a real life version for her—minus the blonde hair.

My friends all wanted the big gowns and fancy parties, but I only cared about the right guy at the end of the aisle waiting for me.

"We can have that. I'll give you whatever wedding you want."

I rest my hands on his chest and grin up at him. "Oh! What about rings and a marriage license?"

I didn't even think about those things until just now.

Trent tucks my hair behind my ear and brushes my cheek. "I already called Judge Wheatley. He said we should come by the courthouse after the ceremony and he'll officially marry us there. As for the rings . . ." He touches my face before admitting, "I don't have them, but we can pick out anything you like tomorrow."

"You thought of it all." I lean in and press my lips to his. "And in a few hours, you're going to be my husband."

"You're never getting rid of me now."

I snort. "If I haven't done it yet . . ."

"You tried, sweetheart."

"And I'm glad I failed."

He kisses my nose. "I am, too."

"I need to get to the hospital."

"Wait!" I say grabbing his hand as he lets me go. "What about a cake or food?"

"Don't you worry about that." He tugs me back against him. "I've got all this taken care of. You worry about getting yourself dressed so we can go. Everyone is headin' there now."

He kisses me again and then heads off to the other room. Married. I'm getting married today.

A knock on the door causes me to jump. It opens a little and Presley peeks her head in. "Hi, honey."

"Pres!"

"Can I come in?"

"Yes! Please!"

She enters the room, and I tighten my robe around me. "Let me see the ring!" She rushes over and takes my hand. "Oh, he did better than I thought! When Zach told me a few months ago, I was a little skeptical."

"You knew?"

She shrugs. "I knew he bought a ring. He told Zach about it."

"But—" I pause for a second. "If you knew that Trent had a ring before the wedding, why would you tell me to date Cooper?"

Presley sits on the bed and pulls me next to her. "Because I hoped it would set things back the way they should go. Maybe it makes me a shitty sister, but I know you belong with Trent and I know my brother, he needed to see that, too. Zach warned me not to meddle." She waves a hand dismissively and smiles. "I guess the apple doesn't fall too far from the tree. God, I hope I'm not as bad as my mother. Can you imagine? We're the next generation of old busy bodies."

"Oh, God."

Presley waves her hand dismissively. "We'll worry about that later, I knew Cooper would always wonder if you guys would work, and I thought you'd always regret not trying to see if there was life beyond Trent. If you hadn't dated Coop, you never would have known for sure. And Trent would've kept thinkin' he could act like an idiot and you'd take it."

"But what about Coop?"

"I think we both know who Cooper likes, but he would never let himself go there. Not as long as he thought there was a chance with you and him."

I sit back and try to think who she's talking about. There's only one girl he ever asked out when we were kids. I remember him telling me about it, but I can't remember who. He just mentioned a blonde girl who stole his heart. There are only a few blonde girls we went to school with. One of them is . . .

"Emily?" I ask when it hits me.

She smiles.

"Our Emily? If he likes her why the hell would he ever try to date me?"

"Because you were safe. Because Emily scares the shit out of him." She laughs. "He's a good guy, but his life is here. He can't leave the farm, even with him and Wyatt and Zach talkin' about becoming more of partners. Imagine allowin' himself to love a girl outside of Bell Buckle!"

I'm not sure what to say. Emily made a few comments about him, but I always brushed them off because that's Em. She says whatever she wants.

"Wow." I shake my head with a smile. "So, you had this big

plan to get me to date Cooper, not fall in love with him, and end up marryin' Trent?"

Presley slaps my leg and grins. "I had a plan to get Trent to see his way out of his ass. You to see that your heart will always be Trent's, and for Cooper to figure out he needs to take risks. I did good, right?"

I roll my eyes and laugh. "Yes, our mamas would be proud."

"Now, enough about all that. You're gettin' married, and we need to get you ready!"

"We?"

The door opens and Angie comes through. She's wearing the same pale yellow as Presley.

"You guys!"

"Emily is about fifteen minutes out. That gives us enough time to get your makeup done and get started on your hair." Angie walks over and touches my arm. "I'm so happy for you. We're all sisters!"

I've always been a part of this family, but it hits me . . . I'm going to be a Hennington.

Mrs. Trent Hennington.

chapter
TWENTY-THREE

O NE BY ONE, MY FRIENDS head into the hospital room. Rhett got his transfusion very early this morning, but the doctor explained he could not handle being out of bed. So, this was the only way we could ensure he'd be present.

I don't feel anything but complete joy. I'm going to marry Trent in front of our family and friends.

Presley braided my hair and then pinned it up. Angie found a pretty white short dress that I forgot I had. It was buried in the back of my closet, but it's perfect. It comes right above my knees and we swapped out the dark brown belt for a yellow scarf I had.

Emily arrived a little bit after we started and changed into a yellow skirt I had. I have my matron of honor, Presley, and my two bridesmaids. Trent asked Rhett to be his best man and Zach and Wyatt are his groomsmen. We have a full bridal party, a reverend who works at the hospital to marry us, and everyone who matters ready to see us say "I do."

Daddy holds my hand outside the room and turns to look at me. "You okay, Daddy?"

He smiles, and his eyes fill with tears. "I'm givin' my last little girl away."

"I'm not goin' anywhere." I kiss his cheek. "I'm right here."

"Trent's a good man. He loves you and he'll take care of you."

I don't doubt that anymore. Trent has shown that he's changed. He changed before I even knew, but I was too hurt to see. I know that we'll always have our challenges, but with him by my side, I know we'll endure.

"I love him, too."

"Then take care of each other. Marriage is hard, and lovin' someone for all their faults isn't always easy, but it's always the right choice. You'll have days where you want to walk away and then times when you'll hope the day will never end. It's a give and take, and sometimes . . . you have to shoulder the burdens for both of you. But you and Trent are strong enough to do that for each other." Daddy touches the side of my cheek. "Your strength will be what gets you through the muck."

"Thank you for bein' my Daddy."

"Oh, baby girl," he says before he kisses my cheek. "It has been my honor."

I wipe the tear and try to fan my cheeks. "I don't want to cry already." I let out a nervous laugh.

"Well, let's get you to the man waitin' for you."

"Okay." I nod.

We start walking, and I hold on tight to the man who's always held me up. He's been the best father a girl could ask for. He loved my sister and I with every part of him. I think about what it was like for him to lose Scarlett. I think about how my sister's story mirrors Macie Hennington's. I wish she were here today, and it breaks my heart she didn't have a man like Trent.

He would never do what his father did to his mother. He fights for women who are in relationships like that. Trent wouldn't raise his hands in anger, he's a protector. Learning about the type of man he came from was hard for him. Knowing that his own father tried to kill him and possibly his mother isn't something he's accepting of. But if anything, it showed him how much he's like Rhett. How much he truly is a Hennington, because he's Rhett's son.

Daddy and I step through the doorway and Trent stands next to his father's bed. I walk toward him with tears in my eyes. His blond hair is pushed back the way I love it, he has on khakis with a blue button-up shirt, and has a yellow rose in his hand. His eyes don't move from mine as I move closer.

My father takes my hand and puts it in Trent's. "Be good to her," he says.

"I will," Trent promises.

My father kisses my cheek and moves over to stand behind my mother.

Rhett clears his throat. "Can I say somethin' before we start?"

"Of course," I say quickly.

"Grace," he says as his voice trembles. "You've been my daughter in my heart for a long time. I've never seen someone love another with such conviction. I want to thank you."

I release Trent's hand and move over to the side of Rhett's bed. "Thank you for raising the man I love."

"Thank you for loving the man I raised."

I kiss his cheek, and he touches my hand before looking at Trent. "Marry that girl before she runs out of here."

"You got it, Pop."

The Reverend smiles at both of us and begins the ceremony. They're words that have been spoken a million times, but they sound different to me. I listen to him talk about love and acceptance, and I gaze at Trent. We've come so far. Our relationship has changed and grown in so many ways. Two years ago, he never would've opened up to me. He would've kept it in and suffered. Our relationship felt like it was always teetering on the precipice of disaster. Now, I have nothing but hope for where we'll go. We've learned that we're stronger together than we are apart.

We turn to face each other, and I say the words I've waited to recite for a long time. My eyes fill with tears and my voice trembles. "I, Grace Louise Rooney, take you, Trent Milton Hennington, to be my wedded husband. To have and to hold from this day forward, for better or worse, for richer or poorer, in sickness and in health, till death do us do part."

Trent squeezes my hands, and he clears his throat. My heart pounds as he repeats the same pledge to me. "I, Trent Milton Hennington, take you, Grace Louise Rooney, to be my wedded wife. To have and to hold from this day forward, for better or worse, for richer or poorer, in sickness and in health, till death do us do part. And long after that."

I smile through the tears and everyone chuckles.

"I think after a lifetime with you, she should get a free pass," Wyatt jokes.

"Because you're a walk in the park?" Angie tosses in.

"Can I kiss her now?" Trent asks The Reverend.

"By the power vested in me by the state of Tennessee, I now pronounce you husband and wife. You may kiss the bride."

"Kiss me, wife," Trent says as he tugs me against him.

"Whatever you say, husband."

Our lips touch, and I throw my arms around his neck. I hold on as he kisses me with so much love, I can't feel the ground. Standing in a hospital room while surrounded by family, I just married my best friend.

I walk around and hug everyone, thanking them for being there as happy tears find their way past my eyelashes. Doctor Halpern urges us all to leave and let Rhett get some sleep. He's had a very exciting morning, and even though there are a dozen people in his room, his eyes are heavy with sleep.

We head to a small break room that the nurses were nice enough to let us borrow for a few hours. There isn't any music or decorations, but there is food. Sort of. We have jello, milk, and I don't even know what kind of pie that's supposed to be on the table.

This is what I get for tasking Zach and Wyatt with food. It's not as if Wyatt's wife owns the bakery in town.

Idiots.

Mrs. Hennington enters the room and heads straight to me. There are tears in her eyes that match my own. "Oh, honey, don't cry." She squeezes me in her arms. "You were always my daughter. Even before you loved my son."

Things between his mother and Trent have remained a little tense. He's managed to forgive his father, but he's still holding anger toward her. I, on the other hand, want to hug her. She's the survival story my sister wasn't. She fought through abuse, found real love, and gave me my husband.

Her eyes travel to where Trent is standing, talking to my parents.

"You know he'll come around," I say as I glance at him.

She waves her hand. "Oh, I know. He's a stubborn ass, but he needs to be mad at someone, and I'll be it for now. You know what you got yourself into with marryin' a Hennington?"

"I think I have a good idea." I smile.

"I'm glad he has you, honey."

"I hope I have a sliver of the love you and Rhett have."

Her eyes turn sad as she looks back at the door. "I don't know how I'll live without him. I've spent my entire life takin' care of him. I thought I was prepared, but lookin' at him today, so weak." She sighs. "I know that I'll never be ready to live in a world without him."

"Did the transfusion help?" I ask with a little hope.

She shakes her head. "It's like putting bubble gum on a slashed tire. It's been a lot of patchin' holes and there's nothing more we can try."

"But he looked better today."

Mrs. Hennington's voice is filled with despair. "It's temporary, sugar. He looked better because he'd gotten the blood his body needed, but in a few hours, he'll be back to the way he was. This was probably the last transfusion he'll do. He doesn't want to prolong the process." A tear falls down her face and she wipes it away. "I'm so sorry I'm talkin' about this, it's your weddin' day."

"Mrs. H.," I touch her arm. "I don't know what to say."

She touches my face. "First, you call me mama like my other daughters do. Second, you be happy today. Because if you saw the smile on my husband's face, you would know it was because of you and Trent. He's wanted to be at his boy's weddings. And after what occurred the other day, to be his best man, I know it gives him great peace."

Trent walks over and wraps his arms around my shoulders. "Mama," he says with restraint.

Macie smiles at her son and touches her throat. "I'm so happy for you, Trent."

"I'm glad Dad got to see this."

"He is too, honey."

"Trent," I look at him from over my shoulder, "why don't you talk to your mother for a bit? I'm going to talk to my new brothers."

They need to work this out. There's no better time to put your crap aside than at a wedding. His grin tells me he knows exactly what I'm doing. He kisses me, and I extricate myself from his hold.

Wyatt holds his arm open, and I lean in. "Who knew it would take this long to be officially family?" He smiles down. "I'm happy for you."

I wrap my arms around one of my oldest friends and squeeze. "Thank you. For everything."

Wyatt has been there through it all. He's given me more advice than he's probably ever wanted to and wiped a lot of tears, but he never judged me. "Listen, there's no give backs on that one. You bought him, so you have to fix whatever is defective."

I laugh and slap his back. "Is that so?"

"Well, we'll of course be happy to kick him around if he needs it," Wyatt says as he looks to Zach for confirmation, which comes in the form of a nod and smile.

"Good to know." I kiss Wyatt's cheek and continue to talk to everyone.

It may not be a real wedding setting, but you'd never know it. Everyone talks, eats crappy hospital food, and smiles. This is one of the times I'm grateful for all the meddling and crazy small-town living. We don't worry about the little things. It's the people in my life that matter. They're the foundation of the house I'm building in life. When things go bad, I know if I fall, I'll be okay.

chapter
TWENTY-FOUR

~ Fourteen months later ~

"THE RULES ARE SIMPLE," WYATT stands on the table as he goes over the rules of the Rhett Hennington Annual Family Competition. "We have seven events. The family with the most points at the end, brings home the trophy."

Trent pulls me close and clears his throat. "Grace and I got this in the bag."

"Dream on." Zach cracks his neck. "The boys and I are going to make you all cry like little—"

"Hey now!" Mrs. Hennington steps forward. "Your daddy would not like any trash talkin'."

"Did you know Dad at all?" Wyatt asks. "He talked more shit than a toilet."

"Wyatt Hennington, you do not curse around your mama!" She scolds him. "Your father prided himself on raisin' men. Act like it."

"Yes ma'am." He drops his head but looks over at Angie and winks.

We've been spending the last six months planning and getting ready for today. It's been one year since we said goodbye to Rhett. A year of adjusting and finding ways through life without him. Trent took it hard, but instead of running away, he leaned on his family.

After a while, Macie asked the girls to think of a way to honor Rhett that would keep the family together.

It didn't take long for us to come up with an extended version of their yearly fishing expedition. Plus, the boys never turn away a chance to compete.

"Now," Mama hoists Felicity in her arms, "your daughter is watchin' you, Wyatt. She wouldn't like it very much if her father lost, would she?"

Wyatt looks at my beautiful niece and smiles. "No, and she'll never see it happen. Daddy's bringin' home that trophy."

"Not so fast, little brother." Trent walks forward. "Don't go counting your chickens before they hatch."

"Boys, boys, boys." Presley steps in the middle. "Are we gonna stand around all day or are we going to compete? Because *this* family is bringing that singin' bass home."

"That's right." Zach throws his arm around his wife.

God, this is going to be a shit show.

The last two months Trent has started Operation Kick Their Ass, which has entailed training days. He's woken me at the ass crack of dawn to go fishing, water balloon tosses, three legged races, and all kinds of other crap. I finally put my foot down the other day when he tried to get me up at five in the morning for a three-mile conditioning run.

I don't run.

Not unless something is chasing me, and even then, I might just let it eat me.

"Cooper," Wyatt calls, "you know the rules?"

"Yup." He gives an evil grin. "I can't wait. I'll be in charge of makin' sure none of you cheat. First event . . . shooting."

I don't know how this event got put on the list, but the boys demanded it. There are three teams: me and Trent, Angie and Wyatt, and Zach and Presley. Any of the offspring can compete in one event each. Since Presley and Zach are the only ones with children old enough to compete, we know they're going to use that to their advantage. Felicity is turning a year old in two weeks so we don't have to worry about her yet.

We walk over to the shooting area.

"All right," Cooper claps his hands, "this event is for the girls."

"What?" I yell. "No, that makes no sense!"

He grins and lifts the paper in the air. "It's the rules I got here."

Wyatt and Zach laugh. "I'm so glad we didn't tell Trent about that rule."

"Assholes," Trent grumbles. "It's okay, sweetheart. I'm a cop, I'm highly trained on weapons and you're my wife . . . you got this."

"How does your being trained on guns mean I've got this?"

I don't like shooting. I'd only gone once with my father, and I never agreed to go again. I'm not sure what he thinks he's going to teach me in a few minutes. But the way that Angie and Presley are grinning, it seems they've done a lot of practice.

I glare at them both. "I thought we were family! What happened to all that solidarity crap y'all were spewing?"

"We are family and all that, but Zach promised me a trip if we win." She shrugs.

Angie gives an apologetic smile. "And Wyatt bribed me with a full month of getting up with Felicity."

I shake my head at them both. "Traitors."

"Wait a minute," Angie says, leaning in close. "You have been off in honeymoon world while Pres and I have been babysitting."

"What?"

Presley nods. "Yeah, Mama has practically moved into Angie's. I mean, you haven't had a kid yet, so we've been watching her."

They're insane. I get Mama two days a week. "She's at my house just as much as yours," I whisper. "She reorganized my closet the other day because I wasn't utilizing my space appropriately. I don't need a kid to have her stoppin' by."

I love my mother-in-law. I love her so much, but since Rhett passed away, she's been—bored. Very bored.

Angie has gotten the most attention since Felicity was born two weeks after he passed. "Oh no." Angie shakes her head. "I definitely win."

Presley waves her hand in the air to stop Angie. "She walked in the house when Zach and I were . . . you know . . ."

My hand flies to my mouth and Angie laughs. "That's awkward."

"Tell me about it."

"I'm sure she'll be around us more soon enough." I smile.

"Enough talkin' girls!" Wyatt claps his hands. "Time to show which of the Hennington brothers is the master of the universe."

I roll my eyes, but Angie and Presley laugh at Wyatt. "I swear."

Presley goes first and manages to hit the outer ring of the bull's-eye. Zach, of course, lets her know that she's going to have to step up her game if she wants the trip. Then Angie goes. She's actually good at this. She gets two shots on the paper, and Wyatt lays a fat one on her before slapping her ass.

Now, it's my turn.

Trent goes over a few things on the gun, and I pray that I can at least hit the target. Not that I care if I win, I wasn't thinking far enough ahead to make a wager. I could've gotten the house painted or something good.

"Okay, you hold it like this." Trent lifts the shotgun and tucks it into my armpit.

"Like this?" I ask as I start to spin, but he stops me.

"Okay, what was rule number one, Gracie?" he asks again.

"Down the way or something."

"Keep the muzzle downrange. Downrange means not at me!" Trent holds my shoulders and points at the targets again.

I nod and try to remember I'm holding a loaded gun.

I don't understand why he thinks this is a good idea.

"I don't want to shoot it," I complain.

"Sweetheart, you have to shoot it and hit the middle. We need to win this one since you didn't train for the run."

"Train for the run," I mutter. He's insane. This is a family competition, and they're making it seem as if we're going out for the Olympics.

I frown and try to remember what he said about my feet. Close together or apart? I think it was close together.

I adjust my feet and pull the trigger.

The gun goes off and pushes so hard against my shoulder I almost drop it. Shit that hurt. "Ouch!" I yell as he takes it from my hand. I rub the spot where it tried to take my shoulder off.

Trent laughs as he puts it on the shelf in front of us. "It has a nice kickback."

"I'm going to kick you! And your stupid brothers."

He moves closer and puckers his lips. "Is my sweet wife hurt?"

"Yes," I grumble.

"Do you want me to rub it? We could sneak off now . . ."

I swear, we got married and he became a teenager again. I'm lucky I can walk right now. All he wants to do is have sex. All the time. Three times a day. Sometimes more.

Little does he know that's all going to change soon.

"Aren't you getting old and that part is supposed to stop working?" I say playfully but also a little curious. Those guys on the commercials don't look much older than him.

We may still be considered newlyweds, but we've been together for a long ass time.

"Don't tell me the sex is gone this soon into marriage. Zach told me this crap could happen."

I smack his chest. "I'm worried about breakin' the equipment."

"Don't you worry, there's plenty of lube in my toolbox."

"You're so gross." I laugh and then look at the target.

Cooper is examining the paper and yells "Grace is the winner!"

"What?" I shriek. "No way!"

"Boom!" Trent yells and points in his brothers' faces. "Beginners luck! Losers!"

We move on to the other events. Each of the three brothers got to choose two events, and then Mama thought of the tiebreaker. Every event chosen was definitely to give an advantage, only we had no idea the girls would be competing in the one obviously geared for the guys. Now, though, it was chosen by coin toss. Damn Cooper and trying to switch things up.

"Okay, final event, sweetheart." Trent puts his hands on my shoulder. "We need to win this one."

"A drink off? You idiots picked an event for who can take the most shots?" I can't believe these dumbasses. "Can we redo the coin toss?"

"Nope." Wyatt grins.

"I guess it's a good thing we did shooting as the first event."

He nods and beams with pride. "That was by design."

I'm not drinking. I'm not going shot for shot with freaking Wyatt who has a hollow leg. I've been there, done that, got the week-long recovery to prove it. I vowed that I would never be stupid enough to attempt that again. Plus, there are other reasons.

"Well, we are going to forfeit this event."

"What?" Trent yells. "No way. We're winning. If we get this event, we beat Wyatt and nothing in this world makes me happier than watching him cry."

"Nothing, huh?" I ask as I cross my arms. "Not your wife?"

Trent's expression falls a little. "You know what I mean, darlin'."

Yeah, that he likes watching his brother in misery. I get it. I like watching Wyatt pout too, but not enough to kill myself for it.

"Trent, I really can't drink Wyatt under the table on a good day."

He looks at the amber colored whiskey and then back to me. "I have an idea," he grins and walks off.

His good ideas usually end in some kind of accident. Like the time he thought it would be easier to spray paint the bedroom instead of rolling it. He failed to tape off the places he didn't want paint and ended up having to hire two guys to come undo what he did. Then, last week, he thought we pay too much in electric and wanted to build a wind turbine because he saw it on some Alaska survival show. After an hour of trying to get the three wooden poles to stand upright, he quit.

I'm not sure what energy he thought we were going to get from it, there's no wind.

But, as Mama always says, men are dumb, and we can only say that because we let them continue to try asinine things.

Trent returns with another bottle of whiskey, and now I'm worried. "You don't think the two bottles on the table are enough?"

He leans in close and hands me the bottle. "Swap that out with the one you're sitting by, it's not whiskey."

"Please God tell me this isn't your hunting pee jug," I beg.

He bursts out laughing. "I'll be right back!"

"Trent!" I call him back. "What the hell am I supposed to do now?"

"Baby," he grumbles. "Just drink that and fake being drunk by your third. We all know that's about all the liquor you can handle."

That's not true. "Hey!"

"Gracie, do you remember the wine?"

Whatever.

He leans in and kisses my lips. "I love you no matter how much of a light weight you are."

I smile and go for another kiss. "I'm not going to be all that light."

He laughs and misses my hint once again. I've been dropping them left and right, but he is either ignoring me, or too oblivious to catch on.

Trent and I have been trying to get pregnant for six months. I was told by the doctor to be patient and understand I'm older and it will be more difficult. Each month, I've waited, hoped, and been let down. Trent does his best to comfort me and joke about getting to have more sex, but I see it wearing on him.

Last month, he held me as I cried about all our wasted time. I felt like shit afterward. It's been a long road for us with mistakes on both sides. I should've pushed for what I wanted a long time ago, and he should've faced his fears head on.

It doesn't matter now, though. We're married, and we both love our life together. Oh, and it finally worked.

"You ready, Grace?" Cooper calls me over.

"Keep your pants on, Townsend," Trent replies with a grin.

"I wouldn't want to embarrass you," Cooper jokes and walks away.

"Yeah right," Trent scoffs. "Let me know when you hit puberty."

Cooper flips him off, and I smother a laugh.

Cooper and Trent finally hashed out their issues. I didn't ask questions, but Presley said Trent came over to thank Cooper not too long after we got back together. She said Cooper respects that Trent talked to him man to man. Since then, there have been big changes at the Townsend ranch with Wyatt becoming part owner. Trent has been there helping on the weekends with the upgrades to the barn.

"You ready, little sister?" Wyatt nudges my arm. "Just you and me. Since Presley can't throw a tomahawk, it's between us."

"And this is the game we ended with?" I ask.

"My partner may have swayed the odds to my favor."

"We'll see. Maybe I've been training for this event since there was no way I was runnin'."

Wyatt raises his arms over his head and grins. "I've seen you drink . . . I'll be fine."

I walk over to the side of the table where my special bottle sits. I'm really hoping this is apple juice.

Cooper goes over the rules, and I wonder if the intention of this tiebreaker was to watch someone break their leg.

"One member from each team was chosen by coin flip. You will each take three shots, stand, turn twice, sit back down, and wait for the air horn. At that time, you'll run to the tree, collect the cup with the ping-pong ball, and run back. The person to complete the revolution the most amount of times, wins."

"Really? I can barely walk sober!"

Wyatt sniggers. "I know."

"Get him, Grace!" Presley yells out.

"Yeah, Aunt Grace!" Logan throws his arm up. "Or I can compete for you?" Zach slaps the back of his head, and we all chuckle. "What? I was being helpful."

Macie snorts and rolls her eyes. "Don't let him fool you, honey. Those boys were stealin' our whiskey at your age."

"Ma!" Zach complains.

"What? It's true. You boys thought you were *so* smart. Little did you know your daddy would water that down. We had the moonshine hidin' in my closet."

"All right. Can we not give the already trouble causin' teenagers anymore hints?" Presley asks.

"We wouldn't want their uncle to have to arrest them for underage drinkin'." Trent gives them each a pointed look.

"Yeah, because it's not like he'd hang out and drink with them." Wyatt is laughing as he says it but shrugs when Trent glares.

Unreal. They're all the same as they were twenty years ago.

It's like time froze in their little man brains and kept them as immature teenagers. And then we all married them. I'm starting to wonder who the dumb ones are in this situation.

"All right. Go!" Cooper calls out.

We make it through the first round with me doing shots of apple juice. Wyatt doesn't seem too fazed, and I'm grateful for so many reasons that it's juice in my bottle.

On round number three Wyatt starts to show signs of being drunk. Thank God because I'm not faking it that great. By now, I should be on the floor and halfway dead. Nine shots would put me on my ass for a month.

But here I am, being slow, and wobbly off juice.

The air horn blows, and I wait for him to go. I need to appear as if I'm too drunk to get up.

This is so dumb.

Wyatt gets to the table on the other side and grabs his cup. "Come on, Grace! You gonna let a little whiskey slow you down?"

I give it a believable push when I stumble standing and then misstep as I pass him. I hear Wyatt chuckle, and then, thinking he's won, he throws his drink in the air and screams. The ball flies out, which means he's lost. All I need to do is bring my cup back.

"You idiot!" Angie slaps him. "If we lose because of this, you're still getting up with Felicity!"

Wyatt gives her a salute, and I focus on looking drunk. This is a lot harder than I thought. I don't usually pay attention to what I would do if I was drunk, but from the look on Trent's face, I need to be more believable.

I get back to the table with my cup and yell. "Ha! I win!" I dance around a little and point at Wyatt. His head is dropped on the picnic table.

Trent's arms are around me a few seconds later, and he hoists me in the air. "That's my girl!"

"We beat you!" I point to my family as we celebrate.

"That's right, suckers!" Trent follows in the taunting.

"Wait a minute," Angie says as she comes around the table. "I've been drunk around you many times. I've seen you wasted so badly off five glasses of wine that you couldn't walk. I've seen you after three shots, forgetting how to dance and function. There's no way." She swipes the bottle off the table before I can lunge for it. "I knew it!"

"I won!"

"You drank apple juice!"

Presley gasps and covers her mouth. "Grace, I'm shocked." See, now that's good acting. I know she's not actually upset, she's trying to keep her composure.

"Who swapped the bottles?" Trent asks. When no one pipes up he shrugs and throws his arm in the air. "Well, too bad, we won."

Mrs. Hennington comes over and slaps Trent's chest. "Don't make me put you over my knee. Grace, honey," her kind eyes hold mine, "why ever would you cheat?"

I can't lie to her, but this wasn't how I planned to tell Trent.

"Well," I say slowly, making it a point to look at everyone. "You all know I can't drink much and I wanted to win for Trent . . ."

Mama's eyes narrow. "I don't believe that."

"Give me one minute," I say and rush to the car. I was in charge of getting the cake from Angie. I told her to leave the top blank and I'd fill it in at home. So I did. I figured I would tell Trent first, but it seems it's not going to work that way.

I grab the cake and pregnancy stick wrapped in a box. I walk over, and place it on the table. Everyone looks at me like I'm a little insane, and I want to strangle my husband for making me cheat.

"So," I let out a shaky breath. "Today didn't quite go as I planned, but that's kind of par for the course with being married to you."

"You love it."

"I do," I agree.

"So, you thought we should have cake?" Trent asks.

"Cake is always a good idea."

"Well, at least it's not your nasty black licorice," Angie says, exaggerating a shudder.

"Why don't you read the inscription," I suggest to my husband.

Trent gives me an odd look and then lifts the box and reads it aloud. "Another Hennington is in the oven."

Everyone goes quiet, and I turn to see Trent's face. His eyes are soft as he steps closer. I don't know if he comprehended what it means, because he's still not speaking. "You're pregnant?" he asks.

"Yes."

"You're pregnant?" Presley yells.

"I'm pregnant."

Trent's arms circle around me, and he pulls me close. "We're havin' a baby."

I tangle my hands in the hair on the back of his neck and grin. "We sure are."

His lips touch mine, and I fight back tears.

Before I can get too lost in the moment, everyone crowds around us, squeezing us tight.

"We're havin' a baby!" Macie yells, and we all hug again.

Trent smiles at me and then kisses my forehead. "Yeah, I'm definitely the winner here today."

EPILOGUE

Trent

~ Eight years later ~

"DON'T TELL YOUR MAMA ABOUT this." I point at Hannah as I try to clean up the candy wrappers all over the table.

Hannah has me wrapped around that tiny little finger of hers. My sweet daughter with the blue eyes and blonde ringlets—she's the Devil. At seven, she's able to get me to do just about anything.

My mother warned me about giving in to her, but I had it under control. Now, I'm learning my daughter is the master of mind warfare.

"Okay, Daddy." Hannah smiles. "But so I don't forget . . . maybe you should take me by Nana's and we should groom Sadie."

She might have been the master's trainer. She's that good.

"I already said we have plans tonight and you can't go see your horse."

"But Mama said no candy, you forgot that."

"Who are you?" I mutter as I go back to getting rid of all the evidence.

Grace has a very strict no candy policy in the house. She talks about the kids she teaches and how they're always hopped up on sugar. I usually don't fight her on it, but Hannah had those sweet eyes and pouty lip.

It's the lip. It's always the lip.

I'm in the middle of putting the last handful in the bag when the door flies open. "Hey, bab—" Her eyes zero in on my hand. "Trent!"

"It's not as bad as you think. And she gave me the lip."

Grace rolls her eyes and shakes her head. "She's seven and you're a cop. Unreal."

I'm glad she knows I'm hopeless at this point. Hannah came into our world and flipped it upside down. She was a difficult baby that became a tiny terrorist. She never slept, crapped through more clothes than any human should, and was constantly puking. I swear, whatever went in was coming out one end or the other.

Not to mention Grace's pregnancy was like Angie's.

She was always sick, threw things at me, and told me I destroyed her soul at least once a day. I was never more grateful for my hovering mother. For some reason, she wasn't mad at her. Mama came every day, cleaned the house, did some sort of exorcism on my wife, and made sure I didn't have to arrest Grace for homicide. Although, it would've definitely been me she killed.

Hannah runs out and hugs Grace. "Hi, Mama!"

"Hi, sweet girl. I see you've already had dessert for the week with Daddy."

"Yeah." She smiles and gives me up. "He lets me have candy when you're gone. Says it keeps me on his side."

"Hannah!" I yell at my traitor child as she runs away. "I thought we had a deal."

"You know you're in charge, right?" Grace asks as she leans against the doorjamb. "I mean, you're the parent and there are no sides."

I never know with these women. "You say that now, but one day, she's going to be a teenager, and I'll be really freaking old."

"You're old now." Grace points out.

"You're no spring chicken, either, sweetheart."

I probably shouldn't have said that.

"That's not going to help you win an argument."

"She's just so cute. I can't help it. It's like lookin' at you, I can't say no."

I try to play to her sweet side.

"You say no all the time."

"Not when you give me the lip," I remind her. I'm a sucker for it.

She walks over and does the look I referred to. Her eyes get all gooey, her bottom lip juts out a little, and she tilts her head to the side. I melt. I can't help it. "This face?" Grace asks as she comes closer. Her hands travel up my chest and rest on my shoulders.

I wrap my arms around her and hold her against me. "I'll give you anything you want."

"You're a mess." Grace laughs a bit and her fake pout breaks into a smile.

"But I'm your mess."

"Lucky me."

I kiss her lips and smile. "You had your chance to walk away, but you couldn't resist me. I'm an irresistible man to you, Grace Hennington. You love me and wouldn't trade me for the world."

Life with Grace has shown me so much about myself. I never realized that I could be this happy. I drive her nuts, and she nags me, but I wouldn't trade a minute of it. That isn't to say there aren't times I enjoy escaping with my brothers for a week, but I'm always anxious to get home.

She leans back, and her blue eyes hold mine. "Yeah, I've always had a soft spot for strays."

"This is why people warn you not to feed the animals."

Grace giggles and gives me a kiss. "I love you."

"I love you, too."

And I do. More than I knew was possible. When I promised Grace I would give her my heart, I did. I've tried to make each day with her special. I didn't deserve another chance with her, but she gave me one. I don't take that for granted.

"How did I get so lucky?" she asks completely rhetorically, but I'm going to let her know anyway.

"Well, one day, you realized how perfect I was." She smacks my arm. The only thing that comes to mind is something my father said to me. "I don't know the how or why, I'm just glad that it is. Because if it wasn't, we wouldn't be."

I may not be good at many things, but I try damn sure to be good at loving her.

letter to the
READER

Dear Reader,

Thank you so much for all your love and support! If you'd like to keep up with what I have going on, be sure to sign up for my newsletters. As a subscriber, you'll receive access to exclusives, lost love letters, giveaways, and lots more!

Subcribe here: http://corinnemichaels.com/subscribe/

books by
CORINNE MICHAELS

THE SALVATION SERIES
Beloved
Beholden
Consolation
Conviction
Defenseless

STANDALONES
Say You'll Stay
Say You Want Me
Say I'm Yours

ACKNOWLEDGEMENTS

I SWEAR I KNOW I'LL forget someone, so if you're that person . . . I'm sorry.

To my husband and children. You're the world to me. Thank you for loving me even when I'm mentally checked out.

My beta readers, Katie, Melissa, Holly, Michelle, and Jenn: I love you guys. This book was not my usual process but I can't tell you how much I relied on your support. Thank you!

My publicist, Danielle, I love you. Thank you for dealing with my insanity and still loving me. I'm grateful for you more than you will ever know.

My readers. There's no way I can thank you enough. It still blows me away that you read my words. You guys are everything to me.

My Corinne Michaels Books group on Facebook, I wake up every single day and go there first. You're the bright spot in life. Thank you for everything.

Bloggers: You're the heart and soul of this industry. Thank you for choosing to read my books and fit me in your insane schedules. I appreciate it more than you know.

Thank you to Ashley, my editor, for dealing with my crazy voice messages and making this book everything. It is truly a blessing to work with you. Sarah Hansen, from Okay Creations, for making my covers perfect. Janice, Alison, and Kara for proofreading and making sure each detail is perfect! Christine, from Type A Formatting, your support is invaluable. I truly love your beautiful heart.

Wordcount Sprint, Kristy Bromberg, and Kristen Proby—if it were not for you, this book would still not be written. You pushed me, encouraged me, and made me get my butt in gear. Thank you from the bottom of my soul.

My agent, Kimberly Brower, I am so happy to have you on my team. Thank you for your guidance and support.

Squad, SOS, & Holiday Reads Authors—Thank you for your friendship, love, and the way you push me to step outside of the box. I love you guys!

Christy Peckham, I'm running out of things to say, but the one thing that stays is: THANK YOU! I love you and even if I say I don't, I'm lying. Well, maybe.

Melissa Erickson, you're amazing. I love your face.

Milasy, my brunch bitch. Thank you for keeping my glass filled with Bloody Mary's. I can't tell you how much I cherish our Sunday morning ritual.

Vi, Claire, Mandi, Amy, Kristy, Kyla, Rachel, Mia, Tijan, Alessandra, Syreeta, Meghan, Laurelin, Kristen, Kendall, Kennedy, Ava, Leylah, and Lauren—Thank you for keeping me striving to be better and loving me unconditionally.

ABOUT THE AUTHOR

CORINNE MICHAELS IS THE NEW York Times, USA Today, and Wall Street Journal Bestselling Author. She's an emotional, witty, sarcastic, and fun loving mom of two beautiful children. Corinne is happily married to the man of her dreams and is a former Navy wife. After spending months away from her husband while he was deployed, reading and writing was her escape from the loneliness.

Both her maternal and paternal grandmothers were librarians, which only intensified her love of reading. After years of writing short stories, she couldn't ignore the call to finish her debut novel, Beloved. Her alpha men are broken, beautiful, and will steal your heart.

www.corinnemichaels.com